Book I in the Keepers Trilogy

MUSEUM
of
THIEVES

Lian Tanner

SCHOLASTIC INC.
New York Toronto London Auckland
Sydney Mexico City New Delhi Hong Kong

ISBN 978-0-545-45339-4

12 11 10 9 8 7 6 5 4 3 2 1   12 13 14 15 16 17/0

Printed in the U.S.A.   40

First Scholastic printing, March 2012

CAST OF CHARACTERS

(some quite charming and some quite chilling)

Goldie

Toadspit

The Brizzlehound

Morg

The Grand Protector

The Fugleman

Guardian Hope

Herro Dan

Olga Ciavolga

Sinew

I n those days, the museum had four keepers: Herro Dan, Olga Ciavolga, Sinew and the boy Toadspit. In ordinary times, they would have been enough to keep the museum and its secrets safe. But these were not ordinary times.

Trouble was coming. The signs were unmistakable. The keepers did not know where it was coming from, or when it would strike. But it was clear that it would not be easily stopped.

Using all his skills of Concealment, Sinew set out to find a child who could be trained as an extra keeper. Six of the children he spied on turned out to be unsuitable. The seventh (according to her official file) was disobedient and willful. She had worn the punishment chains three times already, and the year had barely begun.

This was the girl who would eventually become the fifth keeper. The girl who would change the fate of both the museum and the city . . .

—*from* The Museum of Dunt: A Hidden History

SEPARATION DAY

Goldie Roth hated the punishment chains. She hated them more than anything—except perhaps for the Blessed Guardians. As the heavy brass cuffs snapped around her wrists and the weight of the chains fell on her shoulders, she stared sullenly at the cobblestones.

She knew what would happen next. Guardian Hope would quote something at her. Something stupid from the Book of the Seven. Guardian Comfort would probably quote something too, and they would both look pleased with themselves.

Yes, here it came. Guardian Hope tugged on the punishment chains to make sure they were properly fastened; then she raised one plump finger. "An Impatient Child," she said, "Is an Unsafe Child."

"An Unsafe Child," said Guardian Comfort, folding his hands piously in front of him, "puts All Other Children at Risk!"

All I did was try and hurry a little bit, thought Goldie. But she said nothing. She didn't want to get into more trouble than she already was. Not today. Oh no, *definitely* not today . . .

She squinted out of the corner of her eye at her classmates. Jube, Plum, Glory and Fort were looking anywhere but at Goldie, hoping that her trouble wouldn't rub off on them. Only Favor was watching, her eyes serious, her hands flicking together and twitching apart in the small, secret movements of fingertalk.

To the Blessed Guardians, it probably looked as if Favor was picking at the threads of her smock, or twisting the links of her little silver guardchain. But to Goldie, the words were as clear as glass. *Don't worry. Not long now.*

Goldie tried to smile, but the weight of the punishment chains seemed to have dragged all the happiness out of her. *This was supposed to be* good *day,* she signed fiercely. *Now look at me!*

"Was that a *scowl*?" said Guardian Hope. "Did you *scowl* at me, Golden?"

"No, Guardian," mumbled Goldie.

"It *was* a scowl, colleague," said Guardian Comfort. The morning was hot already, and he had pushed his heavy black robes away from his shoulders and was mopping his forehead. "I dis*tinct*ly saw a scowl!"

"Perhaps the brass chains are not punishment enough," said Guardian Hope. "Let me see. What can we do that will make the lesson more memorable?" Her eyes fell on the little blue enamel bird that was pinned to the front of Goldie's smock. "That brooch. Where did you get it?"

Goldie's heart sank. "Ma gave it to me," she mumbled.

"Speak up! I can't hear you."

"Ma gave it to me. It belonged to my auntie Praise."

"The one who disappeared years ago?"

"Yes, Guardian."

"Disappeared?" said Guardian Comfort, raising an eyebrow.

"Praise Koch went missing," said Guardian Hope sourly, "the day after she Separated. She was too bold, of course, like her niece here. Without a guardchain to protect her, she probably fell into one of the canals and drowned. Or was kidnapped by slave traders and carted away to a life of misery and despair."

She looked back at Goldie. "This brooch is important to you and your family?"

"Yes, Guardian," mumbled Goldie.

"And I suppose you think about your *bold* aunt when you are wearing it?"

"Yes—I mean, *no*, Guardian! Never!"

"I don't believe you. Your first answer was the truthful one. You should not have such a trinket. It sets a bad example."

"But—!"

Guardian Hope jerked at the punishment chains. *Clank clank clank,* they went. Goldie bit off her protest. Any other day she would have argued, whatever the consequences. But not today. *Not today!*

Briskly, Guardian Hope unpinned the blue brooch and slipped it into the pocket of her robes. Goldie watched that hopeful little bird disappear into darkness.

"And now," said Guardian Hope, "we must be on our way." Her mouth twisted in a sarcastic smile. "We must not be late for this *important* ceremony, must we. The Grand Protector would be *sooo* disappointed."

She set off across the Plaza of the Forlorn, with Goldie stumbling beside her. *Clank clank clank.* The other children tagged along behind Guardian Comfort, their guardchains attached to his leather belt. Everyone they passed stared at Goldie, then quickly looked away again, as if she was diseased.

People were used to seeing children chained, of course.

Every child in the city of Jewel wore a silver guardchain on their left wrist from the moment they learned to walk until their Separation Day. Whenever they were outside the house, the guardchain linked them to their parents, or to one of the Blessed Guardians. At night it was fastened to the bedhead, so that no one could break into the house and carry them off while their parents were sleeping.

But the punishment chains were different. The punishment chains were fastened to *both* wrists. They were far heavier than the little silver guardchains, and they clanked shamefully so that everyone knew you had displeased the Blessed Guardians. Which was a *very* dangerous thing to do . . .

As they approached the Grand Canal, Goldie heard a dull roar ahead of them. Guardian Comfort stopped and inclined his head. "What's that? Is there danger awaiting us, colleague?"

Guardian Hope shortened the punishment chains even further and dragged Goldie along the narrow street to the next corner. Goldie gritted her teeth and tried not to think about the blue brooch.

"No danger," shouted Guardian Hope. "It's merely a crowd."

Guardian Comfort ushered the rest of the class up to the corner, and they all stared at the throng of people walking along the boulevard that ran beside the Grand Canal.

"Where are they going?" said Guardian Comfort. "The markets aren't until tomorrow."

"I imagine they're going to the Great Hall," said Guardian Hope. She raised her voice. "To witness this *Separation* ceremony. This *Abomination!*"

Several of the passersby turned to see who had spoken. When they saw the two Blessed Guardians, they seemed to shrink a little, as if the mere sight of the black robes and black, boxy hats made them afraid.

Goldie felt a spurt of anger. She hated the way the Guardians made everyone act as if they were smaller than they really were. She shifted her hands so that Favor could see them.

Tomorrow I go catch brizzlehound, she signed. *Hungry brizzlehound. Put in sack, bring back to Guardian Hope. "O Blessed Guardian, here is gift to thank you for years of tender care. Please open without caution!"*

Favor's face remained blank, but her eyes laughed. *Won't work,* she signed. *Brizzlehound die of fright when see Guardian Hope's ugly mug.*

"I don't know what the Grand Protector can be thinking of," muttered Guardian Comfort, peering at the crowd. "Lowering the Age of Separation from sixteen to twelve! If she had any sense she'd *raise* it! To eighteen. Or to twenty!"

"The Protector is a fool. She believes that the city is safer than it used to be. She thinks it's time for a change," said Guardian Hope. She and Guardian Comfort looked at each other and snorted rudely. Then they stepped forward into the crowd, dragging the children with them.

People quickly made way for them, and before long they were walking in a large space. It was as if, thought Goldie, there was an invisible line drawn around them that no one wanted to cross.

"Look at them," hissed Guardian Hope. "They avoid us as if we were dogs. They don't know how lucky they are, having us to protect their children!"

"Perhaps we should remind them, colleague."

Guardian Hope nodded thoughtfully. "Perhaps we should." She raised her voice. "It must be obvious to any *thinking* person, colleague, that the Protector is making a *serious* mistake in lowering the Age of Separation. Do you not think so?"

"I *do*, colleague. A *very* serious mistake."

"Jewel is as dangerous now as it ever was. It is only the vigilance of the Blessed Guardians that keeps the children safe. Take away that vigilance and we will go straight back to the bad old days! Has everyone forgotten how *terrible* those days were? Have they forgotten the *drownings*? The *diseases*?"

"Purple fever," said Guardian Comfort, shivering dramatically. "Suppurating heart scab. *Plague!*"

The people within earshot looked at each other uneasily.

"Have they forgotten the slave traders?" said Guardian Hope.

Have you forgotten your brooch? whispered a little voice in the back of Goldie's mind.

Goldie's eyes widened. All her life she had heard this voice, like a whisper from somewhere deep inside her. Sometimes it got her into trouble; sometimes it got her out again. She had never told anyone about it, not even Ma and Pa. Not even Favor.

She's not going to give it back, whispered the voice. *And you might never get this close to her again.*

Goldie glanced down to where her right hand was pressed against Guardian Hope's robes. *Uh-uh,* she thought, mentally shaking her head. This was *definitely* one of those getting-into-trouble times. Imagine the fuss if Guardian Hope found the brooch gone!

She'll think she lost it, whispered the little voice. *And besides, it's Separation Day.*

Separation Day! The day when Goldie's silver guardchain would be removed forever! From now on she would be allowed to walk the streets by herself, without being tied to one of the Blessed Guardians. It was like the beginning of a new life.

Maybe the little voice was right. . . .

Guardian Comfort leaned toward Guardian Hope. "I am reliably informed," he said in a loud voice, "that the slave traders' ships lie just over the horizon, waiting for us to lower our guard! Natkin Gull, Old Lady Skint, the infamous Captain Roop. What can a twelve-year-old do against such monsters, tell me that?"

A man on the edge of the invisible circle muttered, "The Seven Gods protect us," and flicked his fingers anxiously. Goldie flicked *her* fingers too, just in case.

The Seven Gods of Jewel were not kindly deities. They were violent and unpredictable (except for Bald Thoke, whose main problem was a strange sense of humor). Worshipping them was a tricky business. You couldn't ignore them, because Gods don't like to be ignored. But calling on them for help was risky. If they were in the wrong sort of mood, they might well rain down balls of fire, when what you had actually asked for was warm weather for ripening the mangos.

So, like most people, Goldie called on them in times of trouble. But at the same time she flicked her fingers, which meant, *Don't worry about me! Please go and help someone else!*

She certainly didn't want Great Wooden and his immortal companions taking an interest in her now. She didn't want anyone else watching her either. Luckily, everyone in the slow-moving crowd was staring straight ahead, trying to make themselves small and unimportant so that the Blessed Guardians wouldn't pick on them for anything. No one was watching *her*.

Goldie thought of the little blue bird, lost in the darkness of Guardian Hope's robes. She thought of Auntie Praise. *Bold* Auntie Praise! She drew in a deep breath. She pushed the cuff of the punishment chain as high as it would go up her arm, so it would not clank or get in the way. Then she slipped her hand into Guardian Hope's pocket.

She had always been good at moving quietly. Now she felt her way through the darkness as silently as a falling leaf. The treacherous chains remained quiet. Guardian Hope strode beside her, scowling.

Goldie's fingers touched outstretched wings.

And suddenly she got the feeling that someone *was* watching her. Her hand froze, still in the pocket of the black robe. As innocently as she could, she looked around. She couldn't *see* anyone watching. It was just an ordinary, frightened crowd. Except . . . except for one particular spot that her eyes seemed to slide across . . .

Look harder, whispered the little voice in the back of her mind.

Goldie looked harder. She saw a flicker of black that didn't seem to belong to any of the people around it. For some reason it was hard to fix her eyes on it. The light sort of . . . *slipped* past it, as if it was too unimportant to worry about.

Look harder.

And then Goldie saw him. A tall thin man wearing an old-fashioned black coatee with sleeves too short for his long arms, so that his wrists stuck out at awkward angles. He was keeping pace with the little group of children and Guardians, and staring straight at her.

When he saw her staring back at him, his face went blank with surprise. He ducked behind another man and disappeared into the crowd.

The strength came back into Goldie's fingers. She closed them around the little blue bird and eased it out of Guardian Hope's robe. Its wings seemed to flutter in her hand, as if it was thanking her for its freedom.

Despite the weight of the punishment chains, a wave of excitement welled up inside Goldie. It was Separation Day. An hour from now, she too would be free.

THE GRAND PROTECTOR

Guardian Hope kept Goldie in punishment chains until they were right outside the Great Hall. When at last she unlocked them, Goldie sighed with relief. *Now there's just my guardchain. And soon that'll be gone too!*

Ma and Pa were waiting inside the hall with the other parents. Guardian Hope and Guardian Comfort unsnapped the guardchains from their belts and silently handed the children over. The parents fastened the guardchains to their own belts.

As they walked toward the stage, Ma murmured in Goldie's ear. "Is it true, sweeting? Did she have you in punishment chains on your Separation Day? Oh, I can hardly believe it! She has no feelings!"

"Shhh," whispered Pa. "You know what sharp ears they have."

Now that they were away from the Blessed Guardians, Goldie's classmates were behaving more like themselves. Behind Goldie, Herro Oster growled, "Don't leap around, Jubilation! You nearly pulled me off my feet!"

"Sorry, Pa," sang Jube, not sounding the least bit sorry.

"I expect you'll be p-pleased to have him Separated," said Favor's pa, Herro Berg, who had a slight stammer. "It's a t-trial, is it not, when they reach this age?"

"I don't know how I'd stand another four years of it," said Herro Oster, a little too loudly to be convincing. "I'm all bruises from his flying arms and legs. Blessings upon the Protector for lowering the Age of Separation."

"Indeed, Blessings, Blessings," murmured the other parents. But their faces were pale, and Goldie thought they looked as if they hadn't slept very well.

They lined up at the foot of the stage and waited for the official whitesmith to come and remove the children's silver cuffs. The hall was filled with onlookers. In the front row, a dozen gazetteers were already making notes for tomorrow's gazettes.

Ma patted Goldie on the arm. "Now, you're not to be frightened, sweeting."

"I'm not," said Goldie.

"Of course you're not," said Ma quickly. She hesitated. "But when you're Separated, you *will* watch out for slave traders, won't you?"

Frow Berg leaned toward them. "And poisonous insects."

"Runaway street-rigs," said Pa.

"Sharp knives," said Frow Oster.

Goldie heard a faint *whump* somewhere in the distance. She looked around. No one else seemed to have noticed it.

"Marauding birds," said Herro Oster. "Mad dogs. *Any* dogs at all!"

"D-d-dirty water," stammered Herro Berg. "*Filthy* water. D-d-disease-ridden, child-drowning water! That's the one that worries me. And g-getting lost. Whatever you do, d-d-*don't* get lost."

Goldie had heard these warnings a hundred—no, a *thousand*—times before. She ducked her head and grinned at Favor, but her friend was nodding seriously at the familiar list.

"That reminds me," said Ma. She took a small parcel from her pocket. "We bought you a little something, sweeting, to celebrate."

It was a compass, of course. The traditional Separation Day presents were always either a compass (so you could find your way home again if you were lost) or a whistle (to call for help if you were attacked by slavers).

Goldie made surprised, pleased noises when she saw the compass. But secretly she wished that she had been given a folding knife, so that she could fight her way out of trouble. Or a spyglass for looking at far-off places and dreaming of the day when she'd be old enough to leave the city of Jewel and its Blessed Guardians far, far behind.

Twenty minutes later, Goldie and her friends stood on the enormous stage, along with a hundred other children and their parents. This was to be the biggest Separation Day in living memory. Every child in Jewel between the ages of twelve and sixteen was about to be given their freedom.

Goldie's cuff and guardchain were already gone, and she was tied to Ma by nothing but a white silk ribbon. Her left arm felt hot and strange. Her body buzzed with nervous impatience as the Protector walked up to the podium.

The Grand Protector of Jewel wasn't really very grand. She wore crimson robes and a gold chain, but she was only a little bit taller than Goldie's ma, and her hair was the color of straw. Above her head, the glass dome of the Great Hall was awash with lights. Clockwork birds whizzed from pillar to pillar on silver wires. Clockwork butterflies opened and closed their wings.

The Protector pushed her eyeglasses up onto her nose and

faced the audience. "There was a time," she said loudly, "when there was no such place as the city of Jewel. Instead, there was a nasty little seaport called Dunt, stuck on the south coast of the Faroon Peninsula like a pustulous wart on an old man's chin. And a pustulous wart of a place it was too, full of disease and danger."

Goldie heard a rustling in the audience as everyone settled in to listen to the well-known story. But, for once, the Protector didn't remind them of how their ancestors had come here from Merne to establish a colony. She didn't tell them about the Native Wars and the Beast Wars and the Wars of Independence, and the floods and murders and famines, and the Year of Despair, when children died like flies. She didn't tell them about the heroic struggle of a few people to save the remaining children, and how those people became the first Blessed Guardians.

Instead, she smiled and said, "But that was a long time ago. For more than two hundred years the city has been progressively cleansed of its dangers. The canals have been fenced, the vacant blocks built upon. The animals and birds have been driven away. Vile Dunt has become beautiful Jewel. We no longer need to be so vigilant."

Many people were nodding, but Goldie could see some who obviously didn't agree. In the second row of the audience, Guardian Hope's face was dark with anger.

"These children behind me," said the Protector, "are about to take us into a glorious future."

She paused. Goldie glanced at her classmates. Favor was chewing her fingernails. Fort was smiling, but there was something fixed about his smile, as if he had put it there earlier and forgotten about it. Plum and Glory were white-faced with nerves, and Jube was jiggling from one leg to the other. Goldie heard Herro Oster hiss, "In the name of the Seven, Jubilation, can't you be still for *five more minutes*?"

The audience laughed nervously. The Protector smiled again. "His Honor the Fugleman," she said, "will now deliver the Blessing."

There was silence in the hall. No one moved. "Where's the Fugleman?" Goldie whispered to Ma.

As if in answer, there was a shuffling in the audience. "Make way, make way!" cried Guardian Hope, and she stepped up onto the stage, making a great business of patting her robes into smooth folds and straightening her hat.

The Protector peered at her over the top of her glasses. "Is this a change of plan?" she said. "No one informed me of it. Where is your leader?"

"Your Grace," said Guardian Hope. "His Honor *should* be here, but it seems he has been delayed. Perhaps we should also delay the Separation."

Goldie's heart lurched. But the Protector said mildly, "If

the Fugleman is not here, Guardian, I'm sure *you* can administer the Blessing."

"Oh no, that would not be—"

"*Now*, Guardian," said the Protector in a voice that was no longer mild.

Guardian Hope fussed some more with her hat, then scowled at the long rows of children. "Do you swear to remain vigilant and not endanger yourself or others," she muttered, "even when you are no longer under the care of the Blessed Guardians?"

Goldie's mouth was suddenly dry. She answered in chorus with a hundred other voices, "I swear."

"Do you swear to honor the Seven Gods and their plans for you, as revealed through the Blessed Guardians?"

"I swear."

"Do you swear to avoid Blasphemy and condemn Abomination, wherever you find them?"

"I swear."

Guardian Hope hesitated. Goldie clenched her fists so tightly that her nails bit into the palms of her hands.

The Protector cleared her throat. "Continue, please."

"Then shall you be Blessed." Despite her reluctance, Guardian Hope's voice rose in the old familiar rhythms. She named the Gods one by one, in order of decreasing importance so as not to offend any of them. "May Great Wooden never send his Black Ox to fetch you in the night! May the

Weeping Lady blame someone else for her tears! May Thunderer, Dreamer and the Locksmith forget your name! May Helper never decide you need her help! And may Bald Thoke take his jokes elsewhere."

Goldie flicked her fingers as each name was spoken.

"Blessings upon you, Blessings upon you, thrice Blessings upon you. So it is done!" As soon as the words were out of her mouth Guardian Hope stalked off the stage, as if she wanted nothing more to do with the proceedings.

"Lieutenant marshal?" murmured the Protector.

The lieutenant marshal of militia had been standing to one side. Now he handed the Protector a small pair of scissors. The Protector took a piece of paper from the pocket of her robes, squinted at it and said loudly, "Golden Roth."

A shiver ran through Goldie. She was to be first! She stepped forward with Ma and Pa beside her.

The Grand Protector smiled, her eyes sharp and clever behind her glasses. "Hold out your hand," she said.

Goldie held out her hand. The white silk ribbon stretched tight.

"By the grace of the Seven Gods," cried the Protector, "and in accordance with the Guardianship Act, let this child be Separated!"

She raised the scissors. Ma gave a little squeak of protest, but said nothing. Pa squeezed Goldie's shoulder. In the audience, the gazetteers dipped their pens into their portable

19

inkpots and began to scribble furiously. Goldie held her breath. . . .

There was a terrible thumping from the far end of the hall, where the big wooden doors had been closed to keep out the summer heat. The Protector hesitated.

"Let me through! Let me through!" cried a muffled voice.

Go away! thought Goldie. *Don't interrupt!*

One of the militiamen guarding the doors pulled them open a little way. "Hush!" he said. "Her Grace is just starting the Separations."

A man pushed past him, his black robes torn and dirty, his face streaked with blood. "Disaster!" he cried. "Murder! The children—!" And he fell to the floor in a dramatic faint.

THE FUGLEMAN

The people in the audience surged to their feet and pressed toward the fallen man, all shouting at once.

"What is it?"

"*Who* is it?"

"What children?"

"Don't tread on him, watch what you're doing!"

"What's he mean, murder?"

"Get him a chair! Get him water!" shouted the Protector, and she thrust the scissors into the lieutenant marshal's hand, jumped down from the stage and began to push her way through the crowd.

Ma hugged Goldie close. Pa wrapped his arms around both of them. "The children," he whispered. "What's happened to the children?"

Goldie's left wrist felt as if it was on fire. She put her other hand in her pocket, and her fingers closed around the little blue bird. *Hurry,* she thought. *Hurry up and finish this so we can get back to the Separation.*

One of the militiamen carried a jug of water through the crowd and poured a little of it over the intruder's head. He groaned and sat up. Someone gasped, "It's the Fugleman!"

Goldie stared down at the disheveled figure in amazement. His Honor the Fugleman of Jewel, leader of the Blessed Guardians and spokesman for the Seven Gods, was a tall, handsome man who never appeared in public unless his black hair was as smooth as a raven's wing and the silver braid on his robes gleamed.

But now his robes were in tatters and his forehead was covered in blood. Beneath the blood, his face was white with ash and horror.

The crowd fell silent. The Fugleman looked around as if he didn't know where he was. "There was—there was an explosion," he croaked. "The children—"

He stopped, unable to go on. Goldie remembered the faint *whump* she had heard. An explosion!

"Great Wooden preserve us!" whispered Ma, flicking her fingers and tightening her grip on Goldie.

"Give him a drink," ordered the Protector.

The Fugleman gulped at the water until the jug was empty. He wiped a bloody hand across his mouth. Then, shaking uncontrollably and stopping every few words to catch his breath, he told the horrified crowd what had happened.

"An excursion . . . this morning . . . just four children with their Guardians . . . I had invited them to visit my office before the Separation ceremony. The Seven Gods forgive me."

His voice was little more than a whisper, but it seemed to Goldie that it carried from one end of the hall to the other.

"We were in the . . . library . . . showing them the portraits . . . the Fuglemen who have gone before me . . . great men all of them . . . serving the Seven, taking care of the city's children—"

He stopped again. For an awful moment, Goldie thought he was going to weep. A single tear ran down his face, cutting a channel through the ash. He wiped it away and continued.

"It was like . . . being hit by a great blow. My Guardians . . . threw themselves across the children to protect them. None of us understood what had happened. We were deafened . . . the noise, the falling plaster . . . the walls collapsing about us. The children—"

A groan broke from Pa. Ma was sobbing openly, and she

was not the only one. The Protector held up her hand for silence.

"When we could see again," said the Fugleman, "we found that the children were safe—shocked but safe. All except one—a young girl from—"

He took a deep, shuddering breath. "A young girl from . . . Feverbone Canal. She was . . . dead."

There was instant uproar in the hall. Goldie could hear her own cry of horror echoing from every throat. Ma and Pa clutched her even tighter. Dead? *Dead?* A *child*? In *Jewel*? It was as if everyone's worst nightmare had come true.

The Protector's face was as white as paper, but again she held up her hand for quiet. "When you came in," she said in an almost-steady voice, "you cried *murder*."

"I thought—we thought it must have been a watergas explosion," said the Fugleman. "An accident. But a witness saw . . . two men running away. Strangers. And my Guardians found the remains of a . . . device. By the Seven, Your Grace, it was no accident. It was . . . a bomb."

The next few minutes were a blur of noise and shouting. Goldie felt as if all the breath had been knocked out of her. She saw the Protector wave the lieutenant marshal to her side. He seemed to be arguing with her. The Protector snapped at him, and he marched back up onto the stage and stood next to Goldie, his face a stiff, angry mask.

The Protector hurried out of the hall with the rest of the militia close behind her. The crowd parted to make way for them. Everyone's face carried the same shocked expression. A *bomb*? In *Jewel*?

"Impossible," muttered Pa over and over again. "Impossible!" Ma's tears soaked the shoulder of Goldie's smock.

Down in the body of the hall there was a flurry of movement as the Fugleman rose wearily to his feet. People rushed to help him, but he waved them away and dragged himself up onto the stage.

"My friends," he began in a heavy voice.

Gradually the crowd became quiet again, although many of them were still sobbing.

"My friends. Danger is all around us. Who can tell where it will strike next? We must beg the Seven to shield us."

Goldie murmured a quick prayer, and flicked her fingers. *Don't protect us, Great Wooden! Don't shield us, Weeping Lady! You've done enough! Go somewhere else! Please!*

"The Grand Protector has gone to deal with this tragedy," continued the Fugleman, "as is her duty. But if she was here, I'm sure she'd agree with me. The wishes of the Seven Gods are clear. Now is not the time for change. This Separation is hereby canceled."

For a moment, the Fugleman's words didn't make any

sense to Goldie. She had been waiting for this day all her life. It couldn't be canceled. Not even for a bomb and a dead girl. It wasn't possible.

Was it?

Her hand—the one that held the little flying bird—felt icy cold. At the same time, there was a heat inside her, as if someone had kindled a fire in her innards. "Pa?" she whispered, trying to control her voice. "Can the Fugleman do that?"

It seemed that he could. He was already beckoning the whitesmith back up onto the stage.

Pa sighed. "Dearling, it's too dangerous to go ahead with it now. Perhaps next year the Protector will try again."

"Or the year after," said Ma, trying to cuddle Goldie and push her toward the whitesmith at the same time.

The heat in Goldie's innards was getting worse. In the back of her mind, the little voice whispered, *You can't wait that long. You have to Separate today.*

"I can't wait that long!" said Goldie. The words seemed to burst out of her. "I have to Separate *today!*"

Guardian Hope's head snapped around. "Unnatural child! There's been a murder! Where's your fear? Where's your trembling?"

"She's upset, that's all," said Ma quickly. She put her hand on Goldie's forehead. "It's the shock. She'll feel better soon."

"I *won't* feel better!" said Goldie. She knew that she was

making things worse, but she couldn't help it. "They promised we could Separate today! They *promised*!"

Everyone in the hall seemed to be looking at her now, but she didn't care. All she knew was that she couldn't bear to have the silver cuff fastened around her wrist again, and the guardchain snapped into place.

The Fugleman was staring at her. "Who is this child who questions the holy will of the Seven?"

Guardian Hope smirked. "Her name's Golden Roth, Your Honor. Always a troublemaker. I've only just taken the punishment chains off her."

"Then perhaps you should put them back on," said the Fugleman. "Until she has learned her lesson."

"She hasn't done anything wrong!" cried Ma. "She's just a little upset."

"*Upset?*" The Fugleman spat the word out. "Your daughter is not *upset*, Frow. Your daughter is *foolish*! *Wicked*! If she does not obey authority, then she *deserves* to wear the punishment chains."

"No!" said Goldie, who seemed to have lost all control of her tongue.

"Unless, of course," said the Fugleman, "you would prefer that we take her into *Care*."

"That won't be necessary," said Pa. Goldie could feel him shaking, but his voice was calm. "My wife didn't mean to

27

complain, Your Honor. Our daughter will wear the punishment chains, won't you, dearling? There now, of course you will. That's settled, then."

Guardian Hope climbed up onto the stage with the heavy brass chains in her hand. The Fugleman turned back to the crowd and drew himself up to his full height. "This tragedy makes one thing clear," he said loudly. "We need more Blessed Guardians in this city!"

No! thought Goldie.

"We must have a resident Guardian in every public building!" cried the Fugleman. "Someone who can protect our most precious possession, our children!"

A cheer rose from the crowd.

"Remember," cried the Fugleman. "When We Endanger Ourselves, We Endanger Others."

"It Is Our Duty to Be Safe!" Guardian Hope chanted the age-old response, and the crowd joined with her in a full-throated roar.

Something wild took hold of Goldie then. She didn't want to be safe. She wanted to be free! The silk ribbon seemed to tighten around her wrist. The high glass dome of the Great Hall pressed down on her so that she felt as if she might suffocate.

Look, whispered the little voice. *Look at the lieutenant marshal. Look behind him.*

Goldie ducked her head. The lieutenant marshal of militia

was standing right next to her. Behind him, at the back of the stage, was a small door.

"Danger Can Strike from Any Direction," cried the Fugleman. "It Lurks Amongst Us and Does Not Sleep."

"It Is Our Duty to Be Cautious!"

Goldie swallowed. The sound was so loud in her ears that she was sure everyone else must have heard it. Her heart was beating right up in her throat. The tips of her fingers tingled.

She squeezed the blue enamel bird. *Maybe Auntie Praise* wasn't *taken by slavers,* she thought. *Maybe she ran away because she couldn't bear living here anymore.*

"Beware of the Bold and the Foolhardy, for They Will Bring Disaster upon Us All!" shouted the Fugleman.

"It Is Our Duty to Be Afraid!"

As the last word of the chant died down, Guardian Hope cried, "Three cheers for the Fugleman, holy servant of the Seven! Huzzah! Huzzah! Huzzah!"

The noise rose around Goldie like a tidal wave. She closed her eyes. When she opened them again, Favor was watching her.

Goldie tried to smile, but she couldn't. Without taking her eyes off her best friend, she let go of the blue bird and slipped her hand into the lieutenant marshal's pocket.

Favor stared. The crowd cheered on and on. Goldie sifted her way past a kerchief, past a bunch of keys, her fingers as light as a breath of air.

And suddenly, there were the scissors. She slid them out of the lieutenant marshal's pocket and into her own.

Standing still then was one of the hardest things she had ever done. She was shaking from head to toe. Favor's eyes were wide with shock, but she said nothing.

Goldie leaned back so that her head rested on Pa's broad chest. "I love you, Pa," she whispered. There was so much noise that he probably couldn't hear her. Still, he put up his hand and stroked her hair.

Goldie kissed Ma on the cheek. "I love you too, Ma. Don't worry about me."

"What?" said Ma, putting her hand to her ear. "Say that again, sweeting?"

Goldie could feel the tears starting up at the back of her eyes. She shook them away. She opened and closed the scissors three times inside her pocket to make sure she knew how to use them.

She glanced at the audience. Her eyes slid across a patch of air. She forced them back, and there was the man in the black coatee, watching her . . .

It was too late to care. The little voice in the back of her mind was shouting, *Go! Go!*

Goldie whipped the scissors out of her pocket and cut through the white silk ribbon with one snip. Then, before anyone could stop her, she ran off the stage and out the back door of the Great Hall.

A FEW UNIMPORTANT DOCUMENTS

The Protector limped down the gangplank of the official waterbus. The corns on her feet ached, and she was tired and heartsick. It had been a terrible day.

She had originally planned to leave the Great Hall straight after the Separation ceremony and make a tour of the levees that protected Jewel from the sea. According to the Levee Master, they were in urgent need of repair.

Instead, she had called up the militia to search for whoever had set off the bomb. She had gone to the Fugleman's shattered office and spoken to witnesses. She had visited the dead child's parents, and the children who had survived the explosion.

And now there was this wretched business of the runaway girl—and the Resident Guardians.

She wiped the sweat out of her eyes and shook her head. A runaway! Coming so soon after news of the bomb! The whole city was reeling with shock.

She was shocked too, but for a different reason. She was sorry now that she had left the Hall when she did. She should have guessed that the Fugleman would take any opportunity to stir up the people.

More Blessed Guardians indeed! The Protector wanted to *reduce* the stranglehold that they had on the city, not *increase* it. She'd been planning to cut their numbers by half, once the new Age of Separation was properly in place.

She grimaced. Well, that plan was dead, and it'd be a long time before she could resurrect it.

Slowly she hobbled up the stone steps of the dock and onto the Bridge of Beasts. It was the oldest bridge in Jewel, and its iron sides were wrought in the shapes of quignogs, idle-cats, slotters, slommerkins, brizzlehounds and slaughterbirds. As she passed, their muscles seemed to strain and bunch, as if they might leap into life at any moment.

Despite her tiredness, the Protector stopped in the middle of the bridge. When her ancestors had first arrived here from Merne, these strange creatures had roamed all over the peninsula. They were gone now, of course, extinct for so long that most people thought they had never existed. But they had been real enough, back in the early days of Dunt. The Protector knew that without a doubt.

In fact, there were quite a few things that the Protector knew . . .

Which reminded her. There was something she must tell the Fugleman. Something important.

It was only a short walk from the Bridge of Beasts to the Protectorate. The lieutenant marshal of militia was waiting at the top of the steps. He hurried to open the door for her, his face strained with guilt.

"Your Grace," he said. "The scissors, Your Grace. How can I apologize?"

The Protector's aching corns made her more short-tempered than usual. "A child has been lost because of your carelessness," she snapped.

"I'm sorry, Your Grace. I'll do anything to make up for it. If I could join the search party—"

"Absolutely not."

"Please, Your Grace—"

"Be quiet! You're lucky you're still in the militia. Whether you *stay* there is another matter altogether. Now, I have a message for the Fugleman. I trust you can deliver it without endangering the lives of any *more* children?"

"But the Fugleman's here, Your Grace! He's been waiting for half an hour or more."

The lieutenant marshal darted in front of the Protector and pushed her office door open—and there indeed was the Fugleman, sitting in one of the visitors' chairs. He had changed his clothes and washed away the ash and dust. Now he was as immaculate as ever, apart from the bandage around his forehead.

"Your Grace," he said, climbing stiffly to his feet and bowing. "Blessings upon you."

The Protector dismissed the lieutenant marshal. Then she closed the door and leaned against it. She forced a smile. "Well, little brother," she said.

There were barely half a dozen people in Jewel who knew that His Honor the Fugleman and Her Grace the Protector were brother and sister. It suited both of them to keep it that way. They had never liked each other, even as children.

The Protector limped around the desk to her chair. "Any news of the girl?"

"None," said her brother, settling back with a grunt. "But we'll find her. My Guardians are trained for moments such as this. Unlike your so-called *militia*, who don't seem to be trained for anything. You know that she was standing right next to one of them? Took the scissors from his pocket? Unbelievable! If he was mine I'd have him court-martialed."

The Fugleman was skilled at the ancient art of swordsmanship, and the Protector often felt as if her conversations with him were a running duel. But today she was determined to ignore his jabs. "Why on earth did the child run away?" she asked. "She must be the first in more than fifty years."

Something flickered across the Fugleman's face. "Ah . . . the second."

"*What?*"

"A boy, last year. He disappeared overnight. His parents thought he'd been taken by slavers, but then they found a note. He'd run away."

The Protector could hardly believe what she was hearing. She knew of several children who had gone missing *after* Separation. But *before*? "Wasn't he guardchained?"

"His parents *said* he was. They claimed that he must have picked the lock somehow. But we were quite sure they had left him unchained. It happens sometimes, but we usually catch it before disaster strikes."

"Why didn't I hear about this at the time?"

"*No* one heard about it. Imagine if word got around that there were children left unchained at night. The slavers would be upon us like wolves. For that reason we kept it quiet."

"But still, *I* should have been told!"

"Do you think so, sister?" The Fugleman ran his hand over his chin. "It was obviously a case of Abomination. I saw no need to inform you. After all, *you* wouldn't inform *me* if the Treasury accounts didn't balance. . . ."

The Protector tried to ignore the anger that was rising inside her. "Did you search for the boy?"

"Of course. We searched everywhere, day and night for a week. But there was no sign of him. He's long dead by now. Probably drowned."

"And his family?"

"There was a younger child, a girl. We took her into Care, and the Court of the Seven Blessings sentenced the parents to three years in the House of Repentance and the confiscation of all their possessions."

"You mean *you* sentenced them."

"It's true that the Court chooses to speak through me," said the Fugleman smoothly. "And I am *greatly* honored by it."

"Three years imprisonment, their possessions gone, their daughter taken into Care. A harsh punishment for people who've just lost their son!"

"They broke the law."

"I *don't* think—" began the Protector. But then she stopped. She really didn't want to fight openly with her brother, especially not today. "Why are you here?"

The Fugleman took a sheaf of papers from inside his jacket

and laid them on the desk. "I have a few unimportant documents that need your signature."

The Protector pushed her eyeglasses into place, picked up the topmost paper and frowned. "Unimportant? This is to approve the new Resident Guardians. You've been very quick to draw up the agreement!"

The Fugleman shrugged. "The people were *most* insistent—"

"Don't take me for a fool, brother. You were always able to sway a crowd."

"You flatter me, sister. But you can't deny that these are desperate times. And the people are frightened."

The Protector hesitated. For once her brother was right. These *were* desperate times. More desperate than she had realized. And the people *were* frightened.

With a sigh, she dipped her pen in the inkwell, signed the top paper and turned to the next one. She blinked in surprise and read it twice, in case she was mistaken. "According to this," she said slowly, "these Resident Guardians of yours will be in place by tonight! I thought it would take a month at least!"

"There are dangerous criminals loose in the city. *They* will not wait a month." The Fugleman rubbed his hand across his bandaged forehead, as if his wound was hurting him. "Besides, the new Guardians can help search for the girl.

She'll probably try to hide in some building or other when night falls. This way, we'll be waiting for her."

"But what about their training?"

"Perhaps *you* are happy to wait for an emergency before you train new militia, sister. But I cannot afford to be so complacent. There are new Guardians in training at all times, just in case. Your signature, if you will."

The Protector tapped her pen against her cheek. She *would* sign. But there was something she had to tell her brother first. What was it?

Ah, yes. "The Museum of Dunt," she said. "You know it?"

The Fugleman's handsome brow creased. "I've heard of it. A small building of no particular importance. I believe it's farther up Old Arsenal Hill from my office. What of it?"

"They won't be needing a Resident Guardian. They're exempt."

"But—"

"*Not* the Museum of Dunt."

At that, something in the Fugleman's face seemed to change, and for a split second he looked as sharp and dangerous as a straight-edge razor. Then he bowed his head, and the dangerous look was gone so completely that the Protector thought she had imagined it.

"I'm sure you have excellent reasons for such an exemption, sister. Might I ask what they are?"

The Protector hesitated. Apart from her, the only people

who knew the truth about the Museum of Dunt were the museum's keepers. There was no actual law that prevented her from telling the Fugleman. But it was not the sort of knowledge that she would trust him with.

So she merely shrugged and said, "It's customary to leave the museum to its own devices."

"And this custom, how did it begin?"

The Protector waved her hand in the direction of her bookcases, which were crammed with documents from the early days of Dunt. "I really can't remember. I'm sure there's an explanation there somewhere."

Then, before her brother could ask any more questions, she scribbled her signature on the paper and pushed it toward him.

He bowed. "Thank you for your time, Your Grace. Meeting with you is always *such* a pleasure. Blessings upon you."

His teeth flashed in an insincere smile. Then he was gone.

ALONE

Goldie crouched inside the cabin of a small private water-rig. Despite the heat, she was shivering. Her head ached and her legs were cramped, but she dared not move. The water-rig was moored right up against Beast Dock, and there were barges and waterbuses all around. It was a miracle that she had got this far without being seen.

Now that the wildness had worn off, she was horrified by what she had done. She glared at the remains of the white silk ribbon on her wrist. "Stupid!" she hissed. "Stupid, stupid, *stupid!*"

There was a clattering from the barge next door, and she jammed her knuckles into her mouth. Had they heard her? Were they coming? What would they do if they caught her?

She squeezed her eyes shut and waited. The clattering died away. A man laughed. The water-rig rocked gently from side to side. Slowly, Goldie opened her eyes.

Above her head was the wooden wheel that steered the boat. On either side of the wheel were narrow seats with sheepskin coverlets. The rest of the cabin was empty. No Blessed Guardians. No Ma and Pa.

For the first time in her life, Goldie was completely alone.

Quickly, she shut her eyes again. The *thump thump thump* of her heart was louder than she'd ever heard it before. She wondered if she was coming down with a fever. Her legs and arms shook. She tried desperately to hold back the tears.

But then she remembered Ma's little squeak of dismay when the Protector raised the scissors. She remembered how Pa had stroked the top of her head. She thought of how much she loved them.

The tears poured down her face. Fear and sorrow sat like twin fists inside her.

She didn't know how long she sat there, crying silently in the slowly rocking boat. It seemed like hours. By the time her tears ran out, her lips were dry and cracked with thirst. She shifted position slightly and her stomach rumbled.

41

She tried to distract herself by imagining what Favor was doing right now. But her mind veered off in another direction, and she found herself thinking about murderous bombers.

And mad dogs.

And slave traders.

Her skin crawled. She felt like an oyster that had foolishly prized itself out of its shell and now had nothing to protect it. She took the scissors from her pocket and clutched them so tightly that her fingers cramped.

The day passed unbearably slowly. Water lapped against the hull. Engines rumbled. People on the neighboring barges shouted instructions to each other.

"Easy now! Eeeaasy! That's it, let it down! Not *there*, you moon-blind idiot! Over *here*!"

At last the sky outside the portholes grew dark, and the work noises faded. Somewhere, someone was cooking fish.

The smell made Goldie feel sick with hunger. As quietly as she could, she stretched the cramp out of her legs, grimacing with the pain of it. Then she crawled along the floor of the cabin and peeped out the nearest porthole.

The waterbuses had gone, and so had some of the barges. The ones that remained had their curtains drawn and their lights dimmed.

Slowly, Goldie crawled up onto the small deck, ready to dive back into hiding if anyone appeared unexpectedly. When she was sure that there was no one around, she crept off the end of the water-rig onto the dock, and up the steps to the street.

There was a gate at the top of the steps. Goldie didn't dare open it in case it creaked. She climbed over it—or rather, half-climbed, half-fell. Then she hurried along the old towpath, her heart thumping and galumping like an engine.

The night was dark, and there was a hush over the streets of the Old Quarter, as if everyone was so shocked by the events of the day that they had gone to bed early and pulled the covers over their heads. Goldie left the towpath and began to make her way toward the Plaza of the Forlorn.

Every time she heard a strange noise, her heart almost jumped out of her chest. Her feet tripped and stumbled on the cobblestones, and when she came to a corner, she hesitated, wondering which was the best way to go. She had longed to be rid of the guardchain, but now she found it almost unbearably odd not having someone tell her what to do and urge her this way and that—someone who would pull her back from danger and catch her if she fell. It was like being a baby and having to learn to walk all over again.

Her own street, when she came to it, was as silent as the rest of the city. Goldie crept along it, her eyes fixed on the apartment building halfway down the block.

Beware, whispered the little voice in the back of her mind. For once Goldie ignored it. She was thinking about Ma and Pa, and wondering what they had had for dinner. She

43

imagined them sitting on her empty bed with their arms around each other, crying. She brushed her own tears away.

Beware!

Farther down the street, the shadows seemed to move and whisper. At the same time, a hand shot out of nowhere and closed over Goldie's mouth. She tried to scream. She struggled, her sandals scraping on the cobblestones. But two more hands gripped her and pulled her through an open doorway.

"Sssshhh!" breathed a voice in her ear. A fourth hand that she instantly recognized as Favor's slid into hers. The door eased closed in front of her but didn't shut completely. The hand across her mouth loosened a little.

Goldie knew where she was now; she could smell Herro Berg's shaving lotion and feel the shape of Frow Berg's bracelet pressing into her arm. She stood trembling in the dark hallway.

In the street outside, there was the sudden flash of a lantern and the sound of footsteps.

"Did you hear that? We've got her now!" said Guardian Comfort.

"*I* heard nothing," said Guardian Hope. "But blow your whistle if you must. Alert the others. If she's here, she'll try to run for it."

The single-note whistle of the Blessed Guardians shrilled up and down the street. The footsteps went a bit farther, then circled back again.

"Golden Roth!" cried Guardian Comfort. "We know you're here! Don't waste our time, we're going to catch you anyway."

Herro Berg's hand tightened over Goldie's mouth.

"Give yourself up," cried Guardian Comfort, "and we may treat you more leniently!"

Silence. A trickle of sweat ran down the back of Goldie's neck.

Guardian Hope sniffed loudly. "I do believe you're jumping at shadows, colleague."

"It was her, I'm sure of it. She's hiding somewhere nearby."

"Perhaps," said Guardian Hope. "Or perhaps you're just wasting my precious time."

Their voices faded into the distance. Silently, Frow Berg bolted the door. Herro Berg took his hand away from Goldie's mouth.

"I'm d-doing this ag-gainst my b-better judgment," he whispered. His stammer was much worse than usual. "I d-*don't* want my d-daughter t-taken into C-C-Care. Nor d-do I want the att-tention of the B-B-Blessed G-Guardians to fall up-pon my family in any way. If they c-c-catch you, you mustn't t-t-tell them we helped you."

"I won't," whispered Goldie.

"I'm so glad you're here!" whispered Favor, throwing her arms around Goldie's neck and hugging her tightly. "Where've you *been*?"

"Hiding."

"All on your *own*? What was it like?"

"Horrible! Favor, I'm so thirsty!"

"Ma, she's thirsty!"

"Of course she is, poor chick," murmured Frow Berg. "And hungry too, I expect. I've got a glass of water for her, and there's some bread and cheese here somewhere."

"What d-d-did you think you were d-d-d-doing, g-girl?" whispered Herro Berg as Goldie gulped the water down. "What p-p-possible g-g-good can come of this?"

"Shhh," whispered Frow Berg. "It's done now, and there's no changing it." She squeezed Goldie's hand. "Your parents asked us to watch out for you."

"Are they all right?" whispered Goldie. "What did they say? Are they angry with me?"

"Their hearts are torn. They want you to be safe, but they don't want the Blessed Guardians to catch you and take you into Care. Your mother said you must try and leave the city. Though how a child on her own might do that I can't imagine!"

Goldie couldn't imagine it either. The whole world had turned upside down, and she had no one to blame but herself. "Can't I just go home?" she said miserably.

"I'm afraid that's no longer possible, my dear. Once the Blessed Guardians are involved, everything changes." Frow Berg pushed a slip of paper into her hand. "Your mother has

46

some distant cousins in Spoke who should look after you if you can get that far. Here's their address. Oh yes, and there's a purse. Where did I put it? Is it with the bread and cheese? Oh dear, where did I put the bread and cheese?" She began to fumble around in the darkness.

Goldie looked helplessly at Favor. "How am I supposed to get to *Spoke*?"

"I don't know, but you'll have to try," said Favor. "You mustn't let the Guardians catch you."

"But I don't even know where to start!"

"Goldie," whispered Favor very seriously, "if *I* had to find my way to Spoke all by myself, I'd probably just curl up and die. But you're braver than me. You always have been. You're braver than any of us. And you do things that no one else'd even think of. Like today."

"I wish I hadn't!"

Favor's breath was warm on her cheek. "So do I, because now I won't see you for ages and ages. But if anyone can get to Spoke, you can."

Goldie shook her head. "I'm so hungry I can't even think."

"Ma!" said Favor. "Where's the food?"

"I'm looking for it," said Frow Berg. "I don't suppose we could risk a light?"

"Absolutely n-n-n-not!"

"I wish we could hide you," whispered Favor. "But Pa says the Guardians will be sure to search—"

As if her words had somehow summoned them, there came sudden footsteps and a loud thumping on the front door.

"Open up!" shouted Guardian Hope. "Open in the name of the Seven!"

"Quick!" hissed Herro Berg. "G-get her out the back d-door! And Favor, into your b-bed! Chain yourself, they'll b-be sure to check!"

"Blessings, Goldie!" whispered Favor. "Hundreds and hundreds and *thousands* of Blessings!"

Then she was gone, and Frow Berg was urging Goldie through the dark house. Behind them the thumping on the front door grew louder.

"Yes, yes, I'm c-coming as quickly as I c-can!" called out Herro Berg in a pretend-sleepy voice.

"Oh, I don't know where I put that purse!" whispered Frow Berg frantically. "And there's no time to look now! Forgive me, dear! But here, at least I found a bread roll!"

She thrust something into Goldie's hand. Then she pulled the back door open just wide enough to squeeze through. "Go quickly!" she whispered. "Blessings! Blessings!"

With the faintest of clicks, the door closed on her kind face. And once again Goldie was alone.

THE SLAUGHTERBIRD

Frow Berg's bread roll tasted so wonderful that Goldie could hardly bear it. She finished it in half a dozen bites, and licked her fingers until every single crumb was gone. Then she huddled back in the shadows of Lame Poet's Bridge.

"Leave the city," Frow Berg had said. But how was she supposed to do that? And even if she managed to get out of Jewel onto the Spoke Road, she didn't have any money or food. What was she supposed to do, *walk* all that way? By *herself*?

Her legs started to shake again. The night closed in around

her. For a moment, she was almost overwhelmed with panic. Then she remembered Favor's words.

"You're braver than any of us. If anyone can do it, you can."

She knew that Favor was wrong. She wasn't brave at all. But her friend's faith in her was a small spot of calm in the middle of the panic.

She fumbled in her pocket and took out her compass. The needle glowed a bright luminous green, pointing back the way she had come. That must be north. So the Spoke Road must be *that* way. East.

Goldie climbed to her feet. She could have eaten another five bread rolls. She was still thirsty too, and the rippling of the water beneath the bridge was like torture. But she knew that the canals were salty and disease-ridden, and she made herself walk away from the sound.

The streets of Jewel at night were very different from their daytime selves. The houses seemed to loom over Goldie like living creatures. She kept thinking she heard footsteps, or the sinister sound of someone breathing close behind her. Her skin prickled, and she took out the scissors again and turned this way and that, trying to catch any sign of movement. But all she saw was shadows.

She was approaching one of the bridges over Dead Horse Canal when she heard someone whistling a tune. She froze. On the far side of the bridge, half hidden by the parapet, stood a man with his back to her.

As quietly as she could, Goldie tiptoed away. There was another bridge farther up the canal. She would cross there.

But when she reached the second bridge, she saw a dark figure leaning against the stone arch. A low whistle reached her ears. It was the same man!

Goldie shrank back into the shadows, holding the scissors out in front of her like a knife. Who was he? She could not see him clearly, but she thought perhaps he wore a black coatee, like the man who had been watching her in the street, and at the Separation ceremony. *Was* it him? Was he following her? What did he want with her?

She remembered the stories she had heard about the slaver, Captain Roop. About how clever he was at luring Separated children into his traps. About how innocent he seemed—right up until the last minute.

This man looked innocent enough. He had his back to her, as if he didn't know she was there. But he *did* know. She was sure of it. He was listening for her footsteps, even while he whistled, and for the breath in her lungs, and for the frightened beating of her heart. . . .

She slunk away, trying not to breathe. When she looked back, the man hadn't moved. Her heart settled a little.

But when she came to the next bridge, *he was already there*.

Suddenly, the night took on an even more sinister tone. Every shadow seemed to hide one of Captain Roop's men. Every sound was the scrape of Natkin Gull's oars. The man's whistling—had it changed? Was it a signal? Was Old Lady Skint closing in on her at this very moment?

Goldie crept back the way she had come. She wasn't going east anymore, but she didn't care. She just wanted to escape from the man in the black coatee.

But every time she thought she had got away from him, he appeared again.

On the other side of a plaza.

Or in a doorway.

Or in the middle of a street.

Not once did he turn and look at her. Not once did she see him move. But bit by bit he drove her through the dark city.

Goldie leaned against the wall of a cul-de-sac. She had been walking for ages, and she was too tired now to be afraid. Which was just as well because there was no way out of the little dead-end street, except the way she had come. And the man would surely be waiting for her if she tried to turn back.

With a groan, she slid down until she was sitting on the ground. She had no idea where she was. She remembered trudging up a hill, with rich-looking houses on either side of the road. But there were several hills in Jewel, and this could be any one of them.

Goldie didn't really care. She just wanted to lie down and sleep. If the slavers came, they'd have to carry her. She wasn't going a step farther.

But no sooner had she closed her eyes than a wisp of night breeze touched her face. Clinging to it was the unmistakable smell of freshly cooked almond cakes.

Goldie's eyes snapped open.

At the far end of the cul-de-sac was a small, ugly stone building. The grand houses on either side loomed over it, as if they were trying to cram it out of existence. But the ugly little building had a stubborn look to it, like an old man refusing to move from his favorite chair. The smell of the cakes seemed to be coming from its open doorway.

Goldie dragged herself to her feet and stumbled down the cul-de-sac and up the steps of the little building. The smell drew her onward like a promise. Through a dimly lit entrance hall. Under a stone archway. Up to the door of what looked like an office.

She had just enough sense left to pause on the threshold. The watergas lamps were lit, but the office was as deserted as the entrance hall. There was a rickety old desk in the middle of it, and there, piled high on a plate, were the almond cakes, with a bowl of milk next to them. Goldie stumbled forward and picked up the bowl, feeling as if she might die of happiness.

She gulped half the milk straight down and ate six cakes,

one after the other. Then she drank the rest of the milk and ate another three cakes. All the while, her eyes scanned the office.

It was small and cluttered. Bits of paper lay on every surface, weighed down with rocks and lumps of colored glass. Shelves overflowed with books and old coins and cracked porcelain statues. In one corner there was a small harp. And above the open door . . .

Goldie nearly choked on the cake she was eating. On a perch above the door sat an enormous stuffed bird. It was at least twenty times as big as the clockwork birds in the Great Hall. Its feathers were as black as sin, and its beak was cruel. Its yellow glass eyes seemed to glare at Goldie as if it blamed her for its death.

Goldie gasped aloud. "It's a slaughterbird! Just like the one on the Bridge of Beasts!"

Fascinated, she circled around underneath it. The bird stared into space. *If I reached up, I could touch its feathers!*

She shivered and backed away. She knew that she mustn't linger in this strange place. She took one last look around the office, and her eyes fell on the coins. There were so many of them, and they were in such untidy heaps that she was sure the owner wouldn't miss a few. And they would make her trip to Spoke so much easier.

I'm already a thief. I might as well steal something else.

She hurried over to the nearest shelf. Her fingers closed

around a small pile of coins. She slipped them into her pocket.

There was a rustling sound from the perch above the door. Goldie spun around, her heart banging against her ribs. The slaughterbird—the stuffed slaughterbird, the *dead* slaughterbird—unfolded its enormous wings and blinked down at her. Then it opened its beak and began to screech in a voice like rusty iron.

"Thie-e-e-ef!" screeched the slaughterbird. "Thie-e-e-ef! Thie-e-e-ef! Thie-e-e-ef!"

There was a thunder of footsteps in the corridor outside the office. A man's voice cried, "Got you!" And the door slammed shut, trapping Goldie and the slaughterbird inside.

Goldie was not the only thief in the city that night. As the Great Hall clock struck one, a man wearing a hooded cloak hurried down Old Arsenal Hill and slipped through the canal gate.

There was a small private water-rig moored at Old Arsenal Dock. The hooded man clambered into it and turned keys and gas switches until the motor came to life. The water-rig edged away from the dock and chugged quietly down the middle of the canal. When it came to Beast Dock, the man cut the motor and tied the rig to an iron ring.

Then he hurried up the steps and climbed the safety fence.

The Protectorate, when he came to it, was in darkness. He slipped around the side of the building and stopped at a small window. He took out a wafer-thin knife and eased it into the crack between the window and its frame. As gently as if he was tickling a baby, he wiggled the blade backward and forward. He swore under his breath at the slowness of it, but his hand remained steady.

There was a faint click, and the window swung outward. The man straddled the sill and dropped down into the storeroom below. He fumbled past shelves and boxes to the open door, and then along the lightless corridor and up a short flight of stairs. He bumped his shins a dozen times before he found the room he was looking for.

When he *did* find it, he closed the heavy curtains and felt his way around the walls to the nearest watergas lamp. He took a tinderbox from his pocket, lifted the mantle of the lamp, turned the gas wheel and lit the wick. With a hiss, the lamp sprang to life, revealing the well-worn furniture of the Protector's office. The hooded man hurried over to the bookcases and began to inspect the rows of documents that lined their shelves.

It was almost dawn before he found what he was looking for. By then he was getting worried. The cleaners would be on the streets soon, and he must be gone before they saw him.

With a curse, he replaced the book he had just inspected,

and put his hand on the slim blue volume that sat beside it. It was called *The Dirty Gate*, and he had already passed over it several times because of the nonsensical title.

But now he was running out of choices. He flicked the book open. Expecting nothing, he began to read the first page. . . .

THE CRIMINAL CHILD

Goldie sat in the corner of the office, as far away from the slaughterbird as she could get. She had a chair wedged in front of her and the scissors in her hand. Her head ached, and she was sick with fear and exhaustion.

No one came for her. She kept expecting the door to burst open and admit half a dozen slavers, or perhaps Guardian Hope and Guardian Comfort. And by the time the small window above her head began to lighten with the coming dawn, she would almost have welcomed them.

The slaughterbird had slept for much of the night. But

now it was awake again, clacking its beak and peering down at her with its wicked head tilted to one side. "Thie-e-e-ef. Thie-e-e-ef," it muttered.

At last Goldie heard footsteps outside the office. Someone whistled a horribly familiar tune. Goldie struggled to her feet, clutching the scissors. "If it's slavers, I'll fight!" she whispered to the slaughterbird, although she had no idea *how* to fight.

The door swung open, and a tall, thin man in a black coatee stepped into the room. Goldie's fingers whitened on the scissors. It *was* the man from the Separation ceremony. The one who had been watching her. The one who had driven her through the city against her will. And now he had her trapped.

The man's face was as forbidding as stone. "You've stolen something," he said. "What was it?"

"Nothing!" said Goldie quickly.

Above the doorway the slaughterbird shifted on its perch. Goldie flinched. The man looked up. "Morg," he said. "Come here."

The slaughterbird peered down at him. Then, with a great clumsy hop, it dropped onto his shoulder.

Goldie gasped. The man called out, "Olga Ciavolga, if you please!"

An old woman appeared beside him. She wore a knitted jerkin and half a dozen skirts, each one brightly colored and clashing with the ones above and below it. Her gray hair floated around her face. She looked sharply at Goldie, and held out her arm. The slaughterbird hopped onto it and she carried it away.

The man turned back to Goldie. "The bird has an instinct for thievery. She can sense it at a thousand paces, or through heavy fog. She's never wrong. I ask you again, what have you stolen?"

Goldie's face grew hot. "The cakes," she mumbled. "I was hungry."

The man raised an eyebrow as if the cakes didn't matter in the slightest and he was surprised that she had mentioned them. "What else?"

"Nothing else!"

The man's eyes were merciless. "Turn out your pockets."

The skin on Goldie's face felt like glass. Slowly, she put her hand in the wrong pocket and pulled out first her kerchief, then her compass, and finally the bird brooch.

"Your *other* pocket," said the man.

Goldie stared at the floor. She put her hand in her other pocket—and pulled out the coins.

The man's tongue clicked in satisfaction. "*Those*," he said, "are five-hundred-year-old gold sovereigns."

Goldie gasped again. The man folded his awkward arms across his chest. "Well, now—"

There were footsteps in the corridor outside. A loud voice

cried, "Hello? Hello?" A second, deeper voice shouted, "Is there anyone in this forsaken place?"

It was Guardian Hope and Guardian Comfort! Goldie shrank back into the corner. There would be no mercy now. This strange man would hand her over to the Blessed Guardians and tell them about the coins. She trembled at the thought of how they would punish her.

But to her astonishment, the man put his finger to his lips. "Shhh!" he breathed, and pointed to the narrow space under the desk. It was only when she was safely hidden that he called out, "In here!"

Goldie held her breath. All she could see were the man's long trousers and scuffed brown boots. The footsteps came to the door and stopped.

"Welcome to the Museum of Dunt!" cried the man. His voice was completely different now. All the severity was gone, and he sounded slightly foolish. "My name is Sinew! Are you after a guided tour? You've come to the right place! Here you can trawl to your heart's content through the city's long and glorious history." He coughed in an embarrassed sort of way. "Well, most of it. We *are* missing a few years here and there, and the labels seem to have gone astray—we have a veritable *plague* of silverfish! But our keepers are always happy to—"

Guardian Hope interrupted him. "Who's in charge here? I wish to see your Resident Guardian."

"Alas, we don't have one."

"*All* public buildings have a Resident Guardian, by order of the Fugleman. As from last night."

"Oh, the fortunate creatures," burbled Sinew, sounding sillier than ever. "If only we could be so privileged! Alas again, we are not. By order of the Protector. Perhaps we're simply too small and unimportant to bother with such things."

There was a moment's silence. Then Guardian Hope said, "We're searching for a runaway child. A criminal child. A girl."

Goldie pressed herself against the cool wood of the desk. Above her head Sinew said, "Great whistling pigs! A criminal? In our glorious city? Who'd have thought it? A murderer perhaps? An arsonist? A . . . thief?"

"Being a runaway," said Guardian Comfort in his most mournful voice, "is a criminal act in itself. Her parents will go before the Court of the Seven Blessings this morning. They'll be tried and sentenced for bringing up such a child. There's no question of their guilt. Their possessions will be confiscated and they'll be sent to the House of Repentance."

Underneath the desk, Goldie nearly cried out in horror. Ma and Pa on *trial*? Ma and Pa going to *prison*? Because of *her*?

The floor of the office seemed to fall away beneath her. What had she done? She must go to them! She must go now and tell the court that it wasn't their fault at all, it was hers, and hers alone!

But before she could scramble to her feet, one of Sinew's boots came down firmly on her leg. She put her hand over her mouth and swallowed her cry.

"You're not interested in thieves, then?" said Sinew. "Not interested in a smash-and-grab raid on almond cakes?"

"Have you seen this girl?" said Guardian Hope impatiently. "You must inform us immediately if you do."

"What'll you do if you catch her?" said Sinew. "Flog her? Cut off her fingers? Brand her on the forehead? That's what they would've done once. Ah, the old days, the good days!"

Goldie's eyes widened. *Cut off my fingers?*

"Don't be ridiculous," snapped Guardian Hope. "We won't harm her. We'll simply . . . reeducate her."

"Aha! Brainwashing! Glad to hear the city is in such kind hands." Sinew's big feet moved away from the desk. Goldie heard him say, "Well now, plenty of places on Old Arsenal Hill where a runaway might be hiding. Some of the nearby mansions—"

"Oh, we're not finished here," interrupted Guardian Comfort. "The Fugleman has instructed us to search all public buildings *thoroughly*."

"Then we are honored indeed!" said Sinew. He sounded as if he was bowing. "Allow me to escort you in your search."

"We don't need an escort," said Guardian Hope.

"Are you sure? Well, you know best. Call for help if you need it. I'll show you where to start. Here we go, turn left, then right, and you're in the first display room."

His voice faded as he ushered the two Blessed Guardians out of the office.

Beneath the desk, Goldie stared at the remains of the silk ribbon on her wrist. How could she have been so stupid? Of *course* the Blessed Guardians would blame Ma and Pa for what she had done! Of *course* they would punish them! She should have realized. She should have *thought*!

In a fit of revulsion she tore the scrap of ribbon from her wrist. The Fugleman was right. She was foolish and wicked. She *deserved* to be in punishment chains.

"Ssst!" It was Sinew, back already. He bent down so that his long nose was just in front of hers. "The museum will keep them busy for a while," he whispered. "Come with me!"

Goldie dragged herself out from under the desk and followed him from the office. Halfway down a dim corridor, he stopped and called softly, "Herro Dan? We have her." Then he strode back the way he had come.

"So we found you, lass," said a voice in Goldie's ear. She spun around. An old man with a broad nose and skin the color of nutmeg was standing behind her. He wore a tattered blue coat with brass buttons down the front, and he was smiling.

"Come along and I'll show you a place to sleep," he said. "Come on now, stay close!"

Goldie was too tired and heartsick to wonder why these people were willing to take the risk of hiding her. She followed the old man through the museum in a daze.

There was no sign of the glorious history that Sinew had promised the Blessed Guardians. Instead, the rooms seemed to be full of nothing but rubbish. There were torn paintings and cracked chairs. There were clocks with their pendulums missing and their hands stuck in some far distant past. There were broken bottles and rocks and empty jars.

It was the most uninteresting place that Goldie had ever seen, which was good. She didn't *want* to be interested. She wanted to worry about Ma and Pa and blame herself for what had happened to them. She wanted to feel unhappy and worthless.

And yet . . .

The old man stopped outside a water closet and waited while she had a pee and splashed cold water on her face. It was as she was coming out again that the strange thing happened. Suddenly the whole building seemed to . . . *shift*. As if a huge sleeping beast had woken up, turned around and gone back to sleep again.

Goldie stopped in her tracks. There was a wooden cabinet full of glass jars in front of her. A moment ago they had been empty. But now each one held the fat, scaly coils of a dead snake. She blinked at them in astonishment.

Behind the glass, one of the snakes raised a narrow eyelid and blinked back.

"Shivers!" Goldie squeaked with fright.

Herro Dan patted her arm reassuringly. Then he laid his hand on the nearest wall and began to sing. His voice rumbled up and down in odd sliding notes that made the hair on the back of Goldie's neck stand up.

"*Ho oh oh-oh,*" sang the old man. "*Mm mm oh oh oh-oh oh.*"

Curious, Goldie laid her own hand on the wall. . . .

The moment she did so, she heard—no, she *felt*—music. Deep, wild music. It seemed to rage up from the center of the earth and pour into her like boiling water. She snatched her hand away, feeling as if she had been scalded.

In their jars, the snakes floated in a sea of yellow liquid. Their eyes were closed, and their scales were peeling. They had obviously been dead for a long, long time.

I must've imagined it, thought Goldie. *But it looked so real. . . .*

The old man stopped singing and took his hand off the wall. His cheerful face was serious. "Trouble's taken a step closer," he murmured. "Can you feel it, lass?"

Without waiting for an answer, he led the way through another couple of rooms to a closed door with STAFF ONLY written on it in faded letters. He took a key from his pocket, unlocked the door and ushered Goldie through it.

Behind the door there was a mattress and a pile of quilts. "You'll be safe here in the back rooms," said the old man. "This door's always locked. Guardians won't catch you here."

Goldie wasn't at all sure that a locked door would be enough to keep Guardian Hope out. But she was too tired to argue. With a sigh she sank down onto the mattress. Then she crawled under the thinnest quilt and fell instantly asleep.

A MISSION FROM HIS HONOR

Guardian Hope did not know why the Fugleman wanted them to search this ugly little building. "Tell them you're looking for the missing girl," he had said when he called them to his office earlier this morning. "But keep your eyes open for anything suspicious. Anything out of place, or strange."

No offense to His Honor, but the only out-of-place thing that Hope was interested in was the runaway girl, and *she* was probably holed up somewhere in the Old Quarter of the city, near where she lived. Which meant that one of Hope's colleagues would have the pleasure of catching her, when it should have been Hope herself.

But when Sinew confessed that the museum didn't have a Resident Guardian, a worm of curiosity uncoiled inside Hope. She didn't let her interest show on her face. She was too cunning for that, oh my word, yes. Instead, she kept questioning Sinew about the girl, as if that was the true reason for their being here and not just a pretense.

And now she was on a mission from His Honor! She could hardly wait to carry out his instructions. She stalked through the drab rooms, peering into every corner, poking behind the broken display cases, looking for things that were *out of place,* or *strange.*

At the same time, she allowed a corner of her mind to slip into her favorite daydream, the one where she was part of the Fugleman's inner circle, where she had power and importance and influence. If she did this job properly, that dream might well come true. . . .

"Haven't we been through this room already?" said Comfort.

"What?" said Hope, jolted out of her fantasy.

"Look at that cupboard with the smashed doors. We were here just a few minutes ago."

"Nonsense," said Hope, glad of the excuse to needle him. "We haven't retraced our steps, have we, colleague? We haven't turned aside at any point? We haven't been *spirited away* by *demons?*"

She laughed briefly at her own wit, then settled back into seriousness. "I think you'll find I have an excellent sense of direction. Keep your mind on the job."

Comfort's face closed in a barely concealed sulk, and he strode through the nearest doorway without waiting to see if Hope was following.

Twenty minutes later, Hope found herself standing in front of the broken cupboard once again.

"There," said Comfort smugly. "I told you so."

"Self-righteousness," said Hope, "is a sin. I'd hate to have to report you, colleague."

"I wasn't being self-righteous, colleague," smirked Comfort. "I was merely pointing out that we're going in circles. That's a fact, is it not? It's clear enough to me."

"What's clear to *me*, colleague, is that you have brought us astray. It *was* you who led the way out of this room, was it not? You must've taken a wrong turn. Perhaps you weren't concentrating."

Comfort's sallow face reddened. "I'd like to see you do better, colleague."

"And so you shall, colleague. So you shall."

Hope fully intended to take them back to the office. Despite what she had said to Comfort, she found the rooms confusing. If she could get hold of a floor plan, it would help them to be more efficient in their search.

She didn't realize straight away that they were lost. She led the way through room after room, retracing the way they had come. But somehow, instead of reaching the office, they ended up back at the broken cupboard.

Hope snorted in surprise and annoyance. She set off again, back through the gloomy rooms with Comfort hurrying along behind her. Around the glass cases. Through this doorway. Through that doorway. Turn right here. Turn left there. . . .

And there was the broken cupboard again! Hope glared at it, suspecting that it was mocking her in some way.

Comfort cleared his throat. "Perhaps it's time to summon help—"

"Ridiculous," said Hope. "Ridiculous!" And she set off once more. Back through the gloomy rooms. Around the glass cases. Through this doorway. Through that doorway. Turn right here. Turn left there. . . .

In the end, she let Comfort shout for help. She wouldn't normally have given up like that, but they were wasting time, and so she was not displeased to see Sinew hurrying toward them.

"These rooms!" he cried out as he approached. "They all look the same! Don't feel bad, Guardians. Even the keepers get lost almost daily. Sometimes I think we should paint little tracklets on the floors, all in different colors, and then we could follow them to wherever we were going. But what if we got lost while we painted the tracklets, and *they* went around in circles? Ha ha ha!"

The man was even more of a fool than Comfort, but at least he managed to get them back to the office. Hope commandeered the chair behind the desk and, with Comfort at her shoulder, began to ask questions.

At first she tried to make them sound casual. How old was the museum? Who started it? Where did the exhibits come from?

But Sinew's answers were so vague that she quickly lost patience with him and began to snap out questions one after the other, as if she was conducting an examination.

Exactly *how many* rooms were there? What was in them? How many of them were locked? Who had the keys? Where did *this* door lead to? Where did *that* door lead to? How many employees did the museum have? How long had they been here? Where did they sleep? Where did they eat?

At last, irritated beyond measure by Sinew's useless answers, she said, "I wish to see your records."

"Our what?" said Sinew.

"In the last couple of hours," said Hope, "I've seen broken glass. I've seen loose rocks that any passerby could pick up and throw. I've seen chairs that would collapse under the first person who sat on them. This building is a death trap, and there may well be an unSeparated child loose on the premises. If I'm to find her, I'll need your records. Your pay sheets. Your floor plans."

Sinew nodded uncertainly. "Will the records for the last five years be enough?"

"That'll do for a start. Go and fetch them. Quickly now."

Sinew wandered out of the office, looking as if he had already forgotten what he was about. Comfort leaned down and murmured in Hope's ear. "Under the desk."

Hope slid her chair out a little way and peered beneath the desk. And there, tucked into a corner, so grubby that it was almost (but not quite) beyond recognition, was a scrap of white silk Separation ribbon.

"Ah!" said Hope. And she pressed her lips together so that Comfort wouldn't see how pleased she was.

THE BRIZZLEHOUND

"Why are they asking all those questions? What do they want? Here, wake up, I'm talking to you! What do they *want?*"

Goldie yawned and mumbled, "Go away, Jube! What are you doing in my bedroom, anyway?"

She stretched, expecting to feel the tug of the guardchain. It didn't come. Her eyes flew open. . . .

Kneeling beside her was a boy. His face was dirty. His black hair stood up in spikes. And on his shoulder—so close that Goldie could see its wrinkled eyelid, could smell the musty stink of its feathers—sat the slaughterbird!

She tried to scramble off the other side of the mattress, but the boy grabbed her arm. "Why do your Guardians want to see our records?"

"Let *go* of me!"

The boy shrugged and let go. "Suit yourself," he said. But the slaughterbird on his shoulder blinked its wicked eyes at Goldie as if she had no *right* to suit herself. No right at all.

Goldie stumbled to her feet. "Well?" said the boy. "Why are they so interested in our records?"

"Reco-o-o-ords," croaked the slaughterbird. Its great beak was only inches from the boy's face, but he hardly seemed to notice.

Goldie tried to gather her scattered wits together. "I—I don't know!"

The boy shook his head in disgust. "They've never taken any notice of us before. But they're here now, and it's all your fault."

When she heard those words, the last scraps of sleep fell away, and Goldie remembered what she had done. . . .

For a moment, she couldn't move with the awfulness of it. Ma and Pa were to be tried and sent to the House of Repentance. And it was all her fault.

She swallowed. "I'll have to go back," she whispered, feeling sick at the thought.

"Back where?" said the boy.

"Whe-e-e-e-ere," croaked the slaughterbird.

75

"To—to the Guardians. I—I'll tell them that it was just me." Goldie bit her lip. "They should imprison *me* and let Ma and Pa go."

She tried the door that led to the museum's front rooms, but it was locked. "Have you got a key?"

"Maybe," said the boy. "Maybe not." And he turned and walked off.

Goldie ran after him, keeping well away from the slaughterbird. "Didn't you hear me? I'm going to give myself up."

"Oh, that'll *really* help," said the boy sarcastically.

Goldie flushed. "You can't keep me here, not against my will."

"No one's keeping you anywhere," said the boy.

"Yes, you are. The door's locked!"

"Can't you get past a little thing like a locked door?" The boy snorted. "I don't know why Sinew thinks you're going to be so useful."

Goldie stopped dead. She had almost forgotten that she wasn't here by chance, that she had been led here. *Driven* here. "Useful?" she said. "What do you mean?"

"Nothing," said the boy over his shoulder.

"Why did Sinew bring me here? Why did he hide me? What does he want?"

"No-o-o-o-o-o-o-o-othi-i-i-i-ing," mocked the slaughterbird.

"I *am* going back," Goldie called after them.

The boy heaved a loud sigh and turned around. "Look," he said. "You can do what you like, for all I care. If you love your precious Guardians so much, go and throw yourself on their mercy—"

"I *don't* love them! I hate them!"

"— but it won't do your parents any good." His voice was bitter now. "They'll still be sent to the House of Repentance. And it'll only make things worse for them, knowing that you're in Care."

"Ca-a-a-a-a-a-a-a-a-are."

Goldie didn't want to believe him. But deep in her heart she knew that he was right. Once the Blessed Guardians got their hands on someone, they did not let go.

Oh, Pa! Oh, Ma! I'm so sorry!

She could have wept then, out of fear and guilt and fury, but the boy and the bird were watching her. So she said, as calmly as she could, "Well then, I—I—I'll go to Spoke."

"A lot of good that'll do," said the boy, turning away again. "At least if you stay here you might be able to help." He sniffed. "Though I doubt it."

"Help?" said Goldie. "You mean help Ma and Pa? How?"

The only answer was a derisive croak from the slaughter-bird, and before long the boy and the bird were out of sight, hidden by rows of cabinets and display cases.

Goldie tried the door again, though she knew it would not

open. She felt as if she was teetering on the blade of a knife. On one side of the blade lay Spoke, and Ma's relatives, and safety, if she could reach it. On the other side was the museum with its unanswered questions and its dangers (a *slaughter*bird!)—and the possibility that she might be able to help . . .

When she caught up with the boy, he didn't seem at all pleased to see her. The bird on his shoulder looked bigger and blacker and more terrifying than ever.

"Um . . . what's its name?" said Goldie.

"She," said the boy. "Morg is a *she*, not an *it*."

"Mo-o-o-o-o-o-o-org." The slaughterbird ruffled its feathers and glared at Goldie.

She took a step backward. "Does it—does she bite?"

The boy's mouth twisted in an unpleasant smile. "Yes. She likes eyes especially. If you were lying on the ground with a broken leg, she'd wait until you were too weak to fight her off, then she'd peck your eyes out one by one. Plop. Plop."

He's trying to scare me, thought Goldie. *He doesn't know that I'm scared half to death already.*

"That sort of thing doesn't happen," she said. "Not nowadays. Not here."

The boy shook his head as if he couldn't believe how stupid she was. "You think you're still in Jewel," he said, "but you're not. You're in the museum now—and *anything* can happen."

78

The back rooms of the museum were very different from the front. The ceilings were high, and the walls were lined with huge gilt-framed paintings of soldiers with long side-whiskers, and fat-faced queens in old-fashioned dresses.

One of the paintings seemed to stand out from the others. "Who's that?" said Goldie, pointing to a young girl in brightly polished armor with a sword and longbow in her hands. On a banner above the girl's head, a black wolf snarled.

"Some old princess," said the boy.

"She's not old."

The boy rolled his eyes. "I meant olden days. She was some sort of warrior, hundreds of years ago."

Goldie looked closer. The painting was cracked with age, but the girl seemed to stare proudly back at her. "Princess Frisia?"

"Who's she?"

"You know, the children's story. The warrior princess of Merne."

"How should I know?" The boy shrugged and kept walking.

Goldie hurried to keep up with him. "Where are we going?" she said.

"None of your business."

"How am I supposed to help?"

"None of your business."

"What's your name?" She looked more closely at him. "I've seen you somewhere before, haven't I? Didn't you use to live in the Old Quarter? Near Gunboat Canal? What are you doing here?"

"None of your business."

The display cases that they passed held suits of armor and skeletons and whips with knotted lashes. Between them were piles of whaling pots and boneshaker bicycles and old wooden carts. Everything was coated in a thick layer of dust. Spiderwebs hung from the rafters.

Goldie had never imagined that such a place could exist within the boundaries of Jewel. She thought of her parents' warnings and shivered. *Poisonous insects . . . dust . . . purple fever . . .*

"What's that?" she asked, pointing at something made of iron, with cruel, spiky jaws.

"Mantrap," said the boy, and he grinned at the look on her face.

Above Goldie's head a whale skeleton groaned as if it was dreaming of the sea. The hair of a stuffed water rat stirred. Something flapped leathery wings. With each movement, with each sound, her skin prickled.

But at the same time the blood surged through her veins, and she had never felt so alive. *I've been asleep!* she thought. *I've been asleep all my life, and now I'm waking up!*

The rooms seemed to go on and on. Goldie knew that the museum couldn't possibly be this big, but still it stretched in front of her. The doorways that they passed through were as wide as boulevards. The glass cases formed a never-ending line.

And then they went through a doorway, and it was as if they had stepped out into the very middle of a road. Except that the ceiling was still there, high above them. And there were no roads like this in Jewel.

Directly in front of them was a vacant block. It was covered in thornberry bushes and deep shadows. In the middle of it was an enormous tree, and cradled in the branches of the tree was a little wooden house, with a rickety ladder leading up to it.

Goldie had never seen anything quite so interesting. She took a step toward the tree—and stopped. Right at her feet, so close that Ma and Pa would have had heartstroke if they had seen it, was a ditch.

A huge ditch, more than twice her height, with water in the bottom.

Dirty water.

Filthy water.

Disease-ridden, child-drowning water . . .

And suddenly everything that had happened to Goldie in the last day and a half caught up with her. Her excitement drained away, and all that was left was fear. She stood staring at the ditch with her mouth open and her head awash with warnings.

"What's the matter?" said the boy, who was already scrambling down one side of the ditch and up the other. "Are you scared?"

"Um . . . no."

"Yes, you are."

"I'm not!"

"I knew you'd be useless," the boy said. And, without a backward glance, he disappeared into the shadows of the vacant block, with Morg on his shoulder.

Goldie didn't know what to do. At first she thought she'd wait there until he came back. Then she heard a faint creaking noise, as if someone was tiptoeing toward her, and she decided that it would be better to go and find Sinew or Herro Dan.

But the thought of walking all by herself through the dim rooms, with the creaking sound trailing along behind her, made her feel sick. So in the end she stayed where she was.

The roaring seemed to come from nowhere. Bright headlights sprang out of the shadows at the far end of the road. A horn wailed. Goldie stared in astonishment. It was a streetrig. And it was coming straight toward her.

Time seemed to slow down then. Goldie could hear the boy shouting in the distance, but she didn't move. She felt as if she was dreaming—as if this was happening to someone else, and she was watching it all from far, far away.

The boy shouted again. And out of the shadows of the vacant block rose—something. Something that took one look at Goldie and began to lope toward her. Something with red eyes and slavering jaws. Something that opened its mouth and bayed! The sound joined with the wail of the street-rig's horn and crashed off the high ceiling like thunder.

This is silly, thought Goldie, in a dreamy sort of way. *The street-rig's going to kill me. I don't need a brizzlehound as well.*

In the same dreamy way, she wondered which of them would get to her first. She wondered which would hurt more. She wondered if this was her punishment for trying to steal the gold coins, and if Sinew had been planning it all along.

The street-rig was almost upon her now. So was the brizzlehound. It took the ditch in one great leap. Its eyes burned. It opened its awful jaws—

In that moment, Goldie came to her senses. With a desperate cry, she tried to throw herself out of the way. But she was too late. The brizzlehound swerved to meet her. Its teeth snagged in her smock. Its weight knocked her flying. Her knees crumpled and she fell sideways, down, down, down into the ditch.

The last thing she heard before she sank into unconsciousness was the sound of the street-rig rumbling past above her. The last thing she felt was the hot breath of the brizzlehound on her face. . . .

83

DOG GERMS

The Fugleman was smiling. He had a particularly charming smile that he used whenever he wanted to persuade people to do things that they really shouldn't do.

He was using it now on the lieutenant marshal of militia.

"I wish to congratulate you, sir," he said, "on your fine work searching for the bombers who took the life of one of our children. We humble citizens of Jewel are grateful for your devotion to duty."

The lieutenant marshal flushed and stared at the floor of

the Fugleman's temporary office. "I—I regret, Your Honor, that I haven't taken part in the search."

"Nooo?" The Fugleman raised his eyebrows. "I would have thought that *every* man of value would be called upon in such desperate times!"

"The Protector . . . she no longer trusts me, Your Honor. Because of the runaway girl. And the scissors. It seems there's a good chance I'll be—" He bit his lip. "I'll be court-martialed. It looks as if my career is . . ." His voice trailed off.

"But surely the Protector does not blame *you* for what happened?"

"She does, Your Honor. And so she should. It was my fault—"

"How could it be *your* fault?" cried the Fugleman. "Are you in charge of the city's children? Can you, a military man, be expected to act as nursemaid? No, I won't hear of it! If it's anyone's fault, it's mine! I should have expected such a thing to happen. I should have been watching more closely."

"That's very generous of you to say so, Your Honor, but—"

"But it's true! When is this court-martial to be? I shall come along and speak on your behalf."

The lieutenant marshal looked up, his face filled with unexpected hope. "Would you, Your Honor? That could make all the difference!"

"Consider it done." The Fugleman waved his hand. "The city can't afford to lose such valuable men."

"I can't thank you enough, Your Honor! If there's ever anything I can do to repay you—"

"No need, no need. It's my pleasure—"

The Fugleman broke off, as if something had just struck him. "Although, now that I think of it," he said, arranging his face into a thoughtful expression, "there *is* something you could do. In my position it's not easy to find a man I can talk to. An intelligent man who won't broadcast my thoughts to the world . . ."

"You can say what you like to me, Your Honor," said the lieutenant marshal eagerly. "I'm as close-mouthed as a stone."

"Are you indeed? Well, then . . ." The Fugleman traced the edge of his desk with his finger, letting the moment stretch out. "Her Grace the Protector," he said at last, "does an *excellent* job of running the city."

"She does, Your Honor! I have every respect for her."

"But sometimes I fear—" The Fugleman broke off and shook his head. "No, I shouldn't say it. I'm sure it's nothing. I'm sure her judgment is as good as ever—"

He stopped again. The lieutenant marshal blinked at him. The Fugleman sighed inwardly. It seemed that he was going to have to spell the whole thing out.

"The thing is," he said, "I don't think the Protector

understands *quite* how much danger the city may be in. Some of the militia are out searching for the bombers, it's true. But what are the rest doing? Opening doors. Forming an honor guard. Helping old ladies across the road."

The lieutenant marshal nodded uncertainly. "Her Grace believes that it's important to keep things as normal as possible. To reassure the people—"

"This is no time for normal!" cried the Fugleman, suddenly thumping the desk. "Forget honor guards! The day is fast approaching when the Seven Gods will require *real* service! The sort where you and your men march home covered in wealth and glory, with the crowds shouting your name from one end of the city to the other!"

By now, the lieutenant marshal's eyes were as wide as a baby's. He licked his lips. He opened his mouth to speak—

The Fugleman held up his hand. The charming smile slipped back onto his face, as smooth as a conjurer's trick. He stood up and walked around the desk.

"Of course we hope that such a day never comes," he said, putting his hand on the lieutenant marshal's shoulder. "After all, despite yesterday's bombing, we are still at peace, and long may we stay that way! But if there *should* turn out to be a serious threat to the city"—he raised his smile another notch—"then I will need men about me whom I can trust."

With that, he pushed the lieutenant marshal out the door.

"Come and see me again when you have thought about this," he said. "Take your time. No hurry."

He turned back to his desk, humming with satisfaction. The militiaman was a fool, like all of his sister's minions. But he was also ambitious. And there was nothing more useful than an ambitious fool.

Goldie was wet and cold, and every part of her body ached. She lay very still, trying to remember what had happened.

Somewhere nearby, the boy was talking. "She could have been killed! Why didn't she get out of the way?"

"You were like that when you first came here," said a deep, gravelly voice. "You could not take care of yourself. You waited for someone to rescue you."

"I was never that stupid!"

"I remember the time when you—"

Goldie shifted her leg, and her sandals squelched in the mud.

"Shhh!" said the boy. "I think she's awake!"

There was a brief scuffle and the sound of running feet. Then Sinew's voice said, "Great whistling pigs! What happened, Toadspit? Is she hurt?"

Slowly, Goldie opened her eyes. She was lying under the

tree in the middle of the vacant block, with Sinew and the boy crouched beside her. There was no sign of the person with the gravelly voice.

"Are you all right?" said Sinew, his face lined with concern. "Have you broken anything?"

Goldie moved her arms and legs carefully. "I —I don't think so," she said.

Sinew helped her sit up, then he took off his coatee and put it around her shoulders. He looked severely at the boy. "Toadspit, I thought we told you to take care of her."

"She was all right when I left her," protested Toadspit. "Then the Shark came roaring out of nowhere, and she didn't have the sense to get out of the way!"

Despite Sinew's coatee, Goldie had suddenly begun to shiver so violently that she could hardly speak. "It was a s-street-rig," she said, "not a sh-shark! And there was a b-b-b-brizzlehound! A real, live *b-brizzlehound*! It tried to k-kill me!"

"Not *a* shark," said Toadspit. "*The* Shark."

"It's the name of Herro Dan's street-rig," said Sinew. "But it's not like Dan to drive so carelessly."

"He wasn't driving," said Toadspit. "There was no one in it at all."

Sinew raised a startled eyebrow. "Are you sure?"

"I'm not blind, Sinew. The Shark was roaming around on its own!"

Goldie stared at them both in disbelief. "Didn't you *hear* me? There was a *brizzlehound*!"

Before anyone could answer her there was a puff of wind, and Olga Ciavolga and Herro Dan came hurrying across the vacant block. Between them, to Goldie's amazement, trotted a dog. A little white dog with one black ear and a curly tail that waved over its back like a flag.

Goldie had never seen a real live dog before. Dogs carried diseases, and quite often they went mad and bit people. There hadn't been a dog in Jewel for more than two hundred years.

Toadspit must have seen the expression on her face, because he frowned and said, "That's Broo. He saved your life. You should be grateful."

Goldie looked at him blankly.

"He knocked you into the ditch," said Toadspit. "You were just standing there! The Shark would've run you over."

It seemed to Goldie that the boy was talking in riddles. She shook her head in angry confusion. "It was the *brizzlehound* that knocked me into the ditch. And it wasn't trying to save me. It was trying to *kill* me!"

Sinew cleared his throat. "The shadows are deep in this part of the museum, and the light is uncertain. The noise and the headlights would have made it even worse. A small dog could easily appear monstrous."

"No!" said Goldie. "That's not what happened!"

But when she looked around, trying to remember the moment when that . . . that *thing* had risen up out of the thornberry bushes, she found that it was already fading into a confused blur. The shadows *were* deep. The light *was* uncertain. Could it have been a little dog?

No.

I don't know. . . .

Maybe.

Olga Ciavolga leaned down and patted Broo on the head. "You are a clever boy." She had a slight accent, as if she had been born somewhere other than the Faroon Peninsula. "Tonight you get extra bones."

The little dog wriggled with pleasure and wagged his tail.

"But what's this about the Shark?" Herro Dan's kind face was worried. He squatted down next to Goldie. "Is it true, lass? Did me street-rig nearly run you down?"

Goldie nodded.

"By my life, I'm sorry," said the old man.

"*Tsk,* what good is sorry if she is squashed?" muttered Olga Ciavolga.

"I wouldn't have had this happen for the world," Herro Dan said to Goldie. "The old Shark's never gone off by itself before."

"So why now?" said Sinew.

"Reckon it's this trouble," said Herro Dan, getting to his feet again. "It's stirrin' things up. Old dangers. New ones too, from the look of things. We best be on our guard, all of us."

"You should've heard the Shark's horn!" said Toadspit. "It was howling like a lost baby."

"And lost we shall be," said Olga Ciavolga sharply, "if we do nothing but be on our guard! We must discover where this trouble is coming from, and stop it!"

Herro Dan nodded. "Sinew, tomorrow you go out into the city again. Talk to everyone you know. Ask questions. The bombin', start with that, it has to be part of it—"

Goldie's head was beginning to throb, and the water from the ditch felt as if it had seeped into her bones. She sniffed unhappily. Everyone seemed to have forgotten about her. Maybe they'd decided that she wouldn't be useful after all. If only Ma and Pa were here! A tear trickled down her cheek at the thought of them.

The little dog gazed up at her with his head cocked to one side and his curly tail stirring the air. His black eyes were sympathetic, as if he knew exactly how she was feeling.

Goldie tried to tell herself that she should be afraid of him. But she was already covered in mud and dirty water, and she probably had purple fever or lockjaw. And Ma and Pa were going to prison and it was all her fault.

A few dog germs can't make things any worse.

She put her hand out and the little dog sniffed it. Cautiously, she stroked his ear. It was warmer and silkier than she expected.

"Broo," she whispered, trying out his name. The little dog wagged his tail so furiously that his whole body wagged with it. Then, before Goldie could stop him, he jumped into her lap, put his paws on her shoulders and began to lick her face with his hot tongue.

Goldie closed her eyes and tried not to think about how she had nearly died, waiting for someone to come along and save her. She shivered. *I'll never do that again,* she thought. *Next time I'll save myself.*

"So, did the Blessed Guardians find anything in our records to satisfy their curiosity?" said Olga Ciavolga.

It was late at night, and the three keepers were doing their rounds.

"Dust. Silverfish. A cockroach or two," said Sinew, who carried his harp slung over his shoulder. "Nothing useful. They've gone now. I doubt they'll be back."

He yawned. Olga Ciavolga peered up at him. "You should be asleep," she said, "like the children."

"She's right, Sinew," said Herro Dan. "You got a lot to do tomorrow. Won't be easy, tryin' to track those bombers."

Sinew smiled faintly, but said nothing. The three of them walked on, down a long corridor of marble statues.

· "Maybe it was a mistake," said Sinew, when they were halfway down the corridor, "bringing Goldie here at a time like this."

"*Tsk*, it was no mistake," said Olga Ciavolga. "Where else would she go?"

"It's so dangerous for a child," said Sinew. "It's bad enough that Toadspit's here. I'd send him home if I could."

"You know as well as I do," said Olga Ciavolga severely, "that if we do not find the source of this trouble, and stop it, then both Goldie and Toadspit will be in danger wherever they are. No one in the city will be safe."

"But I don't—"

Olga Ciavolga laid her hand on his arm. Her face softened. "Broo likes her, and that counts for much. Tomorrow I will take her to Harry Mount and let the museum test her."

"Then we'll tell her why we brought her here," said Herro Dan, "and leave the rest up to her."

"Well, of course!" said Olga Ciavolga. "Did you think I was going to force her? Am I a Blessed Guardian now?"

"Ha!" said Herro Dan. "You, a Blessed Guardian? Now, *that* I'd like to see!"

"You think I would not be good at it?" Olga Ciavolga glared at him, but her mouth twitched as if she was trying not to smile.

"I reckon you'd keep 'em all on their toes—"

He broke off. The watergas lamps on the walls suddenly flickered as if their wicks needed trimming. The museum *shifted*. The statues disappeared, and in their place was row after row of ancient cannon, their black muzzles smoking as if they had just been fired.

Herro Dan and Olga Ciavolga looked at each other. "I don't like this," muttered Herro Dan. "I don't like this one bit!"

Sinew said nothing. He unslung his harp and ran his fingers over the strings. Then he squatted down between two of the cannon and began to play with grim concentration, as if the lives of Goldie and Toadspit and everyone else in the city depended upon him.

Which, in truth, they did.

HARRY MOUNT

That night, Goldie slept with Broo curled up against her stomach. She was glad to have him there. When she woke up crying for Ma and Pa, he licked away her tears. And when a great black shadow stalked through her dreams, looking first like a brizzlehound and then like Guardian Hope and then like some horrible combination of the two, the little dog whined softly and snuggled against her.

There were no windows in this part of the museum, so she didn't know what time it was when she woke up properly.

Broo was gone, and she was hungry. She thought it must be morning.

For a little while she sat on her mattress and waited for someone to come and get her. But then she got sick of waiting and went looking for the kitchen where she had eaten supper the night before.

It was not where she remembered it being.

At first she thought she must have taken a wrong turning, so she retraced her steps to where she had slept, and started again. But she ended up back at the same blank wall.

She ran her hand over the chipped plaster. *It was here last night. I'm sure it was.*

She turned in a circle, feeling like an idiot. To her left was the way she had come. To her right was a gloomy corridor that she had never seen before. In the back of her mind, the little voice whispered, *Go that way.*

The little voice was usually right, so, after a moment's hesitation, Goldie tiptoed down the gloomy corridor, listening carefully for the sound of runaway street-rigs or hungry slaughterbirds. When she came to a doorway, the little voice urged her through it, into a room full of wooden masks with cruel eyes. The next room was full of statues, and the one after that seemed to be made entirely of giant bones.

And then, suddenly, there was the kitchen, smelling of scones and jam and hot chocolate. Toadspit scowled as Goldie walked through the door, as if he disliked her this morning even more than he had yesterday. Sinew looked up from his gazette and nodded. Olga Ciavolga and Herro Dan glanced at each other, and an unspoken message seemed to pass between them.

Goldie ate her way silently through a plateful of scones, and drank her chocolate, all the while watching the museum's keepers out of the corner of her eye. She had never met people like this before. People who were bold enough to defy the Blessed Guardians. People who would carry a slaughterbird on their shoulder and think nothing of it. People who thought she might be *useful* . . .

She waited for someone to explain to her what was going on. But no one said anything, so in the end she put down the scone she was about to eat, plucked up her courage and said, "What can I do to help my parents?"

Sinew closed his gazette. "Ah," he said. "A good question. What *can* you do?" He pushed his plate away. "I'll make some inquiries about your parents while I'm in the city today. And if I can get a message to them, I will."

A message! Goldie's throat was suddenly tight. "Tell them—tell them—"

She couldn't get the words out, but Sinew seemed to understand what she meant. He nodded. "I'll meet you later with the news."

"You be careful, Sinew," said Herro Dan. "There's

Guardians and militia everywhere. Don't you go takin' unnecessary risks."

"*Pfft!* Listen to you!" said Olga Ciavolga. "*Life* is a risk! *Breathing* is a risk! Have you forgotten that so easily? Does Sinew need someone to follow him around and keep him safe, like an infant?"

"*Unnecessary* risks, I said. There's a difference, and you know it."

The corner of Sinew's mouth turned up. He bowed awkwardly to Herro Dan. "I'll be careful," he said. Then he bowed to Olga Ciavolga. "But not *too* careful."

It was only after he had gone that Goldie realized he had not answered her question.

"Now, child," said Olga Ciavolga, wiping her hands with a napkin. "Enough sitting around. It is time you learned more of the museum. Toadspit and I will take you to Harry Mount."

Harry Mount turned out to be a staircase. But it wasn't the sort of staircase that was normally found in Jewel. Seen from below, it seemed to curl and twist dangerously, so that sometimes it hugged the wall and sometimes it looped out into midair and teetered there for a dozen steps before going back to its proper position.

Broo was lying on the bottom step, with Morg perched on the banister above him. As soon as the little dog saw Goldie he sprang up and danced around her, his tail wagging frantically. Goldie hesitated, then bent down and patted his head.

"Come along," said Olga Ciavolga. "Harry Mount will not wait for us."

"Where are we going?" said Goldie.

"You will see, child."

No one spoke as they climbed the long staircase. They passed doorways in the walls, and high-ceilinged galleries thick with cobwebs. Dust rose in clouds around them with every step they took. Several times it seemed as if they must be nearly at the top, but then they rounded another curve and Goldie saw that the steps went up and up and up, steeper and steeper, until they disappeared in the gloom.

Soon she was breathing hard. When they stopped on a landing, she sank down with a sigh of relief, her face damp with sweat. Toadspit and Olga Ciavolga sat on the stair above her.

They had been there for only a minute or two when there was one of those disconcerting *shifts*. Without a word Olga Ciavolga and Toadspit stood up and began to climb the staircase again. Goldie scowled at their backs—*why won't they* tell *me anything*—and scrambled after them.

She had not gone far when the little voice in the back of her mind whispered, *Don't trust your eyes.*

What?

Don't trust your eyes.

What on earth did that mean? Goldie looked at the stairs. There didn't seem to be anything wrong with them. She closed her eyes. . . .

She stopped.

"What is it, child?" said Olga Ciavolga.

Goldie knew that if she was wrong Toadspit would sneer at her. So she turned her back on him and whispered, "Do you feel anything strange?"

"Everything in the museum is strange," said Olga Ciavolga.

Goldie bit her lip. "It—it looks like we're going *up* Harry Mount. But when I close my eyes it doesn't *feel* as if we're going up. It feels as if we're going *down!*"

The old woman nodded approvingly and turned to Toadspit. "She feels it."

Toadspit looked annoyed, as if he had been hoping that Goldie *wouldn't* feel it, whatever "it" was.

"That shifting feeling," said Goldie. "What is it? What does it mean?"

Instead of answering her question, Olga Ciavolga said, "Can you whistle, child?"

Goldie nodded. The old woman put her hand in her pocket and pulled out a large kerchief. It was set with sequins, and there were knots at each corner and around the edges. Olga Ciavolga untied the smallest knot.

Immediately a breeze seemed to spring up out of nowhere. It lifted Goldie's hair and ruffled Morg's feathers. Olga Ciavolga pursed her lips and whistled three notes. The breeze disappeared, but on the steps above them the dust rose and swirled in midair before settling again.

Goldie stared. "How did you do that?"

Olga Ciavolga looked at Toadspit.

"She's a windspeaker," the boy muttered. "All the little winds, they tell her stuff."

"They are not always reliable," said Olga Ciavolga, "and there are places where they will not go. But in small ways they do my bidding."

She held out the kerchief. "You may try."

Why? thought Goldie. *Why are you showing me this?* But she took the kerchief and studied it curiously.

The four knots at the corners were big, but the rest were small. Goldie touched one of the small ones. It hummed under her fingers—*hrrrrrmmmmmm*—and she jerked her hand away.

"She won't do it," said Toadspit. "She's scared."

"We were all scared once," said Olga Ciavolga. Toadspit scowled and fell silent.

Goldie touched the knot again. The humming wasn't so bad now that she was expecting it. She dug her nails into the cloth and the knot came free. A breeze blew across her forehead. She whistled the three notes. The breeze tickled her ears, then disappeared. The dust rose and fell.

"Soon those breezes will come back," said Olga Ciavolga, "and tell us if the way ahead is safe."

Goldie felt a lick of excitement. Just two days ago she hadn't even been allowed to cross the road on her own. And now here she was, commanding the wind!

"I want to do another one," she said, and she took hold of one of the big corner knots.

"*No!*" shouted Toadspit and Olga Ciavolga together.

IIRRRRRMMMMMMMMMMMMMMMMMM! went the knot under Goldie's fingers.

It was so loud and fierce that she dropped the kerchief in fright. Olga Ciavolga caught it before it hit the ground.

"That was *stupid*!" said Toadspit. "That's one of the Great Winds! You're not allowed to even *touch* them!"

"He is right," said Olga Ciavolga. "You cannot send the Great Winds to do your bidding. They go where they please and do what they wish. If a Great Wind is unleashed, it will destroy everything in its path. I have never untied one of them, and I would not do so unless there was no other solution."

"I'm sorry," mumbled Goldie.

"There is no disgrace in learning," said Olga Ciavolga. "But caution is a good thing when you travel in the unknown."

She raised her head as if she was listening to something. Her gray hair lifted in the sudden breeze. She tied two small knots in her kerchief and the breeze disappeared.

"I do not like where we are going," she said, "but both my wind and your wind tell me that there is no immediate danger."

She began to climb the staircase again, although really they were still going down. Toadspit hung back and whispered in Goldie's ear, "Don't start thinking you're clever. It's not *your* wind. It's *hers*. They're *all* hers. You don't know *any*thing."

Goldie stuck her tongue out at him and ran down the stairs after Olga Ciavolga.

Now that Harry Mount had decided to take them down instead of up, it seemed in a hurry to get rid of them. The walls on either side began to draw in. They went around one more turn and the staircase ended abruptly.

Goldie found herself on the threshold of a huge, dimly lit room. Brick arches loomed above her head, held up by great square pillars. Watergas lamps burned dimly in small cages at the top of each arch. There was no floor. Instead, all Goldie could see were the wide dark waters of a lake that lapped at the pillars and at the bottom step of Harry Mount.

"This," whispered Olga Ciavolga, "is Old Scratch. We will pass through here quickly. Do not speak unless you must."

There was a narrow brick ledge running around the edge

of the lake. Broo stepped down onto it and sniffed at the dark water. The playfulness had completely gone out of him. He wagged his tail briefly and began to lead the way along the ledge.

Toadspit went second, with Morg hunched on his shoulder. Then came Goldie and Olga Ciavolga. Water dripped from the ceiling and ran down the backs of their necks. The air was as cold as a winter's night.

They had not gone far when Broo stiffened and pricked up his ears. Morg bobbed her head from side to side as if she was trying to see through the gloom. They all stopped and listened.

At first Goldie could hear nothing except the *drip drip drip* of the water, and a scratching sound from behind the nearest pillar. Then, far away across the cavern, something splashed. A second later, the water rose up like a black tongue and lapped at her feet.

"Quickly!" whispered Olga Ciavolga. "We must be gone from here!"

Broo didn't move. He stood staring out over the water, the hair on his back bristling. Toadspit stepped over him and Goldie followed. It was hard to hurry. The ledge was covered in green slime, and she was sure that if she went too fast she would slip.

The splash came again, closer this time. The water rose around Goldie's feet, cold and hungry.

"Toadspit, find the door! Hurry!" shouted Olga Ciavolga, no longer bothering to be quiet. Her voice echoed around the arches. *Hurry! Hurry! Hurry!*

Goldie ran. Her feet skidded on the treacherous bricks. A wave wrapped itself around her ankles and tried to drag her off the ledge. She clutched blindly at Toadspit, and he grabbed her arm. There was a low door in the wall in front of them. Toadspit fumbled it open. They both fell through it with Olga Ciavolga close behind them.

"Broo!" gasped Goldie. "Where's Broo?"

She glanced over her shoulder in time to see the little dog racing along the ledge toward her—only somehow, in the fitful light, he looked bigger. *Much* bigger.

Goldie opened her mouth to cry out. . . .

There was a flurry of movement and shouting. The door slammed shut. Goldie blinked, and looked down. And there was Broo, dancing around her feet, wagging his tail and smiling. Just a little white dog happy to see them all safe and sound.

The shadows had fooled her once again.

AN EXPLANATION OF SORTS

"**S**omething nasty in Old Scratch, eh?" said Sinew, when they met up with him at the end of the morning. He ran his awkward-looking fingers over the strings of his harp. "Dan was right, then. Ancient dangers *are* stirring. We'd best be wary."

In the four hours or so since they had left the underground lake, Olga Ciavolga and Toadspit had led Goldie through room after room. She had seen stuffed dolphins and old dolls' houses and little dark prison cells with the stink of despair embedded in their walls. She had walked past deep pits, and rusty metal wheels that loomed as high as a three-story building. She had gazed up at the hulk of a sailing ship that lay tipped on its side as if it had been stranded inside the museum when the tide went out.

Each room had a name. Dauntless, Lost Children, The Tench. Old Mine Shafts, Rough Tom. And that was just the beginning. The museum was even bigger than Goldie had thought. There seemed to be no end to it.

Right now they were standing on top of a hill called the Devil's Kitchen. It was covered with giant rocks, and the air hummed with the sound of insects. For the first time since Goldie had entered the museum there was no sign of any ceiling, and she could hardly believe that they were still inside that small stone building. The sky seemed to stretch in every direction.

"And what of the other business?" said Sinew. "What of Harry Mount?"

Olga Ciavolga nodded. "She felt it."

A huge smile transformed Sinew's serious face. He grabbed Goldie's hand and shook it vigorously. "Good! Excellent!" he said. He turned back to Olga Ciavolga. "Have you told her the rest of it?"

Goldie pricked up her ears. The things she had seen this morning had fascinated her, but they had not made her forget Ma and Pa and her desperate desire to help them. Ever since breakfast, her impatience had been growing.

Is this it? she thought. *Are they going to tell me what I can do?*

"I am waiting for Dan," said Olga Ciavolga. "He is meeting us here." She looked around. "Where is Broo? He ran ahead."

"I think he went down the tunnels," said Sinew.

"*Tsk*, he is too quick. Toadspit, you take Goldie and go after him. I will follow as soon as Dan comes."

Goldie didn't move. "What about Ma and Pa?"

Sinew hesitated. "There's no good news, I'm afraid. They were sentenced yesterday. Four years in the dungeons of the House of Repentance."

Goldie had been expecting it, but still her whole body went cold and weak, and she had to lean against one of the rocks or she might have fallen.

"I thought I might be able to get a message to them," continued Sinew. "I've done it before. But my contacts are lying low. The bombing has scared everyone."

Goldie hardly heard him. "I have to *do* something," she whispered. "Maybe I *should* go back."

"Do not be foolish, child," said Olga Ciavolga. "It benefits no one if you are also taken. You must be patient." She turned back to Sinew. "What have you discovered about the bombers?"

"They seem to have disappeared completely. I couldn't find a trace of them. But I'll try again tomorrow—"

"Well?" said Toadspit in Goldie's ear. "Are you coming?"

He pushed aside some bushes, revealing a narrow fissure in one of the rocks. He ducked his head and squeezed through it. Goldie heard the scrape of a tinderbox, and a thin beam of light shone out of the darkness. She ducked her own head and slipped through the gap.

She found herself in a small cave with a smooth rock floor. There was a tunnel leading off to the left, and Toadspit was walking down it, with a lantern swinging in his hand. Behind him the shadows were already closing in.

Goldie thought of Ma and Pa. It would be even darker than this, in the dungeons of the House of Repentance. . . .

She bit her lip, and hurried to catch up with Toadspit.

The tunnel ran level for a little way, then it turned a corner and began to slope downward. The air smelled dry and old. In the light of the lantern, the walls glittered like snakes' eyes.

"Where are we?" whispered Goldie.

Toadspit didn't reply straight away. But when he did, he answered a different question altogether. "It's because you're a thief," he said, over his shoulder. His voice was a little friendlier than usual, as if he too was affected by the darkness.

Just then, the floor of the tunnel dipped unexpectedly. Goldie stumbled and put her hand out to save herself. The rock wall sliced into her finger. *"Ow!"* she yelped.

Toadspit stopped and held up the lantern. "What's the matter?"

Goldie had only ever cut herself once before. That was when she was six, and Ma and Pa had rushed her off to the physician for stitches, and kept her in bed for a month afterward. This cut was bigger and bloodier, and the sight of it horrified her. But Toadspit snorted when he saw it, and continued down the tunnel as if there had been no interruption.

"Only a thief can find their way through the museum," he said over his shoulder. "No one's quite sure why. And only one thief in a thousand would notice when Harry Mount turned itself around. That's why we went there. It was a test."

Goldie tried to concentrate on what the boy was saying. But her finger had begun to throb painfully. She did her best to think of something else. "Does that mean you're a thief too?"

"Yep."

"What did you steal?"

For a moment, she thought he wasn't going to answer. Then he said, "Myself."

That didn't make *any* sense to Goldie at all. Her finger felt as if it was on fire. Ahead of her, the tunnel went down, down into the darkness. The rock walls, when she brushed against them, were as sharp as teeth.

And suddenly, out of the blue, she was angry. What was

she *doing* here? She should be trying to help Ma and Pa, not wandering around in some stupid tunnel listening to stupid stories that she didn't understand. It was all very well for Olga Ciavolga to tell her to be patient. She was *sick* of being patient!

She stopped. Toadspit lifted the lantern so that it shone in her eyes. "What's wrong now?"

"I want to go back. I want to get Ma and Pa out of the House of Repentance."

"Don't be an idiot. You can't get them out."

Goldie stared at him. "You said I could! That's why I stayed here instead of going to Spoke!"

"I said you might be able to *help*. I didn't say help them es-*cape*. No one ever escapes from the House of Repentance, not till their sentence is over. You should know that. Now come on, stop wasting time!"

Goldie shook her head in angry frustration. "You don't understand! None of you do! It's not *your* parents who're locked up. If it was, you'd want to do something about it. You wouldn't just hang around here being useless!"

Toadspit stiffened. "You don't know *anything*!" he snarled. Then he hunched his shoulders and began to walk down the tunnel so fast that Goldie had to run to catch up with him, or risk being left alone in total darkness.

The floor was steeper than ever now. The sides were drawing in. Here and there a black hole showed where another tunnel split off from the main one. In front of Goldie, Toadspit's back was hard and unfriendly.

He's sulking, thought Goldie. *Because he knows I'm right. I should be doing something! He told me I could! Otherwise I'd never have stayed!*

In thinking that, she made herself even angrier. Because if it wasn't for Toadspit, she'd probably be in Spoke with Ma's relatives by now, instead of bleeding to death in this stupid tunnel.

The glittering walls seemed to reflect her anger back at her. All she could think of was that Sinew and Olga Ciavolga and Herro Dan were keeping her here against her will. She was furious with them. And furious with Toadspit too, for making her believe she could rescue Ma and Pa when she couldn't.

As if he had heard what she was thinking, Toadspit suddenly stopped. He wasn't sulking now. He was smiling. "Your turn to lead," he said.

Goldie was so angry that she didn't think twice about that odd smile. She snatched the lantern out of his hand. Ahead of her was a huge boulder. She marched around it.

On the other side was the brizzlehound.

THE PLACE OF REMEMBERING

It was as if the boulder itself had suddenly come to life. The brizzlehound loomed up, huge and black and terrible. Its eyes glowed red in the lantern light.

For a moment, Goldie couldn't move or speak. *Someone save me!* she thought desperately. *Toadspit! Help!*

But there was no sound from behind her at all.

He's gone. He's run away and left me here.

Somehow that thought brought the strength back into her bones. And with it came the determination that she would not stand helplessly, waiting to die. She *would not*!

She took a shaky step backward. The shadows cast by the lantern crawled around her. The brizzlehound opened its awful jaws—and *spoke,* in a voice that rumbled like a distant rockfall.

"I have been waiting for you."

Goldie was so frightened that she could hardly breathe. She gripped the lantern harder. If she threw it—if she threw it into the brizzlehound's mouth . . . She was so close that she could hardly miss. She would throw the lantern, and then she would run, back up the long lightless tunnel with her hands stretched out in front of her and her ears straining for sounds of pursuit. . . .

No, don't think about that! Just do it!

She licked her lips. "Say something else," she whispered to the great beast. "Open your mouth."

The brizzlehound cocked its head.

"Do not be afraid," said a voice from behind Goldie.

Goldie almost sobbed with relief. Olga Ciavolga! If anyone could save her it was Olga—

"It is only Broo."

"*What?*" Goldie swung around and stared at the old woman. Then she turned back and blinked at the monster in front of her. "*Broo?*"

"Did you not know me?" said the brizzlehound.

"N-no!"

The brizzlehound took a huge, swaying step toward her.

He was so big that his eyes were on a level with hers, and he moved with a terrible grace. He was completely black, except for one white ear.

"Do you know me now?" he rumbled.

"N-not really."

The great hound looked so disappointed that Goldie felt she must add something more. "I—I expect it's b-because you couldn't talk when you were small."

Broo nodded thoughtfully. "That is the nature of brizzle-hounds. Sometimes we are big and sometimes we are small. When we are small, we speak with our tails and our ears and the hackles on our backs. And when we are big . . ."

He fell silent. Goldie stared at him in awe.

Behind her, Olga Ciavolga said, "Toadspit? Why did you not tell her it is Broo? What is this game you are playing?"

"It was just a joke," muttered Toadspit, who was still there after all. "Because she's new—"

"You were new here once," said Olga Ciavolga coldly. "And I do not remember anyone playing jokes on you. *Tsk!* There are dangers enough in the museum without you making more for your amusement. Go! I am ashamed of you."

Toadspit tried to say something, but the old woman wouldn't let him. "Go!" she snapped again.

The boy's footsteps echoed back up the tunnel. Then Olga Ciavolga was standing beside Goldie in the flickering light. "You see," she said. "There is nothing to be afraid of."

"I—I thought brizzlehounds were—" Goldie was about to say "make-believe," but that sounded rude when one of them was standing right in front of her. So instead she said, "I thought all the brizzlehounds were gone."

"And so they are. All of the great hounds are gone, except for Broo," said Olga Ciavolga. She reached out and stroked the giant head. "Now lead the way, my friend. There are things we must show this child."

The brizzlehound's body almost filled the narrow tunnel, but he turned around in a single fluid motion that took Goldie's breath away. As they wended their way downward between the rocky walls, she edged closer to Olga Ciavolga.

"Is he really tame?" she whispered.

"Tame?" said Olga Ciavolga. "No brizzlehound is ever tame. He is wild and bold and he has his own way of seeing the world. But if you treat him with respect he will not harm you."

"Where did he come from?"

"I stole him from a circus."

"But there hasn't been a circus in Jewel for hundreds of years!"

Olga Ciavolga gave one of her rare smiles. "Some of us are older than we look."

Goldie's head swam. She remembered what Toadspit had said. "Is Broo a thief too?"

"Ah, yes. He is a stealer of lives. In the circus he killed a

117

man who tormented him cruelly. They were going to shoot him, but I stole him and brought him here."

It was hard for Goldie to act normally when there was a stealer of lives so close in front of her. But after a while her heart slowed almost to its normal rate and the clammy feeling in the palms of her hands went away. She gave a little hiccup of scared laughter and wished that Favor could see her, walking behind a real live brizzlehound.

It was warmer in the tunnel now, but the air was still dry. They had been going down for so long that it seemed they must be approaching the center of the earth. And then, suddenly, the tunnel opened up, and they were walking across the floor of a cavern. Olga Ciavolga turned the flame of her lantern up high.

Goldie gasped. The walls of the cavern were lined with human bones. There were thigh bones stacked from floor to ceiling, and arm bones crisscrossed in intricate patterns. There were ribs and backbones and pelvic bones, and skulls piled one on top of the other like loaves of bread, with a lacework of finger bones between them.

"This," said Herro Dan's voice right behind her, "is the Place of Rememberin'."

"Oh!" Goldie spun around. "I didn't know you were there!"

"*Tsk,* he is showing off," said Olga Ciavolga. "What do you think you are doing, Dan, frightening the child?"

"She weren't frightened, were you, lass?"

Goldie looked at the old man's smiling face. "A little bit."

"Ah well, no harm done. Keeps you on your toes," he said.

"We are not here to talk about toes," said Olga Ciavolga severely. "We are telling her about the museum."

With that, all of Goldie's frustration came flooding back. "But *why?*" she burst out. "*Why* are you telling me? Why did you bring me here? Toadspit said that maybe I could help, but I don't know what that *means!*"

Herro Dan sighed. "You're right, lass, it's time we told you." He cleared his throat as if he was about to begin a story. "There was a time, long ago, when the Faroon Peninsula was known as Furuuna."

Furuunaaaaaaaaaaaaa . . . The word seemed to echo around the cave and linger in the corners, as if the bones recognized it and didn't want to let it go.

"Back then," said Herro Dan, "the Place of Rememberin' was sacred. Whenever someone died, their body was given to the slaughterbirds. Then their bones was brought here and stacked in rows so they'd never be forgotten, even when everyone who knew 'em was gone."

"The hill keeps them," rumbled the brizzlehound. "The hill keeps everything."

"The museum was built five hundred years ago," continued Herro Dan, "to hide the Place of Rememberin' from those who would've destroyed it. There was only a few rooms then, and nothin' in 'em but bronze tools and old coins. But

119

as the years passed, and the people of the city started fillin' up the vacant lots and banishin' the animals, the museum started growin'."

"It became a refuge for all the wild things," said Olga Ciavolga. "All the things the city did not want."

"The hill keeps them," rumbled the brizzlehound again. "The hill keeps everything."

Herro Dan laid his hand on one of the skulls. It was yellow with age, and its eye sockets were woven shut with spiderwebs. "But you can't hold wild things in one place. And they won't be tied down. That's why the rooms shift like they do. And if ever the museum or its keepers are under threat, they shift even more. This is their last stronghold and they won't stand quiet and see it destroyed."

The brizzlehound growled suddenly—a sound so fierce that it made Goldie's heart skip a beat. "The museum is under threat *grrrnooooow*! I can *smell* it!"

Herro Dan nodded. "We know there's somethin' comin'— some sorta trouble. The museum can feel it. But we dunno what the trouble is or where it's comin' from. And that makes things tricky." He looked directly at Goldie. "You see, lass, there's great wonders hidden in this place, but there's terrible things too, things that shouldn't be disturbed."

"Like what's in Old Scratch," whispered Goldie.

"Worse than Old Scratch," said Herro Dan. "Much worse.

And if the museum gets *too* restless, there's a danger that some of those things'll break out into the city. . . ."

On either side of him the bones seemed to shiver in the lantern light. Goldie swallowed, trying not to think of Ma and Pa trapped in the House of Repentance with *terrible things* stalking through the streets toward them.

"This is why we do our best to keep the rooms calm," said Olga Ciavolga. "Sinew plays his harp. Dan and Toadspit and I sing. We protect the museum, and we protect the city as well. But despite all our efforts, things are getting worse. The museum knows that something bad is coming."

"The bombing?" said Goldie.

"We think that is a part of it," said Olga Ciavolga. "But there is a greater danger that is still hidden from us. Sinew is doing his best to track it down."

"And when he finds it," said Herro Dan, "well, then we fight. That's where you can help us, lass."

"To *fight*?" squeaked Goldie. "I don't know how!"

"There's fightin' and there's fightin'," said Herro Dan. "How many folks d'you know who question what the Blessed Guardians say?"

"Lots of people," said Goldie. "Everyone I know moans about them in secret."

"Oh, in secret! We're all bold in secret. But to do it out in the open, that takes rare courage."

Goldie wanted to believe the old man, but she couldn't. "It wasn't courage," she said. "I just couldn't bear it anymore. The way they try and squash everyone into the same shape. The way everyone talks so meekly around them, and never dares say what they think. I hate them."

"And so you became a runaway," said Olga Ciavolga. "And a thief."

"Yes." Goldie blushed. "Toadspit said that only a . . . a thief can find their way through the museum."

"That is true," said Olga Ciavolga. "We are not sure why. Perhaps there is a wildness in thieves that speaks to the wildness that is here. Perhaps a thief sees the secret paths, the hidden places."

She looked hard at Goldie. "Listen to me carefully, child. *I do not wish to glorify theft.* There are people in this world who think they are better than others, or deserve more. People who would rob their grandmother of her last coin and laugh as they did it. I have no time for such people. To move quietly, to be quick of hand and eye, that is a gift. If you use it to hurt others, even in a small way, you betray yourself and everyone around you."

She paused. "But there's *some* things—" prompted Herro Dan.

"I was coming to that," said Olga Ciavolga. "Are you taking the words out of my mouth now?"

But she was smiling when she turned back to Goldie. "But

there are some things, child, that you *should* steal. That you *must* steal, if you have enough love and courage in your heart. You must snatch freedom from the hands of the tyrant. You must spirit away innocent lives before they are destroyed. You must hide secret and sacred places."

"Takes a brave thief to do such things, lass," said Herro Dan. "And you're brave, even if you don't believe it. If you want to, you can help us."

"But only if you truly want to," added Olga Ciavolga. "If you do not, no one will blame you. We will send you out of the city to a safe place."

It was only a little while ago that Goldie had been wishing she had gone to Spoke after all. But now, at the thought of leaving, she felt a jolt of dismay. "I'll stay!" she said quickly. "I'll help! I'll even learn to fight if you want me to!"

She thought Olga Ciavolga would be pleased. But the old woman shook her head. "*Tsk!* Do you take time to think about this question? No, you run headlong into the unknown!"

She put her hands on Goldie's shoulders. "Listen to me, child. You have been treated like an infant all your life. Now you must grow up quickly. You are bold, and that is good, but you must also be wise. Think carefully before you make decisions. The museum is full of dangers—"

"I will protect her," interrupted Broo.

"I know you will do your best, my dear," said Olga Ciavolga, "but even you cannot guarantee her safety in this place."

123

She turned back to Goldie. "Think carefully. *Then* make your choice."

Goldie thought. She thought about that first night in the city, and how frightened she had been. She thought about Morg, and Old Scratch, and the moment when she had stepped around the boulder and come face to face with the brizzlehound. *And there's worse.* Much *worse.*

Was she brave? She didn't think so. Could she bear to stay in such a dangerous place?

In the back of her mind, the little voice echoed Olga Ciavolga's words, *We protect the museum, and we protect the city as well.* . . .

Goldie slipped her hand into her pocket and wrapped her fingers around the little blue bird. She still wished more than anything that she could rescue Ma and Pa from the House of Repentance. But Toadspit was right. No one escaped from that awful place before their sentence was finished.

At least if she stayed here she could help protect them from even worse things. She would be protecting Favor too, and Frow and Herro Berg, and all her other friends.

She took a deep breath. "I'll stay," she said. She was amazed at how calm her voice sounded. "I'll do everything I can to help."

FINGERTALK

"There are things you must learn, child," said Olga Ciavolga, next morning at breakfast. "We will all teach you, whenever we have time. But Toadspit will be your main teacher."

Toadspit groaned. "Do I *have* to?"

Sinew glanced up from his gazette. "It's not so long since you learned these things yourself. I'm sure you remember how hard it can be."

Toadspit flushed and looked away. He hadn't spoken to Goldie this morning, and she hadn't spoken to him. She didn't trust him, and was determined not to turn her back on him or let him trick her again.

She wasn't turning her back on Broo either. He was there now, in the kitchen, lying small and white at Herro Dan's feet. But Goldie couldn't forget what lay just beneath the surface.

"The sooner you start, the better," said Olga Ciavolga. "Toadspit, take Goldie to the Shades now and teach her to run."

Toadspit didn't move. "What about Sinew? What's he doing?"

"It's back to the city for me," said Sinew. "There are some—"

"I could come with you," interrupted Toadspit eagerly. "I could disguise myself, pretend to wear a guardchain!"

"No," said Olga Ciavolga. "You are teaching Goldie."

"But I might be able to find out—"

"No!" Olga Ciavolga's voice was sharp, as if she had not yet forgiven Toadspit for the trick he had played yesterday.

Good, thought Goldie. *Neither have I.*

"There are some leads I want to follow," said Sinew. "I'll do it best on my own."

"It's all right for you," muttered Toadspit.

"What?" said Sinew.

"Nothing."

"What did you say, Toadspit?"

Toadspit glared at the table. "It's all right for you. You get to do something useful."

"And you don't think that teaching Goldie is useful?"

"She's hopeless," said Toadspit. "She doesn't know anything."

Sinew pushed his gazette aside and stood up. "Right, I've had enough of this." He turned to Goldie. "I assume you know some form of fingertalk?"

Goldie nodded.

"And you, Toadspit?"

"Everyone knows fingertalk," mumbled Toadspit.

"But is it the *same* fingertalk?" said Sinew. "I doubt it. Even in the Old Quarter I've seen children using five or six different versions."

"So?" said Toadspit.

"So, from now until I tell you otherwise, you and Goldie are only allowed to speak to each other in signs."

Goldie glanced at Toadspit and quickly looked away again. "What if we don't know the same ones?"

"Then you must learn each other's. I don't imagine it will be so difficult to work out a common language. *If* you cooperate."

"But, Sinew—" said Toadspit.

"No! Not another word out of your mouth until you return." And Sinew picked up his harp and strode out of the kitchen.

The Shades was a place of mud and moss and stinking ponds. The ground squelched underfoot like a sponge. Even the air felt damp, and there were little biting insects that circled Goldie's head and tried to settle on her arms.

"This—" began Toadspit. He broke off and scowled. Then he signed, *This is toilet. Don't fly off fish or you rattle.*

Goldie stared at him in astonishment. *What?* she signed.

With a long-suffering expression on his face, Toadspit signed again, very slowly and carefully. *This. Is. Toilet. Don't. Fly. Off. Fish. Or. You. Rattle.*

Not understand, signed Goldie.

Toadspit blinked, as if she had said something odd. Then he shrugged. *Hit me,* he signed, and he turned his back on her and began to walk down the narrow path that ran between the ponds.

It was impossible to resist the temptation. Goldie marched up behind him, clenched her fist and punched him hard on the shoulder.

He yelped and spun around. "What did you do *that* for?" he said out loud.

You told me hit you. Like this, signed Goldie. And she punched him again.

Toadspit narrowed his eyes. *No!* he signed. Hit *me! Like* this*!* And he beckoned her to follow him.

You mean—? Goldie made the sign for *follow.*

No! That means— Toadspit paused, red-faced. Then he wrapped his arms around himself as if he was cuddling someone. *See? I* not *mean that! I mean hit!*

So Goldie hit him again.

Stop it!

Goldie shrugged. *You tell me hit, I hit.*

Toadspit scowled ferociously. He bent down and picked up a stone, and threw it into one of the ponds. Half a dozen bubbles rose up and burst with an ugly *plop.* The stink grew worse.

Toadspit heaved a sigh. Then he signed, Follow *me,* and hurried off, looking back over his shoulder as if he was afraid that Goldie might try to sneak up and cuddle him.

Goldie was quite sure by now that she *had* seen Toadspit before, and that he used to live in the Old Quarter, somewhere near Gunboat Canal. But Sinew was right—the boy spoke a very different kind of fingertalk from the one she knew. The small words like *me* and *you* and *not* were the same, but that was all. And if there was danger coming, like Olga Ciavolga and Herro Dan said, they needed to be able to understand each other.

The farther they walked into the Shades, the hotter the air became. Goldie could feel the sweat trickling down her forehead. It was a relief when Toadspit stopped again and signed, *Now we dance. Along fish.*

Goldie didn't think he really meant either *dance* or *fish*. She signed a question, and they managed to work out, after a lot of eye rolling and scowling, that *dance* meant *run*, and *fish* meant *path*. After a lot more eye rolling and scowling, they agreed that they would use Toadspit's sign for the first word, and Goldie's for the second.

Then, without warning, Toadspit took off. He was almost out of sight before Goldie realized what was happening, and ran after him.

She wasn't used to running, and the Shades made it harder. The sticky mud clung to her sandals and weighed her down. The path turned this way and that for no apparent reason. The ponds plopped and sighed around her.

Ahead of her, Toadspit dodged and twisted with every twist of the path. Goldie gritted her teeth and wished that she could run like that, sure-footed and swift. Her body felt horribly clumsy, and she stumbled and tripped and almost fell off the path several times. But she kept going, although her breath was coming so hard that she thought her lungs might burst.

At last Toadspit stopped and Goldie caught up with him. She bent over with her hands on her knees, gasping. The insects descended on her. They seemed to like her even more now that she was hot and sweaty.

When she had recovered a little, she looked up. Toadspit

was watching her with a superior smile on his face. *Mud?* he signed.

Goldie glared at him. She hated that smile.

Mud? he signed again.

What on earth was he talking about? What did *mud* mean in his stupid version of fingertalk? Maybe he was asking if she wanted a drink. Or something to eat. Or a good long rest.

Then again, he might just mean *mud.*

Goldie stopped glaring and looked as innocent as she could. *You want mud?* she signed.

Toadspit rolled his eyes. *Yes.*

Now?

Yes!

Goldie smiled happily at him. Then she bent down, scooped up a handful of mud and threw it at Toadspit from close range.

She caught him right in the face. The mud splattered over him, and he yelped with shock and disbelief. Goldie laughed out loud, but not for long. Toadspit, his eyes white and furious, scooped up his own handful of mud and plastered it in her hair before she could back away.

Goldie grabbed more mud and flung it as hard as she could. At the same time, Toadspit threw more at her. She could feel it sliding down her face and arms and smock, but she didn't care. She just wanted to *get* him.

Toadspit was far more accurate in his throwing, and stronger too. But Goldie's fury almost made up for it. She scooped up double handfuls and dumped them on the boy, and then ran back for more. And all the time Toadspit was pelting her with the same foul stuff.

They fought for what seemed like ages. And then, just as suddenly as they had started, they stopped. And looked at each other.

They were both black and stinking, and barely recognizable as human. Only their eyes were still visible.

With an effort, Goldie raised her hands. She pointed at the muck that covered Toadspit. *Mud,* she signed.

For a moment, Toadspit did nothing. Then, very slowly, the black mask of his face split open and he began to laugh. He laughed and laughed, and before long Goldie caught it, and she began to laugh too. They laughed almost as hard as they had fought. Every now and then they would stop, and then one of them would sign, *Mud,* and they would start again.

That was how Olga Ciavolga found them. She raised her eyebrows when she saw the state they were in. The corner of her mouth twitched. "I see," she said, "that you have been practicing your throwing."

Which, of course, set them off again.

Things were a little easier between Goldie and Toadspit after that. The boy was still prickly, and sometimes he scowled at Goldie for no apparent reason. But mostly he did his best to teach her what he knew.

They ran every morning. Sometimes Broo joined them, leaping out at Goldie unexpectedly, mostly as a little white dog, but once or twice as a monstrous black brizzlehound, so that her heart almost stopped with fright. She learned to think ahead and watch for signs of him, or for anything else that might be lying in wait. She learned to listen more closely to the little voice in the back of her mind, and be always on the alert for danger.

When they weren't running, Toadspit taught Goldie how to light fires. He taught her how to dress a wound, and how to track someone across rock and scrub and wooden floors, and how to lose someone who was tracking *her*. Between them they gradually worked out a common fingertalk, and practiced it until they were perfect, at which point Sinew finally allowed them to speak to each other again.

And all the time, Goldie wondered about the trouble that was coming, and when it would show itself. And what she would do when it did . . .

As she grew stronger and quicker, she began to learn other things. It was Sinew who taught her the Three Methods of Concealment.

The easiest was Concealment by Sham. This was really

just pretending to be someone else, someone who was a bit foolish, or mad in a harmless sort of way. Someone who wouldn't be taken seriously.

Concealment by Camouflage was harder. Goldie had to study butterflies and moths and see how they blended with their surroundings. She learned to break up her outline with grass and leaves, and paint her face and arms in uneven stripes, so that she merged with the shadows. She practiced crouching without moving, and breathing so quietly that even Broo couldn't hear her.

At first it seemed impossible. But then she got the hang of it, as if it was something she had been on the brink of knowing all along, and had just needed a little push. The first time Sinew walked past her without seeing her, she almost shouted with joy.

The hardest to learn was Concealment by Imitation of Nothingness. Goldie had lost track of how long she had been in the museum by this time, and the world outside seemed like a distant memory.

Still, she thought about Ma and Pa every day. And she dreamed about them nearly every night. In her dreams they were threatened by something much worse than the House of Repentance . . .

"Goldie, are you listening to me?" said Sinew.

"Sorry," said Goldie.

"I said, there aren't many people who can imitate

nothingness. Herro Dan and Olga Ciavolga, of course. They're even better at it than I am. And Toadspit's not bad. I've only ever come across one or two others. But I've got a feeling that you'll pick it up quickly."

He walked a short distance away, until he was in shadow.

"The simplest way to do it," he said, "is to make yourself so uninteresting that even the light slips across you and doesn't stop. It helps if there are deep shadows, or some other sort of camouflage. But it's really a trick of the mind. You've got to be a part of whatever's around you, and at the same time a part of nothing."

He screwed up his long nose. "Funny thing is, your mind seems to stretch a bit when you're doing it properly. You find yourself hearing things that you shouldn't be able to hear. Knowing things that you shouldn't know." He grinned suddenly. "You probably don't need to worry about that for a bit. Let's get you started on the basics first. Here, I'll show you. Turn around for a minute."

Goldie turned around. When she turned back again, Sinew was gone.

No, he was there, but only just. Goldie's eyes kept drifting away from him and she had to force them back again.

"It doesn't work at all well in bright light," said Sinew. As soon as he spoke, she could see him clearly again. "Unless there's a bit of a crowd. Then you can slip through it un-noticed, as long as you don't move suddenly. Sudden movements catch the eye, and they'll give you away in an instant. Now, why don't you have a go?"

Goldie did her best to empty her mind, the way Sinew instructed. It wasn't easy. Thoughts kept creeping back in. She got impatient with herself, and that made it worse.

"Don't try so hard," said Sinew. "Don't *think* so hard!"

But although Goldie practiced for days, she couldn't even come close to Imitation of Nothingness.

"Never mind," said Sinew. "It took us all a while. Keep trying." And he handed her over to Herro Dan.

The old man taught Goldie how to walk so lightly that she could tread on eggshells without breaking them. He taught her how to interpret the sound of other people's footsteps— how heavy they were, and how quick, and whether the person making them was sick or well, man or woman, dangerous or harmless.

He showed her how to hide things in the palm of her hand or up her sleeve. He showed her how to deal with her fear.

"Don't try and push it away," he said. "If you fight it, you make it stronger. You gotta greet it politely, like an unwanted cousin. You can't make it leave you alone, but you can do what you have to do, in spite of it."

Then *he* handed her over to Olga Ciavolga.

From the old woman, Goldie learned how to pick locks and jimmy open windows, and how to tell if someone was lying, and how to make her own lies sound like the truth.

She learned how to steal honeycomb from a hive and fish from a stream. And when to steal secretly and when to steal boldly, and when not to steal at all.

The lessons seemed to touch something deep inside her. She ate them up as if they were food and she had been starving since the day she was born. Every day she practiced. And when night came she dreamed about Ma and Pa. And trouble that was getting closer and closer . . .

One evening, Sinew called them all together in the kitchen. "As you know," he said, "I've been searching the city. I've followed every rumor, every whisper, almost before it was spoken. I've found nothing. The bombers have left Jewel, there's no question of that. If they were still here I would've found some trace of them. As for the Blessed Guardians—"

He looked at Goldie. "Official word is that the search for you has been called off, but I'm not sure I believe it. They haven't crossed you off the register of children, which is odd. But they're keeping their mouths shut as tight as oysters and I couldn't find out more." He shrugged. "I don't know what to think. The shifting hasn't got any worse over the last few weeks. Maybe the danger has passed us by."

Herro Dan shook his head. "The shiftin' hasn't got worse, but it hasn't got better either. Whatever's out there, it's not goin' away. Didn't you find *anythin'*? Nothin' at all?"

"We-ell," said Sinew slowly. "Someone seems to have broken into the Protector's office a while back. No one reported anything missing, but there are some scratch marks that shouldn't be there, on one of the ground-floor windows. It *might* have happened on the same night Goldie came here. But then again, it might not."

"Sounds bad to me," muttered Herro Dan, "though I dunno why. All I know is, the danger hasn't gone. I can feel it in me bones. It's out there somewhere, right now. I think it's waitin' for somethin'. I just wish I knew what."

The Fugleman was practicing with his new sword. It was a fine weapon, especially made for him, with a silver hilt and a straight blade. As he stepped back and forth, parrying with an imaginary foe, he thought about his plans. Things were falling into place nicely. Now all he needed was the lieutenant marshal.

According to the Fugleman's spies, the militiaman had not been court-martialed after all. This did not surprise the Fugleman; his sister had always been weak-minded. Instead of punishing the man as he deserved, she had merely confined him to barracks. He had been allowed back to his duties this morning.

A smile curled around the Fugleman's mouth. If he had judged his man correctly, he wouldn't have to wait long. In fact . . .

A sharp rap sounded on the door of his office. The Fugleman felt a surge of satisfaction. With one final thrust he skewered the office curtains at heart level. Then he pulled out his pocketwatch. Perfect timing. "Come!" he said.

The door flew open and the lieutenant marshal of militia marched in. His uniform was polished and pressed as if he was on parade. There was a sheen of sweat on his face. He strode across the carpet and snapped to attention in front of the Fugleman. "Your Honor! I hope it is not too late to call on you?"

The Fugleman slid his sword into its scabbard. "Lieutenant marshal, what a pleasure to see you again! Too late? Of course not! My staff have gone home but I am here, working into the night as always." He gripped the militiaman's hand. "I am relieved to see you out of detention. I am only sorry that all my pleadings could not free you earlier. But I *did* manage to persuade the Protector not to court-martial you."

"*Thank* you, Your Honor," said the lieutenant marshal, blinking rapidly. "I am in your debt! If it had not been for you, I—"

"No need for thanks," said the Fugleman. "It was my pleasure. We cannot afford to lose men of your talents. Now, have you had a chance to think about . . . ?" He let his voice trail off.

The lieutenant marshal nodded vigorously. "As you suggested, Your Honor, I have been thinking about the security of the city. I hope that we will remain at peace for as long as possible. But if a serious threat *should* emerge, it would be my duty to serve the Seven Gods—" He paused and looked meaningfully at the Fugleman. "To serve the Seven Gods in *any way* that was required of me."

"Very good," said the Fugleman. "*Very* good! And are your fellow militiamen as . . . ah . . . loyal to the Seven as you are?"

"Some of them, Your Honor. I have been sounding them out in subtle ways. I could give you a list of names."

"Very good!" said the Fugleman again. He laid the sheathed sword across his desk and sat down in his chair, watching the militiaman with a ferocious curiosity, the way a cat will watch a mouse that it holds in its claws. "Of course, if such a threat *does* emerge, the city will require a strong leader. . . ."

"Like yourself," said the lieutenant marshal quickly.

"You're *too* kind." The Fugleman opened the door of the wine cabinet that was built into the desk. His eyes flickered over the slim blue book that he had hidden there. "A glass of best Merne claret to drink a toast to the Seven?" he murmured.

The lieutenant marshal nodded. Without being asked, he sat down in one of the visitors' chairs, took off his cap and wiped his sleeve across his forehead.

The Fugleman bent over the wine bottle to hide his contempt. The militia were truly a pathetic bunch. There wasn't a real killer among them. But they would do until he found something better. Which should be quite soon now . . .

SPIES

The next morning, Herro Dan took Goldie to the long balcony called the Lady's Mile. It ran right down one side of an enormous hall full of tattered banners and moth-eaten tapestries. Patches of moss clung to the stone wall beside it, and tiny white flowers grew in the cracks. When Goldie looked over the balustrade, she could see tables below, and chairs that seemed to shift and sigh in the smoky air, as if a crowd of people had just left them.

"It's time you learned the First Song, lass," said Herro Dan. "It's what we sing to quiet the museum when it's unsettled. I couldn't teach it to you any earlier. You have to build up strength to sing the First Song, strength of body and strength of mind—"

He stopped abruptly and inclined his head as if he had heard something unexpected.

Goldie listened. From somewhere far away there came a popping sound. It was so faint that she thought she must have imagined it. But when she looked at Herro Dan, he was staring back at her with worried eyes.

"That's not right," he murmured. "That's not right at all! I better go and take a look."

Goldie wasn't sure how long the old man would be, so she stayed where she was for a little while. But then she grew restless and made her way back to the kitchen. To her surprise Toadspit was waiting for her, his face alight with excitement.

"Your Blessed Guardians are back!" he said, as soon as she walked through the door. "They're in the front rooms! And they've brought a couple of trainees!"

Goldie's heart sank. "I thought they'd given up. Why are they still looking for me?"

"According to Guardian Hope, they're not," said Sinew, pulling out a chair for Goldie. "*She* says they're doing a survey. A *historical* survey. Old paintings, things like that."

Olga Ciavolga snorted. "Do they expect us to believe such nonsense?"

"I don't think they care if we believe it or not," said Sinew.

"So what is their real purpose?" said Olga Ciavolga.

"I don't know. Maybe they're looking for Goldie. Maybe it's something else."

"We could go and see," said Toadspit, jerking his thumb at Goldie. "Her and me. We could spy on them."

Goldie stared at him, appalled. To her relief, Sinew shook his head. "No."

"Come on, Sinew," pleaded Toadspit. "I've done it before, watched people in the front rooms. They won't see us. And we might find out what they're up to."

"I said, no!"

Toadspit gave a *phh* of disgust. "And you're the one who's always going on about overprotective adults."

Olga Ciavolga looked thoughtful. "It might not be such a terrible idea."

"Yes!" said Toadspit.

No! thought Goldie.

"I don't think—" began Sinew.

"The Blessed Guardians are taking an interest in us for the first time in many years," interrupted Olga Ciavolga. "Why? Is it connected with Goldie? Or with the trouble that is coming? Have they discovered things that they should not know about the museum and what it contains? We must find the answers to these questions."

"But—"

"You are concerned for the safety of the children, Sinew, as am I. But Toadspit is right, he has spied on visitors before and never once been seen."

"But Goldie—"

"She has learnt much since she came here. And she does not have to go. No one will make her. It is entirely up to her."

But it wasn't, of course. Not with Toadspit sitting there grinning, as if he knew how much Goldie dreaded the thought of seeing Guardian Hope again. And Olga Ciavolga, expecting her to make a sensible decision when she'd hardly ever made a decision in her *life* before she came here.

And even Sinew, his worried face suddenly reminding Goldie of Pa, so that her stomach clenched with homesickness, and she knew that if she sat there for a minute longer she'd start crying like a baby, and probably never stop.

She stood up quickly. "I'll go," she said, and the look of surprise on Toadspit's face was almost enough to make it worth it.

※

"You," said Guardian Hope, "are *under*-guardians. And I am your *over*-guardian."

The two trainees from the School of Blessed Guardianship gaped at her. They had told Hope their names, but she had already forgotten them. Their faces were equally forgettable. What mattered was that they were *hers*.

Well, hers and Comfort's, officially. But hers really.

It seemed like forever since Hope had reported back to the Fugleman with a description of the museum and its confusing rooms. At the end of her report she had shown him the scrap of silk ribbon and requested permission to cart Sinew off to the House of Repentance and—ahem—*persuade* him to tell them where the Roth girl was.

Instead, the Fugleman had pulled Hope and Comfort out of the museum altogether. For weeks Hope had had to contain her impatience. And all the while the knowledge that the girl was *there*, in the building somewhere (laughing at her, no doubt, and thumbing her nose), had simmered away inside her until she could hardly think straight.

But the meeting with the Fugleman early this morning had reassured her. There was not such a great clash between His Honor's plans and hers after all. If she did what he asked, she should find the girl very soon. . . .

With an effort, she dragged her thoughts back to the under-guardians. Comfort was handing them a large sheet of paper, a pencil and a yardstick. "I believe you already have your instructions," he said.

The trainees continued to gape like idiots.

"Oh, for Great Wooden's sake," snapped Hope. "Get on with it!"

They were not even slightly efficient, of course. They used the yardstick so clumsily and slowly that Hope was forced to shout at them several times. But in the end, they managed to measure the width of the museum's entrance and the distance from the front door to the stone archway. They measured the height of the archway and its thickness. They wrote the numbers down on the sheet of paper, and drew diagrams in thin black lines. Then they moved into the first display room and did the same thing all over again.

It was in the third room that the trouble started. One of them went ahead to make a preliminary survey and got lost for more than an hour. The other made mistake after mistake with the measurements, never getting the same one twice. If it hadn't been for the Fugleman (and the girl tucked away somewhere, thinking herself safe), Hope would have thrown up her hands in frustration and gone home.

Then they lost the sheet of paper. . . .

Toadspit lay flat on his belly behind the broken cabinet. Goldie crouched beside him, her body tense.

She wasn't sure how they had got here. She had followed Toadspit blindly through the Staff Only door into the front rooms, trying not to think about where they were going. She felt as if she had forgotten every single one of her lessons.

146

Once she blundered into a table and Toadspit turned and scowled at her. She stuck her tongue out at him, and that made her feel slightly better.

The cabinet was in a corner, with display cases and tables on either side. Toadspit dragged her behind it and pushed her down. Then he lay next to her. And they waited.

When Goldie heard Guardian Hope's voice, she wanted to jump to her feet and run back the way they had come. Her wrist burned as if a silver cuff might be snapped around it at any moment.

". . . are idiots," said Guardian Hope as she stalked into the room. "Did you hear me? Complete idiots, both of you! Can't you do a simple job without having your hands held like children? How do you expect to get the *scale* right if you can't even measure things accurately?"

"Standards are slipping, colleague," said Guardian Comfort mournfully. "They are not what they were when we did our training."

"With respect, colleague," snapped Guardian Hope, "it's nothing to do with standards. It's basic common sense! Measure this. Measure that. Go here. Go there. What could be more simple? But can these two fools do it? No, they cannot!"

There was a crack in the back of the cabinet. Goldie slid her eye up to it, and the room tilted and came into focus. There was Guardian Comfort! There was Guardian Hope!

And there were the trainees, both young men. The brass punishment chains around their waists were as new and shiny as their faces.

"I—I'm sorry, honored colleague," gulped one of the trainees. "We *will* do better! Won't we, colleague?"

"We will," mumbled his friend.

"Hmph," grunted Guardian Hope. "Get on with it then. This is your last chance, mind! Mess it up again and you'll be sorry."

Goldie watched as the two young men unrolled a large piece of paper and laid it carefully on one of the display cases. They weighed down its corners with rocks. Then they took a yardstick and a pencil from the folds of their robes and began to measure the distance from the doorway of the room to the first corner.

Goldie felt a stirring of excitement. Her lessons were coming back to her now and she could see what needed to be done. *If I crept along the wall* that *way . . .*

Toadspit tapped her arm. *I go see what's on paper,* he signed. *Wait here. Don't move. Don't do anything stupid.*

Goldie's fingers flashed. *No! I go! You wait!* And before Toadspit could stop her, she unfolded herself and slipped away.

She could feel his eyes on her as she slid silently along the wall behind the tables and display cases, but she didn't look back. She thought about what Sinew had taught her. *Camouflage . . .*

The legs of one of the tables were burnt, and she ran her fingers over them and smeared the charcoal on her skin. Her face and arms blended with the shadows and the broken wood. Her heart beat fiercely in her chest.

It seemed to take no time at all to get to where she was going. The display case loomed above her. Her hand crept upward and tilted the rocks. Without a sound, the paper slithered off the case. Goldie caught it before it hit the ground.

"The same measurement twice?" said Guardian Hope in a sarcastic voice. "Can it be true?"

"I—I believe so, honored colleague," said one of the trainees.

"Well, mark it down quickly, idiot, before it changes."

"Yes, yes, of course!"

Goldie slid away just in time. From deep in the shadows she heard the young man's voice change. "Um . . . honored colleagues, the paper—"

"Yes, idiot, on the paper, where else?"

The trainee bent over and peered at the floor beneath the display case. "It's gone!"

Guardian Hope sighed loudly. "Don't be ridiculous! You've put it down somewhere else."

As the young man moved away from the display case, patting the pockets of his robe, Goldie scanned the piece of paper. It took her a moment to make sense of all the lines and numbers. Some of them had been crossed out and redrawn, and she could see where the old marks were.

And then, suddenly, it fell into place and she realized what it was.

She heard Guardian Hope groan dramatically. "By the Black Ox, do I have to do everything myself?"

Goldie's skin prickled. As Guardian Hope's angry footsteps stalked toward her, she crept forward to the very edge of the shadows and launched the paper through the air. Then she froze on the spot and tried to imitate nothingness.

She had never yet got it completely right. But there was no time to practice. She slowed her breathing. She emptied her mind—or at least she tried to. But Guardian Hope's footsteps were nearly upon her. Her wrist was burning. She could almost *feel* the weight of the punishment chains dragging her down. She didn't *want* to be afraid, she didn't *want* to. . . .

Don't try and push the fear away, whispered the little voice. *Greet it politely like an unwanted cousin.*

She swallowed. *Hello, fear! You're not going to go away, are you? Well, stay there then, but let me get on with it!*

She slowed her breathing again. Something seemed to

click inside her head, and suddenly Sinew's instructions made sense.

I am nothing. I am a shadow in the corner of the room.

Her mind drifted outward like motes of dust. She could sense Toadspit behind the cabinet, holding his breath. She could sense the two trainees frantically searching their pockets, and Guardian Hope's rising frustration.

None of it seemed to matter.

Guardian Hope peered over the edge of the display case.

I am nothing. I am a shadow. . . .

"As I thought," said Guardian Hope. "It was here all the time. It just needed someone with a grain of common sense to look for it."

Her eyes flickered past Goldie as if there was no one there. And she reached down and picked up the piece of paper.

"They're trying to make a floor plan of the museum," said Goldie.

Sinew raised his eyebrows. "Are they just?"

Goldie's heart was still pounding at the memory of what she had done. She had imitated nothingness! She had spied on the Blessed Guardians and got away with it! The Fugleman was right, she *was* wicked! And she didn't care!

"Did they see you, or suspect anything?" said Olga Ciavolga. Toadspit sniffed. "Nearly."

"No, they didn't!" said Goldie.

"Good. But this floor plan, that is not good. We must tell Dan and see what he thinks of it. Where is he?"

"He went to check something," said Goldie. "When we were up on the Lady's Mile."

"Did he say what?"

Goldie shook her head. "He heard a noise. I don't know what it was."

"Never mind," said Sinew. "I expect he'll be back soon. And then we'll tell him, and work out what to do."

But Herro Dan did not come back soon. They waited for him all day and late into the night, but he did not come back at all.

THE FIRST SONG

I t was supposed to be Guardian Hope's day off. But she could not rest. She had set her idiot assistants to make a floor plan more than a dozen times yesterday, and they had failed on every occasion.

At first she had thought that it was due to their stupidity, and she had poked them in the ribs with the yardstick and shouted at them until her throat was sore.

It made no difference. Gradually, it had dawned upon her that perhaps it wasn't the under-guardians after all. Perhaps it was the building itself. There was certainly something strange about it. Something she couldn't quite put her finger on . . .

But no heap of moldy bluestone was going to make a fool out of Blessed Guardian Hope! The Fugleman had entrusted her with a mission, and she would carry it out—and find the Roth brat into the bargain.

She stalked up the front steps of the museum and hurried through the entrance hall to where Comfort and the two under-guardians were waiting for her. She peered cautiously around the door of the office. It was empty. Good. She didn't want the keepers interfering with her plans.

She took a large ball of string from her pocket and thrust one end of it at the young men. "Hold this," she snarled. "And *don't let go!*" Then she hurried away through the display rooms, unraveling the string as she went.

"We must ask ourselves, colleague," said Comfort, as he strode beside her, "whether a simple ball of string will make our search any easier. After all, it cannot *guide* us, can it? It cannot *leap* ahead and *lead* us, like children, to the *promised land*."

He laughed, obviously pleased to be the witty one for a change. At the same time, the string suddenly jerked in Hope's hand, as if someone had tugged it. She cursed her assistants under her breath. Aloud, she said, "What it *can* do, colleague, is ensure that we do not go around in circles. Like *so* . . ."

She stopped in a doorway. She was as sure as she could be

that they had not deviated from their path, had not doubled back in any way. But the telltale string ran across the room in front of them.

"Now," she said, with great satisfaction, "we know that we must go a *different* way, a way that we have not been before. And so, with the help of this *simple* ball of string, we will explore every part of this cursed building, however slyly it may be hidden."

It was still not easy, of course. The rooms were as confusing as ever. Hope led the way through them with no idea as to where she was going. The string jerked twice more, so viciously that she almost dropped it. And twice more she found that they had somehow turned back on their tracks.

But she kept her head, and at last she was rewarded. They turned a corner, and there in front of them was a door that she had never seen before. Written on it in faded letters were the words STAFF ONLY.

She paused, smiling with satisfaction. Comfort reached for the handle—

"No!" hissed Hope. She put her finger to her lips and pressed her ear against the door. Faintly through the wood she could hear two voices, a boy and a girl.

"Herro Dan still isn't back," said the boy.

"Do you think something's happened to him?" said the girl.

Hope stiffened. "It's the Roth brat!" she mouthed. "Listen!"

"Olga Ciavolga reckons he wouldn't stay away at a time

like this," said the boy. "Not willingly. She and Sinew have gone looking for him. And I have to show you how to sing the First Song. Whatever's causing the problem, it's suddenly got worse again."

"What problem?" mouthed Comfort. "What's he talking about?"

"I know, I felt it just then," said the girl. "The rooms shifted three times."

"And five times last night. *Big* shifts."

Hope's mouth fell open and she beckoned Comfort away from the door. "Is it possible?" she whispered. "Shifting rooms?"

"I've never heard of such a thing." Comfort shook his head in disbelief.

"It would explain why we keep getting lost. And why those two morons couldn't draw two floor plans the same. Oh, His Honor will want to hear about this!"

Hope tiptoed back to the door, as silent as a corpse. But when she again pressed her ear to it, she could hear nothing except footsteps fading into the distance.

"Quick!" she whispered to Comfort. "We must follow them!"

She tried the door handle, but it was locked. She shrugged. Perhaps it was just as well. The ball of string was nearly finished. It was no use going farther if they couldn't find their way back again.

She began to retrace her steps, reeling in the string as she went. "It *was* the Roth girl," she said. "We have her trapped now, do we not?"

"But the boy, who was the boy?" said Comfort.

"First things first, colleague. We must work out how to deal with these shifting rooms, so we can carry out His Honor's instructions. Then we will make inquiries about the boy." Hope smirked. "And *then* we will return, and both of these brats will learn what happens to bad children in the city of Jewel. . . ."

"The museum," said Toadspit, "is like a brizzlehound. Sometimes it growls, deep in its belly. Sometimes it shivers with excitement."

The children were standing halfway along the Lady's Mile. There was no sign of Morg, but Broo had been waiting there as if he was expecting them. When he saw Goldie he wagged his little white tail and bounced around her.

"If you put your hand on the wall," said Toadspit, "you can feel its temper. But don't try and grip it or hold it in one place. The museum hates that more than anything."

Goldie hesitated, remembering the first time she had done this. Slowly, she put her hand on the wall.

It took all her will not to snatch it straight off again. The wild music seemed to swell up from the hot center of the earth and *pour* into her body. It rattled her bones and turned her innards upside down and made her want to shout and cry and fight all at the same time. When at last she took her hand away, she was shaking from head to toe.

Toadspit was watching her with an odd look on his face. "The first time I tried that," he muttered, "I fell over. And it's much worse now." Then he turned quickly back to the wall, as if he'd said more than he intended.

"You have to stroke it," he said. "Like you'd stroke Broo." He ran his hand over the stone, as if he was calming an animal. "Then you sing. Like this. *Ho oh oh-oh. Mm mm oh oh oh-oh oh.* If you do it right, you can get the museum to sing with you, and that quietens it down for a bit. *Ho oh oh-oh. Mm mm oh oh oh-oh oh.*"

His voice slid up and down the scale in a way that made the hair on the back of Goldie's neck stand up.

"That's Herro Dan's song," she said.

Toadspit nodded. "Herro Dan reckons it's the very first song, from the beginning of time. From before humans even existed. He reckons every other song in the world grew out of this one. The museum doesn't take any notice of anything else. *Mm mm mm oh-oh oh-oh. Mm oh-oh-oh mm oh-oh.*"

Goldie put her hand back on the wall. The wild music surged through her, but it was slightly different now. It seemed to be picking up the notes of Toadspit's song and playing with them, like a giant tossing baubles in the air. And in the same way that the giant might be pleased with the baubles, and want to play with them more and more, the wild music seemed pleased with Toadspit's song. Gradually, it changed and settled and, before long, the museum and the boy were singing almost the same notes.

"HO OH OH-OH. MM MM OH OH OH-OH OH," sang the museum. *"MM OH-OH-OH MM MM MM OH-OH."*

The music was still frighteningly big, and every now and again there was a note that seemed on the brink of breaking out. But it no longer made Goldie want to cry and scream and fight.

She stroked the wall gently. *"Mm oh-oh,"* she sang, trying hard to catch that odd sliding sound. Her voice felt puny and ridiculous next to the mighty music that rumbled up from the depths. She stopped, wondering where Herro Dan was, and hoping that nothing bad had happened to him.

Toadspit jogged her elbow. "Keep going."

"Mm mm. Mm mm oh—" She tried again, but it was no good.

Broo was gazing up at her, his head cocked. *He looks so little and harmless,* thought Goldie. *But inside, he's bigger and wilder than anyone could imagine. And the museum's the same.*

Something snagged at her memory. For a moment, she was back in the Old Quarter, wrapped in punishment chains and longing for freedom—and she realized that it wasn't just the dog and the museum that were bigger and wilder inside than anyone could imagine . . .

She put her hand back on the wall. She took a deep breath. *"Ho oh oh-oh,"* she sang, and she let some of the curiosity and longing and frustration that she had felt all her life leak out into her voice. *"Mm mm oh oh oh-oh oh."*

The museum seemed to pause and listen. Then, suddenly, it picked up *her* notes! It tossed them in the air, it wove them into its song! Toadspit grinned in approval. "Keep going!"

So Goldie stroked and sang, and Broo leaped around her ankles yapping the same strange notes, and the music swelled inside her, so that before long she could feel every part of her body fizzing with energy.

This time when she took her hand off the wall, she felt enormous. As big as the museum. As big as the sky. Everything she looked at seemed clear and bright—the tapestries, the moss, the tiny white flowers. It was impossible to believe that trouble was on its way.

"I wish—oh, I *wish* Ma and Pa could come and live here," she said.

Toadspit's face went blank. He took a coin from his pocket and began to roll it between his fingers, making it vanish and reappear and vanish again. "They're locked up," he said, his eyes fixed on the coin.

"You don't have to remind me—"

"You should've known what'd happen to them. You

should've known they'd end up in the House of Repentance." The old bitterness was back in the boy's voice. "How could you run away like that and leave them to the mercy of the Blessed Guardians?"

Goldie opened her mouth to retort. Then she bit her lip. She had the odd feeling that Toadspit wasn't really talking to her.

"Got any brothers or sisters?" he asked, still staring at the coin.

"No," said Goldie, and she looked at him curiously. "Have you?"

"If you did, if you had a little sister, say, would you worry about what was happening to her?"

"I s'pose so."

Silence fell between them. Presently Goldie said, "I *have* seen you before, haven't I? In the Old Quarter?"

Toadspit nodded. "I ran away last year."

"You can't have!" Goldie stared at him. "I would've heard! Everyone would've been talking about it."

Toadspit laughed angrily. "The Blessed Guardians told our neighbors we'd moved to Lawe. They didn't want other children getting ideas."

"So where are your parents?"

"Where do you think?"

"House of Repentance?"

Toadspit gave a brief nod. "And my sister's in Care—"

He stopped. Goldie heard a faint, faraway popping sound. "What's that?" she said.

"Guns! From beyond the Dirty Gate! *Quick!*"

Toadspit shoved the coin into his pocket, put his hand on the wall again and began to sing. Goldie copied him.

The wild music was back, surging under her hand. At first their singing seemed to make no difference to it. Their voices bobbed helplessly in the mighty current of sound. Then Goldie heard a third voice join theirs from somewhere deep in the museum. Not a human voice this time, but the song of a harp. It was Sinew, playing for all he was worth.

For a moment, nothing changed. Then, bit by bit, the wild music began to weave itself to their singing, and to quietness.

Goldie took her hand off the wall. "That popping sound," she said.

"The guns?"

"Yes. I think that's what Herro Dan heard. Just before he disappeared."

"What?" Toadspit stared at her in horror. "He must have gone past the Dirty Gate! Come on!"

And without waiting to see if Goldie was following, he began to run along the Lady's Mile.

THE DIRTY GATE

The Dirty Gate was deeper inside the museum than Goldie had ever gone before. It was made of iron— not a solid piece, but strips welded together like a giant honeycomb. It was brown with rust, and fitted into the wall so carefully that there was no gap above or below it. On the right-hand side there was an enormous keyhole.

Morg was perched on one of the iron strips. She rattled her wings when she saw them. "Wa-a-ar!" she croaked. "Wa-a-a-a-r!"

A shiver ran down Goldie's spine. "What does she mean? Why is she saying that?"

"That's what's on the other side of the Dirty Gate," said Toadspit grimly. "The war rooms. The plague rooms. The famine rooms. All the really awful stuff that happened in the early years of Dunt. It's still here in the museum. Most of the time it's quiet and doesn't cause any problems, but something must have stirred it up. You heard the guns. Come and look."

Goldie sidled up to the gate and stared through the honeycomb holes, some of which were big enough to climb through. At first all she could see was long grass, but then Toadspit pointed to a flash of white far to the left.

"See those tents? That's an army camp," he said. "This is the first of the war rooms."

"Who are they fighting?"

"Anyone. Everyone. I don't know. It's just—war."

Goldie thought she saw a movement near the tents. She took a quick step backward. "Won't they see us? Won't they try and break down the gate? Or shoot us or something?"

Toadspit shook his head. "As long as the gate is shut, they can't see it and they can't come through."

As he spoke, he took a folding knife and a bit of wire out of his pocket. He slid the tip of the knife into the keyhole and pushed the wire in above it. Then he began to wiggle it carefully back and forth. Broo growled softly.

"What are you *doing*?" said Goldie.

Toadspit's face was pale, but there was a stubborn set to his jaw. "Herro Dan should've come back last night." He spoke slowly, concentrating on the keyhole. "I reckon he heard the guns and went through here to see what was happening, and the soldiers caught him. They probably thought he was a spy. I'm going to see if they've got him. And if they have, I'm going to steal him back."

"Shouldn't we go and find Olga Ciavolga first? Or Sinew?"

"There's no time. They might shoot Herro Dan at any moment."

"They might've shot him already!"

"If they had, we'd know— Got it!" said Toadspit. There was a loud click and the lock sprang open. Toadspit slipped the knife and the wire back into his pocket. "Are you coming?"

Think carefully, whispered the little voice in the back of Goldie's mind. *Think carefully before you rush into danger.*

But Goldie didn't want to think carefully, not if Herro Dan might be shot at any moment. "Of course I'm coming!" she said.

The Dirty Gate was so heavy that the two children could hardly move it. They dragged it open just far enough to squeeze through the gap.

"Come on, Broo," said Toadspit. "We mustn't leave the gate open for long."

Broo didn't move. He stood on the other side of the gate, every hair on his little white back bristling.

165

"We'll go without you," said Toadspit.

Still the little dog did not move.

"Stay here then," said Toadspit. "See if I care."

The children dragged the gate shut, and dropped onto their bellies in the long grass. Goldie's heart was thumping in her chest. How could a place like this be a *room*? How could it be *inside* the museum? She felt as if she had stepped into a completely different country. There was no ceiling that she could see, and the sky was pale and distant. High above her head, a dozen ominous black shapes floated in the air like specks of ash.

"Look!" whispered Toadspit, pointing. "Slaughterbirds!"

Goldie heard a soft whine, and turned her head. The Dirty Gate was little more than a shimmer in the grass behind her. She could just make out one of the honeycomb holes, and Broo wriggling through it. She hoped that he had decided to follow them after all, but instead he lay down just inside the gate and put his head on his paws.

"He won't come any farther," whispered Toadspit. "There's no point waiting for him."

He picked up a handful of dirt and smeared it over his face and arms. With shaking hands, Goldie copied him.

Then the two children began to crawl toward the distant army camp.

Before they were even close to the tents, Goldie could smell smoke and sewage and beer and blood and dung and a score of other things that she couldn't name.

She wrinkled her nose in disgust. Out of the corner of her eye, she saw Toadspit do the same. She felt a bubble of silent laughter well up inside her. That made her feel braver, and when at last they came to the edge of the camp she peered through the long grass with almost as much curiosity as dread.

Directly in front of her, the ground was trampled and muddy as if some huge hungry beast had crossed it in the night. There were rough tents and old-fashioned wagons that looked like something from a history book. There were ugly black cannon slung on enormous wheels, and oxen and hens and goats and pigs snuffling across the mud between them.

Next to the tents were fireplaces made out of rocks. Above each fireplace, a cauldron hung from an iron hook. But there was no sign of any soldiers. Except for the slow movement of the animals, and the *peck-peck-peck*ing of the hens, a stillness hung over the camp.

Toadspit put his finger to his lips and wriggled back a little way. Goldie followed him, thinking about the animals and birds, and the bare ground and how they would have to cross it.

"There are no horses," whispered Toadspit. "They must be off fighting or something. If we're lucky we'll be able to search the whole camp before they come back."

"We'll have to be careful," whispered Goldie. "They might have left a few—"

She broke off. There were footsteps marching toward them. "—*sentries!*" she hissed.

She threw herself flat in the long grass. Toadspit did the same. The footsteps slammed toward them, hard and brutal on the bare ground. Left *right* left *right* left *right*. Two men. Both of them extremely dangerous. Goldie pressed her face into the earth and tried to control her trembling.

Left *right* left *right* left *right*. The feet marched toward their hiding place. The grass quivered. Goldie's heart raced. LEFT *RIGHT* LEFT *RIGHT* LEFT *RIGHT*. For a moment, it seemed as if the sentries would march right over the top of them. But instead they went straight past, following the grass edge that marked the boundary of the camp.

Goldie lay still for a long time after they had gone. She had a cramp in one leg and she didn't think she would ever move again. But when Toadspit stood up in a low crouch and ran across the open ground to the shelter of the first wagon, she was beside him.

It was the strangest thing, slipping through that almost-deserted camp. Wisps of smoke rose from the fires, as if they had only just been put out. Flies buzzed around the cauldrons. Oxen stamped and shook their heads as Goldie and Toadspit passed.

As they crept from wagon to wagon, Goldie's skin itched

with the knowledge that the sentries might return at any moment. She tried to tell herself that this was a war from hundreds of years ago, that it was over and done with, that surely it could not hurt her. But the camp around her was as real as anything she had ever seen. Flies settled on her face and arms. Her feet kicked up little clumps of mud. High above her, the slaughterbirds wove a dance of death.

Many of the tents had their flaps pulled back, and the children could see straight away that there was no one in them. But as they got closer to the center of the camp, more and more of the flaps were shut. They dared not open them in case there was someone inside, so instead they put their heads close to the canvas and listened. They heard nothing.

Silently they stole onward. The sun beat down on their heads. Mosquitoes hovered around them and they brushed them away and kept going.

Once they heard the *tramp tramp tramp* of the sentries in the distance. They dived behind the nearest wagon until the sound faded. Then they crawled out again and dusted themselves off—and kept going.

Goldie was pressing her ear against yet another tent when she heard it. On the other side of the canvas, a man was singing quietly. *"Ho oh oh-oh. Mm mm oh oh oh-oh oh."*

"Herro Dan?" she hissed.

The singing stopped. *"Goldie?* Is that *you?"*

"Me and Toadspit."

"What are you doin' *here?*"

"We've come to rescue you!" whispered Goldie.

She waved frantically at Toadspit and he came hurrying back. When he heard Herro Dan's voice he closed his eyes for a moment, and swallowed, as if there was something stuck in his throat.

"I've busted me leg," whispered Herro Dan. "They didn't even bother puttin' a guard on me. They know I'm not goin' anywhere."

"But—"

"You gotta go back. It's too dangerous for you here."

"We'll go back," said Toadspit. "And we'll take you with us." He took out his knife and began to saw at the straps that held the tent door shut.

"Now you listen to me, boy," said Herro Dan fiercely. "You go back and tell Olga Ciavolga that the war rooms are on the move."

"We know. We heard the guns," said Goldie.

"That trouble, I reckon it's stopped waitin'," said Herro Dan. "Now it's gallopin' toward us, full tilt. You gotta find out why. What's changed? What's different? What's stirrin' the museum up like this?"

"It could be the Blessed Guardians," said Goldie.

"What about them?" The old man's voice was sharp.

"They're trying to make a floor plan."

There was a hiss of anger from the other side of the canvas.

"No! The museum won't tolerate that! No wonder the war rooms are movin'! The Guardians have gotta be stopped! Tell Sinew to go to the Protector—"

He broke off. Goldie heard the tramp of heavy shoes.

"Go!" hissed Herro Dan. "Go now!"

This time, the children obeyed him. Toadspit snapped his knife shut, and he and Goldie leaped to their feet and ran. They ran silently, heads down, slipping in and out of the tents and wagons, trying to keep something between themselves and the tramping feet.

There was a shout off to one side. Without turning around, they ran faster, no longer worrying about the noise. Goldie's feet pounded in the mud; her heart hiccuped with fear. They were nearly at the edge of the camp. If they could just reach the long grass, they could disappear into it—

"Hey! Where yoo tink yoo goink?"

Goldie stopped so abruptly that she almost fell over. A soldier had stepped out from behind one of the wagons, directly in their path. He was dressed like someone from the depths of history, with baggy knee-breeches and stockings, and a long-sleeved coat of such a deep gray that it seemed to suck all the light out of the air. His old-fashioned musket was pointed at Toadspit's head.

A second soldier came jogging up behind them. He stared at the children, his eyes blue and hard. "Leedle spice, hey?" he said.

His accent was so heavy that it took Goldie a moment to work out what he had said. When she realized that he thought they were spies, her heart seemed to shrivel within her.

"Who senchoo?" said the first soldier, poking Toadspit with the end of his musket. "You wit de odder spy? De old man?"

Toadspit flinched but said nothing. The soldier leaned toward them and winked, as if he was going to tell them a wonderful secret. His face was filthy and his skin was red and peeling. He stank of tobacco and stale sweat.

"We gonna shoot dat old man soon," he said. "But I don't tink we wait for dat. I tink we shoochoo now."

He wasn't lying. Goldie could hear it in his voice. Could see it in his face. He cared nothing for human life, this man. He was going to shoot them, right now. Unless she could find some way of stopping him . . .

He turned the barrel of his musket toward her. "Who's gonna go ferst?" he said. "De leedle gel—" The barrel shifted back to Toadspit. "Or de leedle boy?"

Goldie was trembling so hard that she thought she might shake to pieces. But at the same time, her mind was racing. These soldiers looked as if they had spent their whole lives fighting. What did they know about children? Not much, probably. So if she acted younger than she was, and a bit stupid . . .

The soldier sighted down the barrel.

Goldie giggled.

It was such an odd sound in the circumstances that both the soldiers and Toadspit stared at her in astonishment. She giggled again, trying to sound as brainless as possible.

"Ooh, you gave me a fright," she said. "Look at those big guns! They're so scary! You must be so brave, being soldiers. I wish *I* was a soldier. Don't you wish you were a soldier, Toadspit? Aren't they wonderful? Aren't they *scary*?"

She grabbed Toadspit's hand in both of hers, as if she was clinging to him in a girly sort of way. Her fingers flicked against his skin. *Concealment by Sham.*

Toadspit's eyes widened the tiniest amount. Then his face split in a foolish grin. "If *I* was a soldier," he said loudly, "I'd be scary too. I'd march!" He swung his arms and thumped his feet up and down. "I'd fight!" He aimed an imaginary gun at Goldie. *"Boom!"* he shouted. "You're dead!"

One of the soldiers lowered his musket slightly and laughed. "Goot boy. Yoo shoot yore sister. Yoo proper solja!"

The second man was still watching them suspiciously. "Whachoo doink here?" he growled. "Dis is army camp, not skool ground."

"We lost our dog and we're looking for him," said Goldie. She blinked up at the man. "Have you seen him? He's small and white. And he's very fat. Isn't he, Toadspit?"

"He's a roly-poly," said Toadspit.

"Our pa says he'd make a good roast dinner," said Goldie.

173

"But he's only joking. No one would hurt Broo. He's so little and sweet. And harmless."

The soldiers looked at each other. Goldie could almost see the thought passing between them. *Little fat dog. Little fat roast dog. Hmm.*

They only hesitated for a moment. "We help yoo find him," said the first man. "We like dogs."

"We like dogs *very* much," said the second man. He licked his lips and they both laughed.

"Ooh, *thank* you!" said Goldie. "I don't think he's far away. We could call him and see if he comes."

"Yoo do dat," said the second soldier. "And when he comes, we welcome him goot." He loosened the knife in his belt.

Goldie took a deep breath. "Broo-oo!" she called. "Where are you?"

"Broo, you naughty boy!" shouted Toadspit. "Come here at once!"

"Come and save us from the scary soldiers!" giggled Goldie.

The soldiers laughed their ugly laugh. The first man slipped his knife out of its sheath and ran his thumb along the edge. "Leedle do-og," he shouted. "Kom here quick! We got a treat for yoo!"

Goldie saw a flicker of movement in the long grass. Her arm felt as heavy as lead, but with a huge effort, she raised it and pointed in the wrong direction.

"Oh, look!" she said. "*There* he is."

Both soldiers turned, laughing—

There was a roar of fury, and out of the grass behind them charged Broo. He was as black as night and as big as a lion. His eyes were red and his great teeth gnashed the air.

The soldiers swung around and saw him. The first one shouted and tried to aim his musket, but Broo was already upon him, bearing him to the ground, his teeth at the soldier's throat.

The second man's face was white under the dirt. He backed away, his hands shaking, his fingers tightening on the trigger. . . .

There was a rattle of wings, and the air around him was suddenly alive with black feathers and a cruel, curved beak. The soldier screamed and dropped his musket.

Broo raised his head. There was blood on his muzzle. "*Rrr–u–un!*" he growled.

Goldie and Toadspit ran.

THE HAMMERING

"You should *not* have gone through the Dirty Gate!"

Sinew had been pacing up and down the office. Now he stopped and glared at Goldie and Toadspit. "You could've been killed! And not just you, but Broo and Morg as well. They're not bulletproof, you know. You *shouldn't* have gone!"

"Of course they should not," said Olga Ciavolga. "They were brave, and very clever at the end. But at the beginning they did not show a scrap of wisdom between them."

Goldie blushed. It was true. She and Toadspit were lucky

to have escaped with their lives. She half-wished that Olga Ciavolga would scold her, but the old woman merely said, "It is done now. And so we must decide. What next to do?"

"Herro D-Dan said Sinew has to g-go to the Protector," said Goldie. She hadn't stopped shivering since she and Toadspit had dragged the Dirty Gate shut behind them.

"And the Protector has to stop G-Guardian Hope and Guardian C-Comfort making their floor p-plan," said Toadspit, who was shivering just as hard.

Sinew nodded impatiently. "Yes, yes, we should've taken the Blessed Guardians more seriously right from the beginning. They're not here at the moment, but I'm sure they'll be back before long. I'll go to the Protector. But what do we do about Dan?"

"And Broo," said Goldie. "And Morg. Do you think they'll be all right?"

"I certainly hope so," said Sinew. His expression softened. "They can look after themselves in most circumstances. I expect we'll see them back here soon enough. As for Dan—" He ran his hand over his face. "Perhaps I should try and get him out."

"After what has happened," said Olga Ciavolga, "the soldiers will be even more on their guard. And Dan's leg is broken. You would have little hope of stealing him without being caught."

"I wasn't thinking of stealing him," said Sinew. "I was

thinking of buying him." He put his hand in his pocket and pulled out a coin. "Blood and gold, that's what those soldiers love more than anything. We won't give them blood if we can help it, but we have gold sovereigns enough to turn their heads. I could have Dan safely back with us by nightfall."

"I think not," said Olga Ciavolga. "You would only stir things up further."

"But—"

"No!" The old woman's face was pale with worry, but she held up her hand. "We shall do what Dan tells us. You go to the Protector and ask her to stop the Guardians and get them out of the museum. I think if she can do this, then the war rooms will calm down a little and Dan will be safe."

"What if the Protector *can't* stop them?" asked Goldie.

"Then," said Olga Ciavolga, "we must do it ourselves."

Sinew pulled on his coatee and left for the Protectorate. Toadspit returned to the back rooms to wait for Broo and Morg.

Goldie didn't want to go with him. "Can I stay here with you?" she said to Olga Ciavolga.

"Very well," said the old woman. "But you must remain close. And if the Guardians come back, you must hide immediately."

She sat down at the desk and began to write in a large book. The midday sun shone through the office window. Goldie leaned against one of the bookcases and pushed her hands deep into the pockets of her smock until she found her compass.

She took it out and ran her fingers over the metal casing. It was hard to believe how much her life had changed since she had come to the museum. She had longed to be free and now she was. And although the museum contained many terrors, she would rather face them all, one after the other, than go back to the way things used to be.

There were different sorts of fear, she realized that now. There was the awful fear of having a musket held to your head, or having black oily water try to snatch you into its depths. There was nothing easy about that fear. It made your heart nearly tear itself out of your chest, and weakened the long bones in your legs so that you could barely stand. It made you want to vomit with fright.

But there was another sort of fear, the fear that you would never be allowed to be who you really were. The fear that your true self would have to stay squashed up, like a caged bird, for the rest of your life. *That* fear was worse than any soldier.

She put the compass back in her pocket and took out the blue enamel brooch. She stroked the little bird's wings. *I'm not really free,* she thought, *not while Ma and Pa are locked up in the House of Repentance. . . .*

Somewhere nearby, heavy feet trod across wooden floors. Olga Ciavolga threw down her pen. "Quickly, child! Hide!"

Goldie scrambled into the space under the desk and pressed herself against the wood. Outside the office the feet stamped to a halt.

"The Guardians have returned," murmured Olga Ciavolga out of the corner of her mouth. "And they have brought many others with them."

"What are they doing?" whispered Goldie.

"I do not know, but they carry coils of rope and wooden planks. I do not like the look of it. Stay here. Do not make a sound."

Olga Ciavolga hurried out of the office. Goldie heard her say loudly, "What is the meaning of this? What do you think you are doing?"

"We are on the Seven's business," said a voice that Goldie recognized as Guardian Hope's. "So you had best keep out of our way, old woman." Her voice rose. "Pay attention, under-colleagues! I want this done quickly and I want it done properly. You, you and you. Hammer duty."

There was a rustle of robes and a shuffling of feet. Goldie pressed herself close to the floor and peeped around the corner of the desk.

She couldn't see Olga Ciavolga, but the corridor was full of young Guardians. They seemed to be laying planks in a horizontal line along the wall at waist height, each one touching the one that came before it.

Goldie heard a cry of outrage, and Olga Ciavolga strode into sight, her eyes blazing. "I do not believe it! You are trying to stop the rooms moving! You *fools*, you will kill us all!"

"We are simply following the orders of the Fugleman," said Guardian Hope.

"Be *damned* to the Fugleman!" said Olga Ciavolga. There was a gasp of horror from the Guardians, but the old woman took no notice. "Your master has no authority here! The museum answers only to the Protector!"

Guardian Hope shook her head pityingly. "My master answers to the Seven Gods. They are greater than any earthly authority."

She crooked her finger, and two of the young Guardians hurried to her side. "Get rid of this *obstacle*," she snapped. "Lock her in the office."

Goldie ducked back beneath the desk. She could hear Olga Ciavolga struggling, then the door banged shut and the key turned in the lock. A moment later, the hammering began.

It seemed to Goldie that, when the first blow fell, the museum cried with outrage, just as Olga Ciavolga had done, but a hundred thousand times greater. She found herself holding her breath, waiting for what would come next.

A second hammer blow fell—then a third.

The whole museum *shuddered*.

"Quickly!" whispered Olga Ciavolga. "Help me, child!"

Goldie scrambled out from underneath the desk and put her hand on the wall. The wild music *exploded* around her. She tried to sing, but the music drowned out her voice. She sang louder, and louder still, until at last she could hear herself. From somewhere deep within the museum, Toadspit's voice joined with hers and Olga Ciavolga's.

I wonder if he can guess what the hammering is, she thought. *I wonder if Broo and Morg are back yet, and if they're all right—*

And then she was swept away by the maelstrom, and there was no time or space to think about anything. The wild music crashed in upon her from every side. Her voice rode it like a tiny boat on a monstrous ocean. She could feel herself bobbing and spinning and nearly sinking, over and over again.

At one point, both Olga Ciavolga and Toadspit ran out of breath at the same time. The music surged up wilder than ever. Goldie clung to it by a thread of sound. She could no longer see the office. She could no longer hear anything except those deep, terrible notes.

But just when she thought she couldn't hold on for a second longer, Olga Ciavolga's voice rang out again. Goldie grabbed it like a lifeline. Then Toadspit was back too, unseen but singing for all he was worth. Gradually the wild music wove itself to their song and began to settle.

Olga Ciavolga took her hand off the wall. Beads of sweat

stood out on her forehead. "We have held it for now," she said. "But I fear it will not last."

Outside the door, the hammers rang. The museum *twitched* like a giant tormented by swamp flies.

"Can't they *feel* it?" said Goldie. "Can't they hear the wild music?"

"Apparently not," said Olga Ciavolga. "But even if they did, I fear they would continue. There is wickedness behind this."

She took her kerchief out of her pocket and tied it around her neck. Then she hurried over to the desk and began to pull out the drawers one by one.

"If the war rooms were on the move before," she said, "they will be seething now. Sinew was right after all. We must get Dan out before it is too late."

She scooped a handful of gold sovereigns out of each drawer and dropped them into her pockets. Goldie looked at the locked door. "How will we get out of here?"

"*Pff!*" said Olga Ciavolga. "Those imbeciles know nothing about this place!"

She patted her bulging pockets, then strode over to the corner of the room and sank to her knees with a grunt. She lifted the edge of the carpet. Underneath it was a trapdoor.

"This tunnel will take us to the back rooms," she said. "We have not used it for many years, so it will be full of dust and spiders." She looked hard at Goldie. "But I do not imagine that a girl who has been through the Dirty Gate will be stopped by a few spiders."

Olga Ciavolga was right. There *were* spiders in the tunnel, and not just a few. Goldie couldn't see them, but the strands of broken webs clung to her face, and whenever the hammering paused she thought she could hear brittle legs scuttling up and down the walls.

Her skin crawled, and she pushed the webs away with a shudder. A little way ahead of her Olga Ciavolga's dry old voice was like an anchor in the darkness.

"The people of Jewel," said Olga Ciavolga, "treat their children like delicate flowers. They think they will not survive without constant protection. But there are parts of the world where young boys and girls spend weeks at a time with no company except a herd of goats. They chase away wolves. They take care of themselves, and they take care of the herd."

She stopped. Goldie could hear the hammers, behind her now, rapping and tapping like someone knocking at a distant door.

"Fools!" muttered Olga Ciavolga. "Imbeciles!"

She began to shuffle forward again. "And so, when hard times come—as they always do in the end—those children are resourceful and brave. If they have to walk from one end of the country to the other, carrying their baby brothers and sisters, they will do it. If they have to hide during the day and travel at night to avoid soldiers, they will do it. They do not give up easily."

The tunnel took a sharp right-hand turn and, for a moment, the old woman's voice was lost. Something dropped onto Goldie's arm, and she opened her mouth to yelp—*and thought of those children carrying their baby brothers and sisters through the night*—and closed her mouth and kept going.

She rounded the corner in time to hear Olga Ciavolga murmur, "Of course, I am not saying that it is a *good* thing to give children such heavy responsibilities. They must be allowed to have a childhood. But they must also be allowed to find their courage and their wisdom, and learn when to stand and when to run away. After all, if they are not permitted to climb the trees, how will they ever see the great and wonderful world that lies before them— Aha, we are here!"

She stopped short and began to fumble with a latch in the roof of the tunnel. There was a shout, then someone grabbed the trapdoor and dragged it open from above. Toadspit peered down at them, Morg on his shoulder.

"What's happening?" he said. "Why did you use the tunnel? What's that hammering sound? Why is—"

A huge dark head nudged him aside. "Someone is doing bad things to the museum," rumbled the gravelly voice of the brizzlehound. "Can I go and kill them?"

WAITING

Olga Ciavolga would not let them go through the Dirty Gate with her. Toadspit protested, but Goldie could tell that he was as relieved as she was.

"You must wait for Sinew," the old woman said. "When he comes, tell him where I have gone. Tell him I will return as soon as possible, and Dan with me."

"What if they—" Goldie bit her lip. "What if they shoot you?"

"I understand the minds of these soldiers," said Olga Ciavolga. "I do not think they will hurt me. And if the Protector acts quickly to stop the Blessed Guardians, the war rooms will calm down and the soldiers will become less dangerous."

"Why will you not let *me* stop the Blessed Guardians?" complained Broo. "I would not kill them if you did not want me to. I would merely pick them up and chew them a little. And when I put them down again, they would run away."

"And then they would come back with nets and guns," said Olga Ciavolga, "to capture the last living brizzlehound. No, my dear, they do not know of your existence, and that is as it should be. We will leave this particular battle to the Protector."

She scratched Broo behind the ear, and stroked Morg's black feathers. Then she smiled at Goldie and Toadspit. "You are bold children and your hearts are good," she said. "But you must both learn to think before you act. Whatever happens, remember that there is always a choice. Think of the consequences, and then do what you must."

She turned away—and turned back again. "Tell Sinew he is not to come after me, whatever happens. He is needed here."

Then, with a whisk of colored skirts and a clink of coins, she was gone.

Goldie sat on the second step of Harry Mount, kicking her heels against the wood. Three steps farther up, Toadspit was playing with his folding knife, palming it and making it disappear. Broo paced the floor below them with long, rippling strides.

"Can I borrow your wire?" said Goldie, after she had watched Toadspit for a while.

Toadspit shrugged, and handed over the wire that he had used to open the Dirty Gate. Goldie took the scissors and a small padlock out of her pocket.

She liked picking locks. Olga Ciavolga had been pleased with how quickly she had learned it. "But you must practice whenever you have the chance," the old woman had said. "There are many locks in this city, and some of them would test even me. One day your life might depend upon your ability to open them."

Goldie slipped one blade of the scissors into the padlock's keyhole, and turned it slightly. Then she poked the wire into the hole above the scissor blade. When she pressed upward she could feel the five little barrels that made up the lock. She pushed at the first one and, after a moment or two, heard a tiny click.

She got the second barrel out of the way too, and the third. But by then the air was growing hotter, as if the whole museum was sickening with a fever, and it was too hard to concentrate.

"Here," she said, giving Toadspit back the wire and jumping to her feet. "Let's go and see what's happening."

Toadspit stood up slowly, as if he had been thinking. "You

know what I reckon? The Guardians are trying to get into the back rooms. Why else would they be nailing the museum down? They're trying to find the Staff Only door."

Goldie nodded. That made sense. "But why?" she said. "What do they want?"

"I don't know."

Broo growled softly. "They will *grrrrnot* come to the back rooms. I will not *let* them. Even when they are in the *frrrront* rooms they make the air smell bad." The hackles on his back rose so that he looked even bigger than usual. "And they *grrrrrhurt* the museum!"

"Don't worry, Sinew and the Protector will stop them," said Goldie, hoping she was right.

The two children wandered through the unsettled rooms, with Morg huddled on Toadspit's shoulder and Broo padding a little way ahead. Every now and again the museum *shuddered*, and Goldie and Toadspit stopped and sang. Before long their throats and their tempers were ragged.

Only Broo seemed unaffected by the waiting. His nostrils quivered, and he growled deep in his chest, but at the same time there was something patient about him, as if he was a coiled spring that could wait and wait until the moment came for action. And the Seven Gods help whoever stood in his way then.

"Broo," said Goldie, who was not feeling at all patient, and wanted something else to think about, "how do you decide when to be big and when to be little?"

Broo cocked his head. "I do not decide, any more than humans decide when to be angry or when to be happy. The big and the little decide for me. Sometimes it is a surprise, even to me."

"Which do you like better?" said Goldie.

The brizzlehound looked thoughtful. "It is agreeable to chase mice and pretend that there is no greater danger in the world. But it is also agreeable to leap upon an enemy and gnaw his bones. . . . Do I have to choose? I do not think I can."

Goldie was going to ask more, but just then the museum *shuddered* again. By the time they had sung to it, in increasingly hoarse voices, she had forgotten her question.

They were passing the stranded ship in Rough Tom when Broo pricked up his ears. A second later, Goldie heard a rumbling sound in the distance. A street-rig horn wailed like a lost child.

"That's the Shark!" said Toadspit. "Do you reckon Herro Dan's back?"

Broo shook his head. "*I* would not howl so miserably if a friend had just returned from beyond the Dirty Gate."

"But you're not the Shark," said Toadspit. "Herro Dan *might* be back. And Olga Ciavolga too! Let's go and see."

Goldie didn't move. "Olga Ciavolga told us to wait for Sinew."

"Yes, but she didn't say *where*."

"She didn't mean chasing all over the place."

"What are you talking about? We've already *been* all over the place! Sinew will find us wherever we are."

Goldie knew that Toadspit was right. But the heat and the worry had worn her temper to shreds, and suddenly she didn't want to take another step. "Well, I'm not going."

"Well, I am!"

"I don't think you should. I think we should stay together."

Toadspit glowered at her. "Who cares what you think?"

"Do not quarrel," said Broo. "If it concerns you, *I* will go." And he bounded away.

With the brizzlehound gone, the waiting was even harder. The two children leaned against the hull of the ship, avoiding each other's eyes. Goldie felt as if every nerve in her body was stretched to breaking point.

"I hope Olga Ciavolga's all right," she said.

Toadspit let out a huff of irritation. "Of course she's all right. Don't be stupid!"

"Who are you calling stupid?"

"I can't see anyone else round here, so it must be you."

Goldie pushed herself away from the ship and glared at him. "*You're* the stupid one!"

"I'm not!"

"You are!"

"If you hadn't come here," said Toadspit, "none of this would've happened."

"This hasn't got anything to do with me! If you haven't worked that out by now, you're even dumber than I thought!"

"I should set Morg onto you. She'd like a couple of juicy eyes. Plop. Plop."

"Oh come on, you think I'm scared of Morg? Here, Morgy, come and sit on *my* shoulder. I'm much nicer than him!"

"She doesn't like you. She'd only like you if you were *dead*, wouldn't you, Mo—"

He broke off, the blood draining from his face. Far away, in the depths of the museum, Goldie heard something groan, as if a high wind was rising.

"*A-a-a-a-ah!*" Morg launched herself from Toadspit's shoulder. At almost the same moment, the wind hit them. It wasn't one of the Great Winds, but it was strong enough to snatch the slaughterbird out of the air and blow her past them like a bundle of black rags.

Goldie staggered against Toadspit and they clutched each other, trying to stay upright. The wind wailed around their ears like a warning—and then it was gone.

In the sudden silence, the two children stared at each other in horror, their argument forgotten. They both knew what the wind had tried to tell them.

Something had happened to Olga Ciavolga.

INSURRECTION

Goldie barely had time to gather her wits together before Sinew was hurrying toward them. His face was white.

"I felt the wind," he said. "What's happened? What are those fools doing in the front rooms? Where's Olga Ciavolga?"

"She went through the Dirty Gate," said Toadspit.

"No!" cried Sinew. And he turned on his heel and ran.

"Wait!" shouted Goldie. "She said that you mustn't—"

But Sinew was already gone.

The children took off after him. Through the long rooms

they ran, with Morg flapping heavily above them. Through Vermin, through Broken Bones. Up Harry Mount and down again. Through Dark Nights, Lost Children and Stony Heart.

Several times they glimpsed Sinew ahead of them. Once the rooms *shifted* just as they were about to catch him, and Goldie and Toadspit found themselves on the Lady's Mile. On the opposite side of the hall, far out of their reach, Sinew was running along an old wooden gallery that Goldie had never seen before.

"Sinew!" shouted Toadspit. *"Stop!"*

But Sinew didn't even turn his head.

When at last the children stumbled, panting, up to the Dirty Gate, he was already there. His harp was slung over his shoulder and he was dragging the Gate open, inch by inch. On the other side of it, the long grass shivered, as if there was a storm coming. The air was heavy with the smell of gunpowder.

"Sinew!" cried Goldie. "Olga Ciavolga said you mustn't go after her!"

But by then Morg was flapping around their heads and Sinew's harp strings were sobbing and his face was as dark as the coming storm. Goldie wasn't even sure that he heard her.

The children threw themselves against the Gate and tried to hold it closed. But Sinew was too strong for them. Gradually they were forced backward.

Suddenly, Toadspit stopped pushing and slipped through the widening gap. From the other side of the Dirty Gate, he glared at Sinew. "If you go, I'm going too!"

Sinew stopped dead. He shook his head, like someone trying to wake up from a nightmare. "Don't be stupid, Toadspit. It's too dangerous. Besides, you're needed here."

"So are you!" said Goldie. "Olga Ciavolga said you mustn't go after her!"

Sinew's harp *ping*ed angrily. "I'm not going to leave her there. She saved my life once."

"Then you should listen to what she tells you," said a deep voice, "and not go rushing off like a thoughtless pup."

It was Broo. He loomed in the far doorway, looking as dangerous as Goldie had ever seen him.

Sinew flushed and opened his mouth to reply. Then he looked down at his hands, and the anger seemed to drain out of him. Toadspit slipped back through the gap. In silence, the three of them put their shoulders to the Gate and pushed it shut. Sinew took a key from his pocket and turned it in the lock.

No one seemed to know quite what to do then. Sinew leaned against the Dirty Gate, his harp silent, his hands dangling awkwardly at his side. Toadspit kicked at the wall, his whole body lost and angry.

"Sinew, what did the Protector say?" asked Goldie.

Sinew's face went blank for a moment, as if he had forgotten where he had just come from. "Oh," he said. "She's going to send for the Fugleman straight away and order him to stop the Blessed Guardians. I told her it was urgent."

He unslung the harp from his back and began to pace up

and down, plucking at the strings. "Of course, I didn't know about this latest madness then, the planks and the hammers." He shook his head. "Great whistling pigs, it's not *urgent* anymore, it's *desperate*! What are they thinking of? Who's behind it? Are they *mad*? Are they *vicious*? Do they have *any* idea what they're messing around with?"

The notes that he plucked seemed to twang and snap at the air. The grass on the other side of the Dirty Gate rippled. The stink of gunpowder grew stronger.

"Sinew," rumbled Broo. "You are making things worse."

Sinew's head jerked up. He listened to the fading notes and his face went pale. Quickly he put his hand on the harp strings to mute them. Then he folded his long legs, slid to the floor and leaned back so that his shoulders were pressed against the wall.

And he began to play the First Song.

It seemed to Goldie that the notes of the harp floated through the room like sunlight. Gradually, the grass on the other side of the Dirty Gate settled back to a shiver. The air cleared a little. The sense of danger remained, but it wasn't quite so close.

"The museum's still listening to us," whispered Sinew. "We can be grateful for that at least."

Toadspit snorted. "It's listening for now. But what happens if the Protector can't stop the Blessed Guardians?"

"She can," said Sinew. "She has to."

"What if she can't?" said Goldie.

Sinew chewed his lip. "Imagine a kettle coming to the boil. If you hold the lid down and don't let any steam escape, the pressure will build and build. Eventually the whole thing will explode."

"You mean the museum will just *blow up*?"

"Not exactly. But if the pressure gets too great, everything on the other side of the Dirty Gate will break out into the city. War. Famine. Plague. All the old evils. There's nothing on this side that can stand against them. Thousands of people will die. The city will fall."

Goldie felt as if a cold hand had touched the back of her neck. She thought of Ma and Pa in the House of Repentance, with the soldiers from behind the Dirty Gate marching toward them. She shivered.

"The museum should never have become so full of wild and dangerous things," said Sinew. "But the people of Jewel are like Guardian Hope, with her planks and hammers. They tried to nail life down. They wanted to be completely safe and happy at all times. The trouble is, the world just isn't like that. You can't have high mountains without deep valleys. You can't have great happiness without great sadness. The world is never still. It moves from one thing to another, back and forth, back and forth, like a butterfly opening and closing its wings."

As he spoke, the music seemed to twist and twine around

his words so that Goldie wasn't entirely sure who was talking, the man or the harp.

"Many years ago," said Sinew, "Olga Ciavolga and Herro Dan and I made a promise to each other. That one day we'd bring some of the wildness back to the city. Not the big stuff. Not wars and famine and plague. Just vacant blocks and dogs and cats and birds. And secret places for children to hide when they want to escape from the eyes of adults."

Broo rumbled his approval. Morg clacked her beak. Sinew took his hands off the harp strings, and the music continued on its own for a few bars, curling around Goldie like a waking dream.

"We'll do it too," said Sinew. "One day."

"If we survive," muttered Toadspit grimly. "If the city is still here."

The Fugleman took a long time to answer the Protector's summons. An *insultingly* long time. When at last he arrived, he strode in the door, sat down and put his boots up on the desk.

The Protector flushed with anger. She felt like throwing him out on the spot. But the news Sinew had brought was critical, so she promised herself that she would put up with her brother for now. She would make sure that the Blessed Guardians were stopped. *Then* she would throw him out.

"I believe I told you," she said in a cold voice, "that there was to be *no* Resident Guardian in the Museum of Dunt."

The Fugleman smirked. "And I took your instructions to heart, dear sister."

"There are Guardians there right now!" snapped the Protector. "And they are causing untold trouble!"

"But they arrive in the morning and they leave at night. They could hardly be called *resident*."

The Protector banged her fist on the desk. "Don't play word games with me, brother! I want your people out of the museum immediately."

The Fugleman leaned back in his chair and yawned. "No," he said.

"That was not a request. It was an order. There are forces in the museum that are not to be trifled with. You will withdraw your Guardians at once!"

"No," said the Fugleman again.

The Protector's scalp prickled and, for the first time in years, she found herself remembering her seventh birthday. Her father, a talented whitesmith, had made her a mechanical dog. When she wound it up with a tiny key, it whirred along behind her, wagging its tail.

She had loved that dog the minute she saw it. And so had her brother—loved it even more because it was hers. Loved it *especially* because it was hers.

He was only five, but by nightfall he had somehow

persuaded their father that the dog was really meant for him. With an awkward apology to his daughter, their father handed it over. Within a day the dog was broken, and the clever little key lost forever.

A chill ran through the Protector. She stood up, knowing that she must do something that no Protector before her had ever done. And, for the sake of the city, she must do it quickly. "Guard!" she shouted.

The door opened and the lieutenant marshal of militia marched into the room. His back was straight. His eyes were shadowed by the peak of his cap.

The Protector nodded toward her brother. "Arrest him."

The lieutenant marshal didn't move.

"Are you *deaf*?" said the Protector. "Arrest him!"

Still the lieutenant marshal didn't move. The Protector thought she saw his eyes dart from her to her brother and back again. A trickle of fear ran down her spine.

"What is this?" she said, as calmly as she could.

Slowly, her brother got to his feet. He sighed, as if he regretted what he was about to do. He put his hand on the Protector's shoulder.

"You've been looking *tired* recently, Your Graciousness," he murmured. "The Seven Gods think it's time you had a nice long rest. . . ."

STRANGERS IN THE BACK ROOMS

Goldie was asleep when it happened. The song of the harp had lulled her so well, and she was so tired that, despite everything, she had slumped down next to Sinew, closed her eyes and drifted off into a dream.

She was in the Great Hall of Jewel, and the air above her was full of clockwork birds, every one of them as blue as the distant horizon. But instead of twittering sweetly, the way they were supposed to, they squawked, "Pla-ague! Pla-a-a-ague!" Then they tumbled out of the air and lay broken on the floor.

She bent down and picked one of them up. Its eyes were bright with fever. "There are strangers in the back rooms," it growled.

And then the growling was all around her, and someone was shaking her awake. "Goldie! Goldie!"

She sat up quickly. Toadspit was kneeling beside her. Above him loomed Broo, as big as a bear and as black as night. The growling came from deep within him.

"There are strrrrangers in the back rrrro-o-oms!" he said again, in a voice that rumbled like a volcano on the brink of eruption.

Sinew was already on his feet with his harp slung over his back. "It must be the Blessed Guardians. Quickly! We must—"

But before he could say more, there was a great creaking and groaning of hinges, and the Dirty Gate swung open.

Goldie, Sinew and Toadspit threw themselves against it. But although there was no one on the other side, they couldn't force it shut. It seemed to be pushing against them, like an animal that has tasted freedom and refuses to go back in its cage. It was only when Broo added his great weight to theirs that the gate creaked back into place.

Sinew took the key from his pocket and turned it in the lock. "I did this before," he muttered. "I *know* I did. How could—"

"How could it open by itself?" whispered Goldie.

On the other side of the Dirty Gate, the long grass surged and rattled. Sinew shook his head in frustration. "The

Protector should have acted by now! I *told* her how important it was!"

"We cannot wait for her any longer," growled Broo.

"No," said Sinew. "We must stop these intruders ourselves."

They ran back through the dusty rooms even faster than when they had come. Morg flew ahead, crying, "Sto-o-o-op them! Sto-o-o-o-op th-e-e-e-em!" in a voice like the scraping of dry bones.

Broo was only seconds behind the slaughterbird. He would have outrun them all, but Sinew shouted, "Broo! Wait!"

The brizzlehound slowed just enough for them to catch up.

"I want you to stay out of sight," panted Sinew. "All of you. I'll deal with this on my own."

"No!" said Goldie.

"We'll all go!" said Toadspit.

"The children are *rrright*, Sinew," growled Broo. "The Guardians play with the lives of everyone in the city. I will *shake* them like *rrrrats*. They deserve no better."

Sinew shook his head. "Toadspit and Goldie mustn't be seen. And I'd rather they didn't know there's a brizzlehound in the museum."

They argued with him as they ran, but Sinew wouldn't change his mind. And so, just before they came to the Staff Only door, Goldie and Toadspit ducked behind a cabinet. They took Morg and Broo with them, although the brizzlehound shivered and growled in his desire to defend the back rooms against strangers.

Sinew strode forward alone, unslinging his harp. Goldie peeped around the side of the cabinet. What she saw made her gasp in dismay.

Beside her, Toadspit muttered, "I'm going to kill them."

The Staff Only door hung half off its hinges. Its frame was crisscrossed with planks, nailed into place to stop it shifting. Guardian Hope, Guardian Comfort and their young assistants were milling triumphantly through it.

Sinew strode toward them. "Stop!" he shouted. "You must go no farther!" At the same time, he played a string of notes on his harp. The combined sound seemed to freeze the Blessed Guardians in their tracks.

In the sudden quiet, Sinew spoke—and played—again. "There are things in this museum," he said, "that are more terrible than you can imagine. If you keep going, you will all die. And so will your brothers and sisters, your mothers, your fathers and your children."

The young Guardians stared at him, open-mouthed. So did Guardian Hope and Guardian Comfort, but only for a second. Then Guardian Hope's face twisted into a sneer. "Lies!" she cried. "He's just trying to protect his little secrets."

"He's trying to protect *you*!" whispered Goldie. "He's trying to protect all of us!"

"I'm going to kill them," muttered Toadspit again.

"We are on the Seven's business!" said Guardian Comfort loudly. "We won't be stopped by these pathetic threats!"

"Indeed we will not!" snapped Guardian Hope. "Advance!"

The young Guardians looked at each other uncertainly. None of them moved.

Sinew's fingers plucked a ringing note from the harp strings. "It's true that there are secrets here. But they won't bring you wealth or fame or glory, if that's what you've been told. They'll only bring death, to you and to everyone you love."

"Rubbish!" screeched Guardian Hope. "Abomination! Don't listen to him!"

"Turn back now," said Sinew. "Turn back and you'll be safe."

"Turn back," whispered Goldie.

"No!" Guardian Hope's face was purple with rage. "Move forward at once! I order you! Anyone who doesn't move forward will suffer the awful displeasure of the Seven!"

The young Guardians began to mutter among themselves. Even Guardian Comfort looked uneasy.

"Silence!" shouted Guardian Hope.

The muttering grew louder. Feet shuffled nervously. Eyes darted from Sinew to Guardian Hope and back again.

"It's working," whispered Goldie. She turned to Broo and Toadspit. "They believe him!"

She was right. One by one, the young Guardians put down their hammers and nails. They turned their backs on

Guardian Hope and Guardian Comfort. They began to retreat. . . .

"*Stop—right—there!*" cried a deep voice.

Goldie's head jerked up in dismay. She saw the young Guardians shuffle to one side, leaving an open pathway.

Through it strode the Fugleman.

He swept up to the Staff Only doorway like a summer storm. He carried a sword in his hand, and he jabbed at the display cases as he passed, as if he was afraid of nothing.

In his wake trailed a string of gazetteers, clutching notebooks and pens. When they saw the dust and cobwebs that lay beyond the broken door, they rolled their eyes in dismay and muttered to each other.

The Fugleman didn't seem to notice the dust at first. He stopped in the doorway, his handsome face serious. "It is my painful duty to inform you all," he said loudly, "that Her Grace the Protector is unwell."

There was a gasp from everyone listening. The gazetteers unscrewed the lids of their portable inkpots and began to scribble in their notebooks. From behind the cabinets, Goldie saw Sinew's face turn white.

"I'm sure that I speak for the whole city," continued the Fugleman, "when I say that I hope she will be better soon. May the Seven hold her in the glorious cup of their hands."

Goldie flicked her fingers so hard that it hurt. Beside her,

Toadspit was doing the same. One of the gazetteers called out, "Your Honor, can you tell us what's wrong with the Protector?"

"My physician is with her now," said the Fugleman. "He will report back to me soon. We should have an answer in time for tomorrow's gazettes."

Another gazetteer raised her hand. "Sir? Who's running the city?"

"Her Grace has given *me* the honor," said the Fugleman. "And in the short time that I have been in charge—"

The rest of his words were drowned out by a roar of approval from the Guardians.

Goldie stared at the Fugleman's handsome, lying face. *What's he done to the Protector?* she signed to Toadspit.

Listen! signed Toadspit.

The Fugleman was talking again. "In the short time that I have been in charge," he said, "I have uncovered a terrible plot. The blackguards who set off the bomb in my office, who so callously destroyed a young life, came from *very* close to home."

He pointed his sword at the high ceilings and the cobwebs. "As you can see, this building contains venomous insects. I suspect that there is disease, as well."

The gazetteers shuddered.

"But," said the Fugleman, "there is something even worse,

something that defies belief. I have proof of it here." He took a thin blue book from his pocket and waved it in the air. "This museum harbors a secret army—an army that plans to take over our city!"

The uproar this time nearly deafened Goldie. The gazetteers and the young Guardians pressed toward the Fugleman, shouting questions. Even Guardian Hope and Guardian Comfort looked startled.

Only Sinew and the Fugleman remained calm. Sinew played a loud *thrum* on his harp. It cut through the shouting like a knife. "Listen to me," cried Sinew. "The museum had nothing to do with the bombing—"

"It is true, is it not," interrupted the Fugleman, "that there is a place within these walls called the Dirty Gate?"

"Yes," said Sinew. "But—"

"And is it also true that on the other side of the Dirty Gate there is an army of ruthless killers?"

"Well, yes. But—"

"You hear him!" trumpeted the Fugleman. "Condemned by his own words!"

"Stop interrupting! Let him explain!" Goldie whispered.

"You're making a terrible mistake," said Sinew. "Talk to the Protector! She'll tell you—"

"Aha!" cried the Fugleman. "It was the Protector herself who insisted that I deal with this awful danger! You are the only one who can save us, Fugleman! she said. You must act quickly before we are all destroyed!"

"The Protector would never have said that!" cried Sinew.

The Fugleman ignored him. He raised his sword in the air. "Guards!" he shouted.

There was a tramp of feet, and a squad of militia pushed through the crowd. The Fugleman pointed his sword at Sinew. "Arrest this man!"

The militiamen cocked their rifles. They eyed Sinew warily as if he might be one of the ruthless killers himself. They began to walk toward him.

No! thought Goldie.

"No!" said Toadspit.

"*Nnnnnnoooooooooooooo!*"

The sudden roar, right in Goldie's ear, almost deafened her. "Broo, stop!" she cried, but she was too late. The brizzle-hound had leaped over her head and was bounding toward the militiamen, bellowing his fury. His teeth were bared and his hackles stood up like spikes. Above his head flapped Morg, a black harbinger of death.

When they saw those twin awful sights bearing down on them, most of the militiamen froze in their tracks. Only the lieutenant marshal seemed to keep his head. His hand shook, but he raised his rifle. Goldie saw his finger tighten on the trigger.

"No!" shouted Sinew, and he threw himself at the lieutenant marshal. The gun went off. The bullet flew harmlessly past Broo's ear.

The sound of the shot seemed to bring the other militiamen to their senses. They raised their guns. But before they could take aim, Broo was upon them, his great teeth snapping.

He mowed the militiamen down like grass. They screamed and tumbled over one another trying to escape. But Morg was waiting for them, with her sharp beak and her tearing claws and the shadow of her wings falling across them like a shroud.

"Broo! Morg! Don't hurt them!" shouted Sinew. Goldie could only just hear his voice above the chaos.

And then, suddenly, she heard another shot. It echoed strangely, cutting through all the shouting and screaming. Time slowed down. The bullet seemed to hang in the air for many seconds before it hit its mark.

Goldie felt herself stand up and walk out from behind the broken cabinets. She could see the Fugleman. In the middle of all the scrambling, he was completely still. His sword was sheathed, and he held a militia rifle pressed against his shoulder. He was smiling.

She began to run. Toadspit was running beside her, but the air was as thick as treacle, and they couldn't move fast enough.

She felt a cry of despair well up in her chest. She saw

Sinew's mouth open in a horrified shout. She saw Morg flap frantically up toward the rafters, leaving a dozen feathers drifting through the air like black snow.

She saw Broo flinch—and falter. She saw him snap one last desperate time at the nearest militiaman.

She saw him fall.

RUNAWAYS

Goldie knelt on the floor beside the great body of the brizzlehound. Toadspit and Sinew knelt beside her. All around them, people were shouting with shock and relief. Blessed Guardians and gazetteers pounded the Fugleman on the back. Militiamen scrambled to recover their rifles and their dignity.

Goldie hardly noticed them. Tears poured down her face and mingled with the blood that pooled around the brizzlehound's head. She stroked Broo's ear with a shaky hand. Her chest felt hollow, as if something big and important had been torn out of it. The sound of the shot still echoed inside her.

"He was just trying to protect us," whispered Toadspit. He looked up at Sinew, the tears streaming down his cheeks. "Why did they have to shoot him?"

Sinew shook his head helplessly. He lifted one of the enormous paws and held it in both hands. On the floor beside him, his harp sobbed.

Goldie rested her hand on Broo's neck. She was amazed now that she had once been afraid of him. Toadspit was right. All he had ever wanted to do was protect them.

Above her head, a voice said, "Your Honor! Look! There are children here! And they are *unchained*!"

For a moment, Goldie didn't understand what the voice was talking about. By the time she looked up, there was a circle of appalled faces staring down at her and Toadspit. The Fugleman was shaking his head sorrowfully.

"Ladies and gentlemen," he said. "*This* is what happens to children when they are not properly protected. Look at them. Look at their wild hair and filthy, desperate faces. Look at the scratches on their arms and legs. How could this have happened? How could they be here, unchained and unsupervised?" He paused. "Well, I will tell you. This one—" He pointed an immaculate finger at Goldie. "This is the girl who ran away from the Great Hall on the day of the bombing!"

A shocked murmur ran through the watching gazetteers.

They scribbled frantically in their notebooks. Goldie looked down at her hands. What did it matter if she had run away? What did anything matter? Didn't they understand that Broo was dead?

"Guardian Hope!" called the Fugleman. "Are you there?"

With a flurry of importance, Guardian Hope pushed her way into the circle, closely followed by another Guardian, a stocky, red-faced man whom Goldie had never seen before.

"Oh no!" groaned Toadspit.

"Guardian Virtue," said the Fugleman to the stocky man. "Is this the boy?"

"It is, Your Honor," said Guardian Virtue, peering eagerly down at Toadspit. "*He's* a runaway too, name of Cautionary Hahn. His parents are locked up in the House of Repentance at this very moment."

Cautionary? Goldie looked at Toadspit in astonishment. He was staring at the floor, his face set and angry.

"Dear me!" said Guardian Virtue, his Adam's apple bobbing with excitement. "I can hardly bear to look at the boy! Such a mess he's got himself into! Riddled with purple fever, no doubt, and only Great Wooden knows what else. He's a risk to himself and everyone around him!"

Toadspit's head snapped up. "It's not us that's the risk!" He glared at Guardian Virtue and the Fugleman. "It's you! You're murderers, the lot of you! And if you don't leave the museum alone there'll be worse things in Jewel than purple fever!"

The Fugleman didn't seem to hear him. "Here we have two children," he said loudly. "Both of them criminals. Both of them obviously mentally disturbed—"

"We're *not* mentally disturbed!" cried Goldie. "We're trying to warn you—"

At that moment, under her hand, something *twitched*. She jerked back in shock. Broo's head lifted slightly from the floor—then slumped down again.

Goldie's heart seemed to leap in her chest. "He's alive!" she whispered. At least, she meant it to be a whisper, but in her excitement it came out louder. "Sinew! Toadspit! He's *alive*!"

There was a split second of horrified silence—then the room erupted. The gazetteers and Blessed Guardians fell over each other in their desire to get away. The militiamen bellowed instructions.

"The brute's alive!"

"Finish it off, quickly! Don't take any chances!"

"Give it a bullet in the head!"

Toadspit threw himself across Broo's body. "Leave him alone!" he shouted. "If you touch him I'll kill you!"

"Someone get this boy out of the way," yelled the lieutenant marshal.

Toadspit kicked and fought, but the militiamen picked him up as if he was a baby. They picked Goldie up too, and carried her a short distance away.

Sinew was not so easily moved. He stood astride Broo.

"This," he cried, "is the last living brizzlehound! If you kill him, you will set terrible forces in motion. You will condemn the city and everyone in it to death."

The Fugleman threw back his head and laughed. "The last living brizzlehound? In that case, we won't just kill it, we'll have it stuffed and mounted and displayed in the Great Hall!"

Goldie felt a ball of red-hot rage well up inside her. "I hate you!" she muttered through clenched teeth. "I *hate* you!"

The Fugleman laughed again. The militiamen raised their rifles and aimed at Broo. Goldie jammed her eyes shut, unable to watch.

But before the militiamen could fire, the air *shuddered*. The floorboards shook. Goldie's eyes snapped open. The water-gas lamps were flickering horribly, and for a moment, she thought they'd go out altogether. But slowly—oh so slowly— they came back to brightness.

Good! thought Goldie. *No one could miss a shift like* that*!*

She was right. The militiamen were looking at each other in confusion. The gazetteers and the Blessed Guardians muttered anxiously.

"Your Honor," said Sinew, bleak-faced. "You have to stop this, now. You must leave the museum and let me take care of the brizzlehound, or we will all perish."

For a moment, Goldie thought that the Fugleman was

listening. But then he smiled and turned to the gazetteers. "A small earth tremor, nothing more. Be sure to tell your readers that it is nothing to worry about."

He turned back to the militiamen. "As for the brizzlehound, perhaps it is more useful alive, for now, at least. Truss it up before it recovers consciousness and tie it to the railings outside my old office. We'll have a public execution tomorrow."

Sinew began to protest again, but the Fugleman interrupted him. "Take this man away," he said. "Gag him so he can't keep spouting his nonsense, and put him in the lowest level of the House of Repentance."

A group of militiamen rushed at Sinew and seized him. He struggled and fought, his face wild with rage and despair, but they tied him, gagged him and dragged him away. Goldie saw one of them pick up his harp and carry it after the others, like an uneasy trophy.

The militiamen who were left behind raised their guns again and aimed them at Broo. Several of the Blessed Guardians edged forward to offer ropes.

"Tie the beast securely, mind," said the Fugleman, "and strap its jaws so it cannot bite. If it tries to escape, shoot it."

"No!" cried Goldie. "Don't you *dare*!"

"What will we do with these children, Your Honor?" said the lieutenant marshal.

Goldie glanced at Toadspit. She could feel the anger

radiating from him, the same anger that was burning in her own body, as hot as a furnace.

"Ah yes, the children." The Fugleman raised his voice so that everyone could hear him. "Ladies and gentlemen, these children may be criminals, they may be mentally disturbed, but we still take our responsibilities to them seriously. My Blessed Guardians will look after them as if they were their own. May the Seven Gods go with them and soothe their troubled souls."

The Guardians in the crowd murmured approval. The gazetteers and the militiamen flicked their fingers.

May the Seven Gods go with you*!* prayed Goldie savagely. And, for the first time in her life, she didn't flick her fingers.

"As for me," continued the Fugleman, "my duty leads me into many dark places, but this may be one of the darkest. Tonight I will accompany the militia to this Dirty Gate. We will take the secret army by surprise. In the name of the Seven, we will destroy these murderous bombers who threaten our beautiful city!"

"Three cheers for the Fugleman!" shouted the lieutenant marshal. "Huzzah! Huzzah! Huzzah!"

The militiamen and the Blessed Guardians joined in enthusiastically. The gazetteers stopped writing for long enough to bang their notebooks against their legs and stamp their feet.

Under cover of the noise, the Fugleman bent down. Goldie

heard him murmur to Guardian Hope and Guardian Virtue, "Take the brats to Care. I want them locked up so securely that they'll never get away again."

Guardian Hope unhooked the punishment chains from around her waist and snapped them onto Goldie's wrists. "Come along," she said. "And don't give me any trouble."

Goldie glanced at Toadspit. Her fingers flicked out a message. *Must stop Fugleman! Must save Broo! Escape somehow!*

Toadspit's fingers twitched in response. *Agree! Meet—meet Fugleman's old office! Midnight!*

"Make way!" cried Guardian Hope. "Make way for the mentally disturbed child!"

The gazetteers and Blessed Guardians made way. At the last minute, just before she was swallowed up by the crowd, Goldie turned back toward Toadspit and wiggled her fingers as if she was waving goodbye. *Agree. Fugleman's old office. Midnight!*

In a small tent beyond the Dirty Gate, Olga Ciavolga was lying on her side, her arms and legs tied, her eyes closed. Herro Dan sat next to her, his fingers entwined with hers.

"You awake?" he whispered.

She squeezed his hand, but didn't open her eyes.

"I've been thinkin'. 'Bout when we was kids. First time I ever saw you, steppin' down off that great big boat as if you was a princess."

Olga Ciavolga snorted under her breath. "A ragged, under-fed princess. With fleas."

A moment's silence. Then Herro Dan sighed. "We've come a long way, you and me."

At that, Olga Ciavolga's eyes opened and she glared up at him. "Is this my funeral speech you are practicing? Do you think I will go to my coffin so easily? We are not finished yet!"

Despite the danger that surrounded them, and the pain of his broken leg, Herro Dan found himself smiling.

"Why are we not singing?" demanded Olga Ciavolga. "Must we leave all the work to Sinew and the children?"

Herro Dan had been singing under his breath for a day and a night, and still he could feel the wild music rising. But he nodded. *"Ho oh oh-oh. Mm mm oh oh oh-oh oh—"* he began. Olga Ciavolga's voice joined his. *"Mm oh oh oh-oh—"*

Suddenly the whole world seemed to—*shudder*.

Herro Dan's mouth fell open. The song stuck in his throat like a fish bone. He looked at Olga Ciavolga and saw his own fear reflected in her eyes.

There was a heavy footstep outside the tent, and the flap was dragged back. A soldier ducked his head and walked in. Olga Ciavolga's kerchief hung half out of his pocket.

He grinned at Herro Dan. "How yoo doink?" he said in his heavy accent. "Yoo havink a nice holiday? Plenty of sleep? Goot food?" He laughed. "If yoo go back home, tell dem about dis nice place, dey all want to kom here. Am I right? Yes? Ha-ha!"

He poked Herro Dan with his shoe. Herro Dan didn't respond. He and Olga Ciavolga had known soldiers like this when they were children. They had been all over Furuuna in those days, looting and killing with no thought for kindness or mercy. From what he had seen here, nothing had changed.

He closed his eyes. He knew that the song was useless, that the museum was no longer listening. But Olga Ciavolga was right. They must not give up. He began to sing again, so quietly that the sound didn't pass his lips.

"Whachoo doink?" said the soldier. "You sleepink? You dreamink about your girlfriend here? Yoo dream while yoo can. Yoo dream plenty. Because tomorrow—"

He walked back to the flap of the tent. "Tomorrow we gonna shoochoo. Yoo and de old lady. At first light we gonna shoochoo both."

CARE

T he massive gate swung shut behind Goldie. The iron bar fell into place with a clang that echoed around the cobblestoned yard. It was barely dusk in the world outside, but here, within the high walls of Care, the air was dark and gloomy.

"Don't dawdle!" said Guardian Hope, jerking at the punishment chains. "I've got more important things to do than hang around while you look at the scenery."

Goldie stumbled toward the tall building that loomed at the far end of the yard. At first glance it seemed welcoming.

The light in the entrance was soft and warm, and the house itself had sweetly curved balconies and high, elegant windows. But as Goldie came closer she saw that those windows were crisscrossed with bars, and the balconies topped with broken glass.

A cold despair gripped her heart. She put her hand in her pocket and her fingers closed around the little blue bird. *I have to escape. I will escape! I will!*

Guardian Hope marched her up the steps and in the front door like an executioner taking a prisoner to the gallows. There was another Guardian sitting in the foyer. He was completely bald, and he squatted behind his desk like a toad.

"Golden Roth, runaway," snapped Guardian Hope. "Chain both legs. No privileges." She unfastened the punishment chains. Then, without another glance at Goldie, she left.

The next half hour was a blur. Goldie was marched out of the foyer and down one long corridor after another, sometimes by one Blessed Guardian, sometimes by two. Along the way, she stopped being Goldie Roth and became Number 67: Runaway.

At the end of one corridor she was pushed into a dank concrete room and told to take her clothes off. As she did so, the little voice in the back of her mind whispered, *The scissors.*

Goldie fumbled with her smock, as if she was having

trouble getting her arm out of the sleeve. One of the Guardians grabbed her and pulled the smock this way and that, all the while complaining about how clumsy children were. Under cover of the fuss, Goldie palmed the scissors, the way Herro Dan had taught her.

She was pushed under a cold shower and scrubbed until her skin hurt, but she kept the scissors hidden in her hand all the while. It was just as well she did. When she was dry at last, and clean, her own clothes were taken away and she was given a gray smock and leggings that smelled as if they had been worn by a hundred children, every one of whom had died of unhappiness.

"Ooh, look, this is nice," said one of the Blessed Guardians, holding up Goldie's blue enamel brooch.

"That's mine!" said Goldie.

"Correction," said the Blessed Guardian, "it *was* yours. Fly away, little bird!" And she dropped the brooch into the pocket of her robes. Then she held out Goldie's compass. "This is yours too, I suppose? Well, you can have *this* one back. Not that it'll do you much good in here."

And she snorted with loud, ugly laughter and continued snorting on and off all the way down yet another corridor, until they came to a solid wooden door with a great black bolt across it.

The Guardian shot the bolt back and pushed the door open. "Silence!" she shouted, although there was not a sound coming from the room. "No talking! Eyes down if you want to keep your privileges!"

The room was long and there were twenty or more beds lined up around the edges. Most of them seemed to be occupied. The Blessed Guardian marched Goldie between them, gripping the back of her neck so that she couldn't look left or right. Halfway down the room, she stopped and pushed Goldie toward an empty bed with gray sheets and blankets. "Welcome to your new home," she said, and snorted with laughter again.

There was an iron staple in the wall above the bed, with chains and fetters dangling from it. The Blessed Guardian took the fetters down and snapped them around both Goldie's ankles, so that her legs were held in a sort of vice and could barely move. She put a padlock through the hole in the fetters. "Double chains!" she said. "You *have* been a bad girl!"

She pulled a plaque out of her pocket and hung it on a hook above the bed, next to the iron staple. Then, with a sweep of her robes, she strode back to the door.

"Night night, sleep tight," she said. "Mind the tarantulas don't bite!" And with one final snort of laughter she slammed the door, shot the bolt and was gone.

Goldie sat on the bed, clutching her compass in one hand and the scissors in the other. Her whole body felt cold and numb. The fetters on her ankles seemed to be trying to drag her through the floor. On the other side of the room, someone began to sob, a desperate, frightened sound.

"Hush, Rosie," murmured a nearby voice. "There aren't really tarantulas. You know she just says that to scare us."

"I wish there *were* tarantulas," said a different voice. "We could train them to bite Guardian Bliss."

Quiet laughter rippled across the room and was gone. Somewhere a chain clanked. The sobbing stopped.

"What's your name?"

It was the same voice that wanted to train the tarantulas. Goldie peered around the room. The only light came from a feeble lamp that guttered and smoked as if it might go out at any moment. *I feel just like that lamp,* thought Goldie.

"She's a runaway!" hissed another voice. "It says so on her plaque!"

"A runaway? I don't believe it."

"It says so, look!"

"I *still* don't believe it."

"We've never had a runaway before!"

"Do you think she's got any food on her?"

"Oh, if only! Hot banana bread!"

"Mango custard and cream!"

"Almond cakes!"

The whispers darted back and forth across the room like mice. Goldie's eyes were getting used to the dim light now, and she counted twenty-three girls sitting up in bed, staring

226

at her. The youngest was no more than three or four, and the oldest seemed to be about fifteen. They were all terribly thin and wretched-looking, but their eyes were curious and they didn't seem unfriendly. All of them wore guardchains, and several of them also had fetters on their ankles.

"What's your name?" The questioner was a small, dark-haired girl, four beds away on the opposite side of the room.

This time Goldie made herself answer. "Goldie Roth."

"Goldie Roth." "Goldie Roth." The information was passed down the room, whispered from girl to girl until it disappeared into the shadows at the far end.

"Did you really run away?" The dark-haired girl seemed to ask the questions for the rest of them. She wasn't the oldest by some years, but even in the feeble light there was something bright and stubborn about her face.

"Of course she didn't, Bonnie," said the girl in the bed on Goldie's right. She was one of the older ones. "No one runs away, it's impossible."

"It's *not* impossible," said Bonnie. "I've told you before, Candor. And this proves it."

"What does it prove?" said Candor. "The Blessed Guardians made a mistake, that's all. Or maybe they're just sick of writing 'Unsafe.'" She waved her hand at her own plaque.

Wearily, Goldie shook her head. "It's not a mistake. I *did* run away."

227

There was a hiss of satisfaction from Bonnie. "I told you!"

"I didn't mean to," said Goldie. "I just—I was going to be Separated and then they changed their minds because of the bomb. So I ran."

She found herself wondering why she had bothered. It had made no difference in the end. Here she was, chained more tightly than ever. Broo was probably bleeding to death, Sinew and Toadspit were captured, there was a strong possibility that Olga Ciavolga and Herro Dan were already dead—and if Sinew was right, the rest of them were going to die very soon.

Around her, the whispers were starting up again.

"Guardian Bliss told us about the bomb. Twenty children were killed!"

"And another twenty lost their arms and legs!"

"And *another* twenty were blinded!"

"Guardian Bliss said the bomber will probably come back soon—"

"—and he'll be looking for a new target—"

"—somewhere with lots of children who he can kill all in one go!"

"Somewhere like Care!"

There was another anxious sob from Rosie, the little girl who was afraid of tarantulas. "Is it true? Is the bomber coming here?"

Goldie didn't want to talk anymore. "No," she said shortly. "And there was only one person killed."

"See, I told you," said Bonnie again, looking around the room. "It's like the tarantulas, we can't believe anything they say. There's nothing horrible coming to get us. Or at least nothing more horrible than Guardian Bliss."

Another murmur of laughter.

How can anyone laugh in this place? thought Goldie. She dropped the scissors and the useless compass onto the bedside table and dragged her fettered legs up onto the bed. Then she lay down on her back, closed her eyes and tried not to listen to the flurry of questions directed at her.

"So how did you get away?"

"Where did you go?"

"What was it like being out on the streets by yourself?"

"What did you eat?"

"Yes, what did you eat?"

"Did you miss your ma? Did you cry?"

"*I* would've cried."

"How long were you on the loose?"

"I want to know what she *ate*!"

The girl called Candor laughed disdainfully and said, "Don't tell me you all believe her? I think she's making the whole thing up."

Goldie felt a flash of irritation. She did her best to ignore it. What was the point in being angry? She couldn't *do* anything.

"No one runs away," continued Candor. "The first person who saw you would turn you in. You know they would, they're all terrified of the Guardians. *I* think she's some sort of spy. I think the Guardians have put her in here to find out our secrets."

Goldie didn't want to move. She wanted to lie there and feel numb and not think about anything important. But the anger was flaring up inside her again, like a not-quite-extinguished spark.

She sat up. "Why should I care about your stupid secrets?" she snapped. "There are things happening that you don't know anything about! And there *is* something horrible coming."

She paused, remembering Sinew's words. *Everything on the other side of the Dirty Gate will break out into the city. War. Famine. Plague. Thousands of people will die. The city will fall.*

"At least," she said, "it'll come if someone doesn't stop it."

"What do you mean, something horrible?" said Bonnie.

"Like the bomber?" whispered Rosie. "But you said the bomber's not coming!"

"And who's going to stop it, whatever it is?" said Candor sarcastically. "You, I suppose."

Thousands of people will die. The city will fall.

Goldie took a deep breath. "Yes, me," she said. "Me and Toadspit. We *have* to stop it."

As soon as the words were out of her mouth she knew that she was right. This was no time for despair. Sinew and Olga Ciavolga and Herro Dan would expect more from her. She must be like those children who carried their baby brothers and sisters through the night. . . .

"Toadspit?" said Bonnie, with an odd expression on her face. "Who's Toadspit?"

"A boy," said Goldie. "Another runaway."

"What's he look like?"

"Oh, sort of smallish. And dark. Same age as me, I think. And he's got a horrible temper, but he's loyal and fierce too, which is good if he's on your side. His real name's Cautionary, which doesn't suit him at all."

When she heard those words, Bonnie's face opened up like the brightest of suns. "I told you!" she said, beaming around at the other girls. "My brother is still alive!"

THE PADLOCK

"**G**uardian Bliss told me he was probably dead," said Bonnie. "Or taken by Natkin Gull or Captain Roop, which is almost the same thing. But I always knew he'd be all right." She laughed. "And he changed his name, like he said he would! Toadspit! It's just the sort of name he'd choose. Where is he? Oh, I wish I could see him!"

"He's here somewhere, in Care," said Goldie. "He was caught at the same time I was. Where do the boys live?"

"Right at the back," said the girl in the bed to her left. "My brother's there. Sometimes we see each other across the yard, but that's all. We're not allowed to talk to each other, or wave or anything."

"*I'm* going to wave," said Bonnie. "I don't care what Guardian Bliss does to me. I'm going to wave and shout and call him Toadspit. I'm going to practice saying it so I don't forget. Toadspit Toadspit Toadspit! And I bet he waves and shouts back at me."

Goldie could see the similarity between the two children now. She was surprised that she hadn't noticed it before.

"That's all very well," said Candor, "but I want to know more about this danger. And how *she*"—pointing at Goldie— "thinks she's going to do anything about it when she's stuck here in double chains!"

"Um . . . ," said Goldie. "I'll have to escape—"

"Oh yes? How?" said Candor, sitting back with a skeptical expression on her face.

Goldie looked at her fetters, and at the heavily bolted door and the dark, barred windows. Her heart sank. She didn't know where to start. What would Olga Ciavolga say in these circumstances? Probably something sensible like, "First things first, child. Get out of your fetters, then worry about the rest."

Goldie wriggled her feet. The padlock on her fetters was enormous and looked quite different from anything she had tried to pick before. She wasn't even sure if it worked the same way.

Somewhere outside the building, a bell began to ring. The sound was muffled by the thick walls, but it was still recognizable as the Great Hall clock. *Ting-ting ting-ting. Ting-ting ting-ting.* Down the scale and up again.

There was a moment of silence, then the heavy chimes began to tell the hour. *Bongggg. Bongggg. Bongggg.* Goldie counted them. *Four, five, six. Seven, eight, nine. Ten . . .*

She waited for the next one, but it didn't come. It was ten o'clock. If she was going to meet up with Toadspit, she had exactly two hours to escape from Care and get to the Fugleman's office.

She took a deep breath and did her best to push all doubts out of her mind. "I'm going to pick the lock on my fetters," she said. "I've got a pair of scissors—"

There was a gasp from the beds around her. "She's got *scissors!*"

"—but I'll need something else. Something thin and tough that I can put a bend in, like a bit of wire."

Everyone looked at her blankly. Candor muttered, "And *I'll* have a roast haunch of quignog on a silver platter."

"No, wait," said Bonnie. She peered toward the far end of the room. "Lamb, what happened to your hairpins?"

Lamb was a pale-faced girl with long blond hair. "Oh, Guardian Bliss took them away ages ago. She counted to make sure she'd got them all."

Bonnie's face fell.

234

"But," said Lamb, digging under her mattress, "she doesn't count very well." She held something up, grinning widely.

"Pass it down!" whispered Bonnie, and the hairpin was handed carefully from one bed to the next, all the way down to Goldie.

It wasn't quite what she wanted, but it would have to do. She straightened it out, then pressed one end against the side of her bed to put a bend in it. It took her a while to get it right, but at last she was satisfied.

She slid one blade of the scissors into the hole in the padlock. She turned it just a little way, and felt the inside part of the lock turn with it. Then she slipped the bent end of the hairpin into the hole above the scissors and set to work.

None of the girls said a word while Goldie tried to pick the lock. Somewhere on the edge of her consciousness she could hear them breathing, but all her attention was focused into a tight little circle that centered on the hairpin.

She pushed it right to the back of the lock and dragged it forward, the way Olga Ciavolga had shown her. Then she did it again, trying to get at least one of the barrels to stay up out of the way. She poked and jabbed at them, feeling as if she was trying to find her way through a dark tunnel full of holes and traps, and all the time the Great Hall clock was ticking its way toward midnight.

After a while, she closed her eyes. Somehow that made it easier to feel what was happening inside the padlock. She stopped dragging at the barrels and settled down to pushing on them one by one. At last she felt the first one swoop upward—and heard a faint click.

She grunted with satisfaction. Someone whispered, "Has she done it?" Someone else whispered, "Shhh!"

The second and third barrels were slightly easier. *Click. Click.* But the fourth and fifth wouldn't move, no matter how hard she pressed them.

By now her left hand, holding the scissors, was beginning to shake. Goldie opened her eyes—and realized that she hadn't taken a breath for at least half a minute. She heaved the air into her lungs and out again. Nearly every girl in the room was watching her with an expression of astonished hope, as if it was *their* fetters that were under assault.

"I need some help," Goldie whispered to Candor.

Candor hesitated. She didn't look as hopeful as the others, but after a minute she swung her legs to the floor and shuffled across the gap between the two beds. Halfway there, her ankle chain pulled her up short. Carefully she turned around and, keeping her chained leg stretched out in front of her, sat awkwardly on the edge of Goldie's bed.

"What do you want me to do?" she whispered.

"Hold the scissors," whispered Goldie. "And keep them turned. If you let them go I'll have to start all over again."

As carefully as she could, she inched her fingers back along the scissors so that there was room for Candor to grasp them.

"I've got them," the older girl whispered. She grinned at Goldie, encouraging now. "Go on! I want to see Guardian Bliss's face when she finds out someone's escaped."

Once again, Goldie set to work. It was a little easier now that she didn't have to think about the scissors as well, but the last two barrels of the padlock remained stiff and stubborn. She poked and prodded at them, with her teeth biting into her lip and the end of the hairpin gnawing at the palm of her hand. But still they wouldn't move.

She almost threw the whole thing down in frustration. Only two to go! How could this be happening? Then she remembered a trick that Olga Ciavolga had showed her.

"You need to let the scissors turn back just the *tiniest* amount," she whispered to Candor. "Not too far!"

Candor's fingers shifted. Goldie pressed with the hairpin. Something moved! She pressed harder. The palm of her hand stung. A trickle of something wet ran down it. She wiped her fingers on her smock and tried again. The barrel rose up. She heard a click.

"One to go," she whispered, and the message flew up and down the room. "One to go!" "One to go!" *"One to go!"*

Now that the fourth barrel had given up the fight, the last one seemed to lose heart. It remained stubborn for a couple of minutes only, then it too clicked into place.

Goldie had to keep reminding herself to breathe. She wiped her hand again—she was bleeding from the scratches that the hairpin had made—and tried to remember what she was supposed to do next. For a moment, her mind was blank. Then it came back to her.

"Now you have to turn the scissors," she whispered to Candor.

"Which way?"

"Clockwise! Wait, maybe this padlock is different! No, clockwise! I think—*clockwise!*"

The knuckles on Candor's hand were white with tension. She turned the scissors clockwise . . .

With a loud *clunk* the padlock on Goldie's fetters sprang open. One of the smallest girls squealed, and immediately everyone else hissed, *"Ssshhhh!"*

Goldie could hardly believe that she had done it. Around her, nearly every face in the room blazed with delight.

But Candor was shaking her head doubtfully. "She still has to open the door. And she can't do *that* with a hairpin."

"Of course she can't," said Bonnie. She grinned at Goldie. "So we'll have to get Guardian Bliss to do it for her!"

A BARGAIN WITH BALD THOKE

Goldie crouched under the bed nearest the door, stiff with tension. In her own bed, pillows and sheets made a vague girl-shape beneath the gray blanket. She wasn't sure if this plan of Bonnie's would work, but she hadn't been able to think of anything better. And time was running out.

She chewed her thumbnail and wondered whether Toadspit had escaped already. She touched the compass in her pocket, and thought about Ma and Pa. Her heart ached with love and worry.

"*Eeeeeeeeeeeeeeeeeeeeeeeeeeeeh!*" The scream echoed up and down the dormitory. It was followed by another, and another, and suddenly nearly every girl in the room was squealing her head off. Goldie put her hands over her ears and hoped that someone would come quickly.

Someone did.

"Be quiet! Be *quiet!*" Guardian Bliss loomed in the open doorway, her face contorted with rage. Goldie hadn't heard the bolt being shot. She could only just hear the Blessed Guardian over the screams, which were now interspersed with terrified words.

"It was the bomber! I heard him at the window!"

"He's come to get us!"

"He's going to kill us all!"

"*Eeeeeeeeeeh!*"

"*Eeeeeeeeeeeeeeeeh!*"

"*Eeeeeeeeeeeeeeeeeeeeeeeeeeeeh!*"

"*Be quiet or you'll lose your privileges!*"

The screaming stopped immediately, but the voices continued, all of them at fever pitch, all of them on the opposite side of the room from where Goldie crouched.

"Keep her attention over this side," Bonnie had said. "We don't want her looking at Goldie's bed too closely, or at the door."

Rosie's voice was the loudest. "I *heard* him!" she squealed. "Right above my head! He said he's coming to kill us!"

Guardian Bliss's angry feet stomped down the room. "What's this nonsense? What did you hear?"

Goldie slipped out from underneath the bed and began to steal toward the open door, as silent as a shadow.

At the far end of the room, Lamb cried out, "I heard him too! He was right up close to the window and he had a deep growly voice and he said he was going to eat us! One bite at a time! Like an idle-cat!"

"Like a slommerkin, that's what he said to me!" cried someone else. "Like the one on the Bridge of Beasts!"

The squealing started up afresh. "Silence!" shouted Guardian Bliss, "or you'll all be in double chains! Now will someone explain to me what is happening?"

Goldie eased past the door and flattened herself against the wall outside. In the room behind her she heard Bonnie say, "Oh, for heaven's sake, they were dreaming! You *were*, Rosie, you were twitching in your sleep, and then suddenly you sat up and started screaming and everyone else just sort of caught it. Now shut up and go back to sleep, why don't you—"

Goldie crept away down the corridor. Despite the danger she was in, she couldn't help smiling at Bonnie's plan.

"We don't want them thinking there's *really* someone out there," the younger girl had said. "Otherwise they'll be on the alert and Goldie'll never get out of the yard."

Goldie suspected that Bonnie had worked out this escape

241

route long ago, but had never had the chance to put it into practice. Toadspit would have been proud of his little sister.

When she was some distance away from the dormitory, she stopped to get her bearings. It wasn't easy. Care was almost as confusing as the museum, except that the museum was alive with a sort of wild curiosity, whereas this place had a grim, muffled feel to it, as if its walls were designed to silence not only voices, but thoughts as well.

Still, the little voice in the back of Goldie's mind didn't let her down. It led her through those grim corridors with barely a hesitation.

This way.

Now that way.

No, not through there, it's dangerous. Go this way instead.

She was searching for a back door, and eventually she found it. But there were two Blessed Guardians stationed in front of it, wide awake and vigilant. Goldie slipped away again without a sound.

She tried the windows next. But although many of them were cracked, the bars were new and strong, and far too close together for even a small child to squeeze through. Before long, Goldie gave up on them and crept toward the front of the building.

The carpets here were thick and luxurious, and the lights were bright. Goldie trod more carefully than ever. The rooms she passed were full of armchairs and comfortable sofas, and many of them held shrines to the Seven Gods. But their windows too were barred and impassable.

When she was close to the foyer, she crept forward and peered around the corner. There was the front door, only a few steps away. But the toad-like Guardian was still moored behind his desk, looking as if nothing could move him, and the foyer was far too brightly lit for any sort of Concealment.

With a sinking heart, Goldie crept back down the corridor, slipped into one of the open rooms and pulled the door shut behind her.

"Just because I haven't found a way out yet," she told herself fiercely, "doesn't mean it's impossible. What would Sinew do? What would Olga Ciavolga do? What's Toadspit doing, right this minute?"

The sofas in this room were enormous, and covered in cushions. The window bars were strong. At the far end of the room, there was a shrine to Bald Thoke, with candles burning around it and a small pile of written jokes and other offerings.

Goldie walked thoughtfully toward the shrine. Bald Thoke was said to be the most trustworthy of the Seven Gods. It was still a risk, of course, asking him for something, but . . .

"Great and Glorious Thoke, baldest of the bald," she whispered, knowing that the Gods liked to be flattered. "I haven't got a present for you—"

She stopped. Actually, she *did* have a present. In fact, she had two. She fumbled in her pocket and took out the compass and the scissors. She looked from one to the other, wondering which one she could afford to lose. The compass had been a present from Ma and Pa, and she hated the thought of giving it away. But the scissors were probably more useful.

Before she could change her mind, she reached out to place the compass on the pile of offerings. Her hand brushed one of the bits of paper. It tumbled from the pile. Underneath it was her bird brooch.

Goldie whipped her hand back, still holding the compass. "I—I haven't got a present," she said again. "But I *would* like to do a swap."

She held her breath, hoping that Bald Thoke wouldn't immediately strike her down. *But he* is *the god of cheekiness,* she thought. *He should be pleased!*

"A swap," she whispered, as firmly as she dared. "You get the compass, I get the brooch. All right? A compass is a lot more useful than a brooch, which means you're getting the better part of the bargain. So I'd be grateful if you'd show me how I can get out of here without being caught."

She felt very strange, trying to bargain with one of the Seven Gods. She reached out again, with both hands this time, put down the compass—and picked up the brooch.

Then she held her breath.

Muffled footsteps sounded in the distance. Goldie heard a shout, and the heavy clank of punishment chains. The footsteps came closer. A boy began to sing in a hoarse, adolescent voice. "Awa-a-a-y, across the ocea-a-an, awa-a-a-y, across the sea-a-a-a—"

There was a slap, and a yell. The singing stopped, but only for a moment. When it started up again, there were a dozen or more voices, all caterwauling at the top of their lungs. "—I'll go-o-o-o where my heart takes me, where my-y-y-y love waits for me-e-e-e-e."

A pause. A furious adult's voice said, "It's not your *love* that's waiting for you, you little villains, it's the House of Repentance! Deliberate destruction of property, putting the lives of others at risk, oh, you're in for it, you are!"

Clank clank clank, went the punishment chains. "I've be-e-e-e-en away so long, dear, I've tra-a-a-aveled far and wi-i-i-i-i-ide—" sang the voices.

Goldie edged along the wall and eased the door open. There was a bustle and a shoving and a clanking, and suddenly the corridor in front of her was full of boys, milling backward and forward, rattling their chains and singing loudly. They were all older than Goldie, but they wore the same gray threadbare smock and leggings. Somewhere in the middle of them were two Blessed Guardians. The smell of burning hung over them all.

There was no time to think. Goldie couldn't see Toadspit,

but she was sure he must be there somewhere. She whispered a quick "thank you" to Bald Thoke, then she stepped out into the corridor and tucked herself between two of the boys.

For a heart-stopping moment the song faltered. The boys on either side of Goldie shot incredulous glances at her—

Then they closed smoothly around her and began to sing louder than ever, their voices bouncing off the high ceilings. "Three yea-a-a-a-ars I rowed the galley-y-y-ys, three yea-a-a-a-ars I was a sla-a-a-a-ave—"

They spilled out into the foyer, a laughing, shouting, singing rabble. The Guardians who led them were shouting too. Only Goldie was silent. She crouched between the tall, raucous boys, her smock blending with theirs, her pulse thundering in her ears.

"What's this?" shouted the toad-like Guardian. "Where are you taking them at this time of night?"

"Set fire to their beds!" shouted one of the other Guardians. "Don't know what's got into them! Marching them off to Repentance!"

"I'll need their names!"

"If I-I-I-I-I could turn back time, dea-a-a-ar, if I-I-I-I-I could start aga-a-a-a-a-in—"

"For Great Wooden's sake, we'll give them to you when we come back. I can't bear this appalling racket a moment longer!"

And with that, the boys, Goldie and the two Guardians

spilled out the front door of Care, across the yard and through the gate.

As soon as they were out on the street, Goldie slipped away into the shadows. The boys had stopped singing now, and were trying to lie down on the footpath, or climb onto each other's shoulders, or do a dozen other things that were impossible in punishment chains. Goldie watched for Toadspit, but there was no sign of him.

At last the Guardians managed to get the boys into some sort of order, and they marched off toward the House of Repentance. Goldie's legs felt weak with relief. She had escaped!

But at the same time she was terribly worried about Toadspit. She was sure that the raucous boys must have set fire to their beds as a distraction, so that he could get away unnoticed. But where was he? Maybe he had already gone. Maybe he was outside the Fugleman's office, waiting for her!

The moon above her head was full. The watergas lamps glowed on their poles. The Great Hall bells began to chime. Half past eleven!

Goldie gritted her teeth. "I'm coming, Broo!" she whispered. "I'm coming, Toadspit!" Then she turned toward Old Arsenal Hill and began to run.

MIDNIGHT

The Fugleman's ruined office was halfway up Old Arsenal Hill. There was a plaza out the front, with a statue of the Fugleman in the middle of it. Goldie crouched behind the statue, peering at the shattered building.

Someone had rigged temporary gaslights, and she could see the smashed doors and the twisted railings. Six militiamen stood halfway up the wide steps with their rifles cocked and their faces wary. At their feet lay Broo, trussed up with so many ropes that his black coat looked brindle. A leather strap bound his jaws shut. Another three or four tied him to the railings.

Despite this, the militiamen seemed nervous. They stamped their feet as if they were cold, and whispered to each other out of the corners of their mouths. The whites of their eyes glinted in the gaslight.

All the way up the hill Goldie had been sure that Toadspit would be here, waiting for her. But away from the steps, everything was still. The only sound was the restless stamping of militia boots. She stared into the shadows until her eyes ached, but there was no sign of Toadspit.

Bongggg. Bongggg. Bongggg. The faint sound of the Great Hall chimes floated up the hill. It was midnight. Across the plaza, the militiamen changed places.

Goldie chewed her lip. "Come on, Toadspit!" she breathed. "Come *on*!"

Her right leg began to cramp. She stretched it carefully, then forced herself to be still again. She could feel her heart thudding in her chest. *Ka-thump ka-thump ka-thump.*

One of the militiamen sneezed, and his companions swore at the unexpected sound. Broo lay as still as death.

Ka-thump ka-thump ka-thump.

Goldie told herself that Toadspit would come before her heart beat sixty times. *One, two, three—*

Just before the count got to sixty, she changed it to a

hundred. Then five hundred. Then a thousand . . .

Still Toadspit did not come.

When she realized that she was going to have to rescue Broo on her own, Goldie's spirit almost failed her. The militiamen weren't nearly as frightening as the soldiers behind the Dirty Gate, but they were big and strong and there were six of them against one of her. How could she get them away from Broo for long enough to cut all those ropes?

She leaned her forehead against the stone plinth and thought back over the things she had learned. Concealment, eggshell walking, interpretation of footsteps. Making a lie sound like the truth. Stealing secretly and stealing boldly.

She had a feeling that this one had to be a mixture. A lie that sounded like the truth. A Concealment. A bold theft . . .

She thought of Lamb and Rosie screaming at the tops of their voices. *"He said he was going to eat us! Like an idle-cat!"* *"Like a slommerkin!"*

Before she could lose her nerve, she got to her feet. As silent as smoke, she crept around the edge of the plaza until she was back on the street that led down the hill. There was a brick wall there, with narrow recesses that she had noticed on the way up. They weren't deep enough to hide her properly, but they would have to do.

Carefully, she tucked herself as far into one of them as she could. Then she thought of the girls in Care—and began to scream.

"*Eeeeeeeeeeeeeeeeeeh!* The slommerkin's got me! The *slommerkin's* got me! It's carrying me away! It's going to squash me! *Eeeeeeeeeeeeeeeeeeeh!*"

She knew that if she had done this the night before, it wouldn't have worked. These days, hardly anyone except children believed in slommerkins, with their enormous bulk and their habit of rolling on their victims to soften them up before they ate them. But hardly anyone believed in brizzlehounds either, or slaughterbirds, and these militiamen had seen them, had been *attacked* by them, just a few hours ago.

And if a brizzlehound and a slaughterbird can come out of the museum, thought Goldie, *why not a slommerkin?*

The militiamen clearly agreed. There was a shout from the direction of the plaza. Boots thudded on the stone cobbles.

"It was a girl!"

"Where did her voice come from?"

"Up the end!"

"She's not here!"

"She must be somewhere!"

"You men go that way, we'll go this way."

"What about the brizzlehound? The Fugleman'll kill us if it gets away!"

"Brizzlehound's not going anywhere! If you see the blasted slommerkin, don't take any chances. Shoot it! But don't hit the girl!"

As the boots pounded toward her, Goldie closed her eyes and forced her breathing to slow down.

I'm a brick wall. I'm a shadow. There's nothing the least bit interesting about me. . . .

The militiamen raced past her, heading down the hill.

Goldie was out of the recess and running up the street before the sound of their boots faded. She dashed across the plaza to the iron railings, the scissors ready in her hand. "Broo!"

The brizzlehound's eyes were open. There was a bloody furrow across the side of his head where the bullet had passed, and dried blood covered his muzzle. He gazed up at her.

"You have to help me!" hissed Goldie. "They won't be gone for long!"

The scissors were sharp, and it took her only a moment to saw through the strap that held his jaws together. As she started on the ropes that tethered him to the railings, Broo tore at the rest of his bonds with his teeth. They fell away like string.

Goldie heard a shout from somewhere down the hill. "Quick!" she hissed. "We have to get out of here!"

Broo's legs were stiff and his muscles were cramped. He staggered to his feet, and fell down again. Goldie tried to lift him, but he was too heavy.

"Can't you make yourself small?" she whispered. "Then I could carry you."

Broo shook his head. "It is . . . not something I can choose," he wheezed. "If the small does not come . . . I cannot make it."

Another shout, closer this time.

"Broo, come *on!*"

The brizzlehound made an enormous effort and managed to drag himself to the bottom of the steps. There he stopped, panting for breath. The wound on his head was oozing blood.

Goldie could hear the militiamen coming back up the hill, calling to each other as they ran. She put her arms around the brizzlehound's neck. "*Please* try again, Broo. *Please!*"

Broo sighed, deep in his chest. He staggered, once, twice, and shook his head. He braced his legs against the cobbles and stretched until his joints cracked. His wound still bled, but some of his old strength seemed to come back to him.

He turned to Goldie, his eyes glowing like rubies. The darkness around him trembled. "If we are to save the city," he rumbled, "we must go *now!*"

TREACHERY

The Fugleman was feeling pleased with himself. Despite what he had discovered on the night when he broke into his sister's office, he had still not been completely sure that the Dirty Gate existed.

But now here it was, right in front of him! And what's more, it was wide open!

Behind him, Hope and Comfort were urging the militiamen to hammer the last few nails into the last few planks.

Your militia have been very helpful, sister, thought the Fugleman. *But I won't be needing them for much longer. . . .*

He raised his hand and beckoned the lieutenant marshal to his side. "We are still quite some distance from danger," he said. "I would like you and your men to go forward another two hundred paces or so and set up an observation post. I will give my Guardians their final instructions, then we'll join you. Just leave one of the lanterns for us, if you will."

"Yes, Your Honor!" The lieutenant marshal snapped out an eager salute and began to muster his men. He did it efficiently enough—the Fugleman supposed that all those parades must have taught them *some*thing. Although *he* wouldn't have marched into hostile territory in quite such close formation.

As the militiamen passed through the Dirty Gate, he saluted them. But as soon as they were gone, he took three quick steps sideways so that he was hidden from anyone on the other side of the gate. Hope copied him.

Comfort, who had always been the slower of the two, didn't move. Even when the first shot rang out, and the second, and the third, and then a great volley of them, he stood there in the light of the lantern, his mouth open in astonishment.

A single bullet knocked him over backward. He gave a choking cry and was dead on the instant. The shooting stopped.

Silence.

The Fugleman reached into the pocket of his robes and pulled out a large white kerchief and a silver ingot. He was surprised to see that his hands were shaking. He forced them to be still. He inched forward and waved the kerchief around the edge of the gate.

Silence.

With his other hand, he held the silver ingot out, and turned it back and forth so that it gleamed in the lantern light.

A guttural voice shouted, "Kom!"

The Fugleman waited another moment or two, to show that he wasn't to be hurried. Then he edged through the Dirty Gate, with Hope close on his heels.

He had gone only a few steps when he tripped over something. He looked down. At his feet lay the lieutenant marshal. His uniform was drenched with blood, and he had a look of astonishment on his face. Scattered around him were the bodies of his men.

The Fugleman's hands were shaking again, and he felt a sudden urge to giggle. "It seems I was wrong about the danger," he murmured to the lieutenant marshal's corpse. "I *do* hope you'll forgive me."

He heard a noise, and looked up in time to see a troop of soldiers striding toward him with flaming torches in their hands. The same soldiers that were described in the blue book.

They were an ugly bunch. Bloodthirsty barbarians, every one of them. Look at their brutal faces and their ancient costumes! Their swords and pikes and muskets! They should have been dead hundreds of years ago. For all he knew, they *were* dead—though he'd never heard of a ghost that stank like this lot.

The main thing was, their primitive bullets were real. He smiled to himself. Everything was going exactly the way he had planned. It was time to make the next move, before Hope did something stupid. He didn't want to lose her, not yet. It was always useful to have at least one disposable underling close by.

With his eyes fixed on the soldiers, he flicked at a speck of Comfort's blood on the front of his robes. Then he drew himself up to his full height and said, "I am the Fugleman of the city of Jewel. Take me to your commanding officer!"

The museum was in turmoil. Goldie could feel the walls straining furiously at the planks that nailed them down, the way Broo had strained at his ropes. The floor rippled underfoot. Piles of broken glass lay everywhere.

The Staff Only door was completely off its hinges. Goldie clambered over it and ran into the back rooms. There she stopped, appalled at what she saw.

Most of the glass cases were broken wide open. The ones that were not broken bulged dangerously, like overstretched balloons. Inside them, everything was in disarray. Costumes and skeletons and suits of armor twitched and rattled as if they were alive. Old surgical instruments scraped at the glass with a sound that made her skin crawl.

Broo raised his massive head and sniffed the air. The hackles on his back rose. "They have breached the Dirty Gate!" he growled. "How *darrrre* they!"

He bounded away and Goldie ran after him. Above her head, the lights flickered. An ominous rumbling came from somewhere beneath her. The walls around her heaved and strained against the nailed planks.

Broo was waiting for her at the edge of the vacant block. Last time Goldie had seen the ditch, there had been no more than an inch or two of muddy water in the bottom. But now the current raced past her, black and foul, cutting away at the edges and spilling over the brim in hungry streams.

Someone had made a bridge out of tables and broken display cases. Broo loped across it, and Goldie followed, trying not to let the foul water touch her. She ran across the vacant block, following the nailed planks. Mud snatched at her feet, and thornberry bushes snagged her clothing. She tore herself away and ran on.

The planks led directly to the bottom step of Harry Mount. Goldie put her hand on the banister, and—

"*Stop!*" growled Broo. He snuffed the air. "Something is not *rrrrright*!"

Goldie hiccuped with frightened laughter. "*Nothing's* right!" But she stopped all the same, and looked at the brizzlehound uncertainly.

Broo's growl rose to a crescendo. Goldie heard a scratching noise. The hair on the back of her neck stood up—

An enormous rat was crawling down the stairs toward her. Its fur was matted and filthy; its head swung from side to side as if it couldn't see properly. As she backed away in horror, it staggered off the bottom step, dragged itself along the floor a little way—and fell over.

"What's the matter with it?" she said in a small voice.

Broo's whole body was stiff with fury. "Plague. The plague *rrrrrooms* are on the move."

After that, Goldie didn't want to go up Harry Mount. But there was no alternative. And so, slowly, carefully, with her head low and her eyes peeled for danger, she began to climb.

There were no more rats. But Harry Mount was even steeper than usual. It rose up high and narrow, like a staircase in a nightmare. Before long, the banister petered out, and in its place was an enormous drop that seemed to go down and down forever. Goldie crawled upward on all fours, keeping as close to the brizzlehound as she could and trying not to look over the edge.

Once, she thought she heard gunfire, and she stopped and pressed herself against the wall. Planks and nails dug into her back. Broo stood over her, trembling with rage.

They were nearly at the top when Harry Mount began to tremble in exactly the same way.

"It's trying to shift!" gasped Goldie.

She was right. The step she was standing on heaved up and down like a ship in a storm. Planks creaked and groaned but did not break. Nails screeched but did not come loose.

"Hurry!" growled Broo. He bounded up the last few steps and loped through a doorway. Goldie followed him.

"Look!" she cried, pointing upward.

They were in the Lady's Mile. But the banners that usually hung from the ceiling were gone. In their place were long hempen ropes, and at the end of each rope was a hangman's noose.

"Hurry!" growled Broo. *"Hurrrrrrry!"*

Goldie raced down the Lady's Mile, ducking her head to avoid the dangling nooses, and ran through the doorway at the far end. And there before her—*much* closer to the front of the museum than it should have been—was the Dirty Gate. It was wide open, and Morg was sitting on top of it. On the ground below her was Guardian Comfort. A little way past him, piled up like logs of wood in the moonlight, were the militiamen.

They were all dead.

Goldie stared, stricken, at the crumpled bodies. Nothing had prepared her for this. "I hope it didn't hurt," she whispered.

Broo growled.

"Shhh," whispered Goldie, as if the dead men were merely asleep and she didn't want to wake them.

Broo growled again. Morg clacked her beak. Her hungry eyes were fixed on Guardian Comfort's face.

"Get out of it, Morg," said Goldie. "Leave him alone."

The slaughterbird gave a disappointed croak and flapped off into the darkness. Broo shifted impatiently. "These men are dead," he growled, "and we cannot bring them back to life. If we want to save the living we must go *on!*"

"But we're too late!" said Goldie. "The soldiers must have broken out already."

"If they had come through the Dirty Gate," growled Broo, "do you think I would not *smell* them?" He shook his great head. "No. This was just a skirmish. They have not yet made their move. But," he snuffed the air, "there is something happening in the army camp. The Fugleman is there."

"What's he doing?"

"I do not know," growled Broo. "But I will not cower here like an unweaned pup while there is a chance we might yet *stop him!*"

There was a brief kerfuffle when the Fugleman and Hope arrived in the middle of the army camp. One of the barbarians disappeared into a large tent with a dozen or so men inside it. The Fugleman could see their shadows on the canvas walls.

A moment later, there was shouting in what sounded like the accent of Old Merne. An officer (judging by the quality of his coat) poked his head out through the tent flap and scowled at them. Then he ducked back inside.

More shouting. The first barbarian came hurrying out again.

The Fugleman drew himself up importantly. He thought about using his charming smile, but decided against it. Among people like these, a smile might be seen as a weakness.

"My good man," he said to the barbarian. He spoke loudly so that whoever was inside the tent would hear him. "My good man, I am here on a mission. Tell your commanding officer that I have a proposal for him. A proposal that will make him an *extremely* rich man."

The barbarian stared at the Fugleman, but didn't move. There was a rumble of voices from the tent, then the flap was thrust aside and a different officer came out.

The Fugleman didn't need to be told that this was the supreme commander. It was enough to see the brutal, intelligent face, the unyielding expression, the way the barbarian soldier straightened up when he appeared.

Hope was biting her lip nervously. The Fugleman was afraid too, though he was not so foolish as to show it. For a moment, he wished he had brought his new sword with him, instead of leaving it hidden in the House of Repentance. But then he pulled himself together. This was the moment he had been waiting for, the moment that all his plotting had been leading up to.

He paused for just a second to savor the taste of success. Then he took a step forward and held out his hand. "I am the Fugleman of Jewel," he said. "And I want you to invade my city."

SHADOWS

Goldie lay in the long grass and stared at the army encampment. Her face and arms were blackened with mud; her belly was pressed against the ground. Broo was no more than a shadow beside her.

It was still at least five hours till dawn, but the camp was buzzing like a beehive. By the light of scores of campfires, men pulled on their shoes, strapped leather water bottles around their waists and shoveled food into their mouths. Somewhere a horse whinnied. The smell of war was everywhere.

Directly in front of Goldie, across the stretch of trampled mud, was a grindstone. A bare-chested giant of a man turned it around and around, his muscles glistening in the firelight. One of the soldiers held a sword against the stone so that sparks flew and the steel took a fine, sharp edge. His companions waited their turn, jostling each other and laughing in voices that brimmed with violence.

There was a sudden flap of wings overhead. Goldie flinched. Morg's harsh voice drifted down from the night sky. "Betra-a-a-a-ayed! Betra-a-a-a-ayed!"

The soldiers muttered uneasily. In the darkness beside Goldie, Broo's hindquarters quivered. "Morg is *rrright*," he growled. "I too smell *betrrrayal*. I smell the hunger for *rrriches*, and for *bloooood*!"

He half-rose out of the grass, his voice trembling with fury. "*I* will give them *bloooood*! I will *rrrrun* through their stinking camp! I will *brrrrreak* the Fugleman's neck before he destroys us all!"

Goldie could feel the same fury welling up inside her—the urgent need to *do* something, to do it *now* before the world fell apart around her. Her breath caught in her throat. Her muscles tensed.

In the back of her mind the little voice whispered, *Think carefully before you rush into danger!*

Goldie shook her head in frustration. How could she think carefully at a time like this? It was like trying to swim against an enormous current, except the current was inside her, sweeping her along.

Think! Think carefully!

She bit her lip until it hurt and forced herself to be still. "Broo, wait!"

"We must act before it is too *late*," growled Broo.

"They'll shoot you!" whispered Goldie. "You'll never get anywhere near the Fugleman."

"I will *rrrun* like a shadow. They will not see me until their *death* is upon them!"

"But there are hundreds and hundreds of them! And they're real soldiers, not like our militia. They'll kill you! We have to think of another way of stopping them."

The brizzlehound turned his head to stare at her. His eyes burned so fiercely that she had to look away. "Think, then," he rumbled. "But do not take too long. The end of *everything* is almost upon us!" He sank back onto his haunches, but the low growl in his chest did not stop.

"Sinew said the museum's like a kettle full of steam," Goldie whispered, half to Broo and half to herself. "The Guardians have nailed the rooms down so they can't move, and now the pressure is building up. So what we need"—she hesitated, working it out as she went—"what we need is something that'll reduce that pressure. Like lifting the lid of the kettle and letting out some of the steam. I think—I think that means we have to let some of the wildness loose. Let it out into the city."

"Not the soldiers," growled Broo. "Not the plague. Not the creature that lies in Old *Scrrrrratch*."

"No. Something else. Something that's not as dangerous. But—but it has to be big or it mightn't work."

A shout from the encampment distracted her. One of the soldiers had been drinking from a leather bottle, and someone had bumped him and splashed liquid all over his sleeve. His companions crowed with laughter. The soldier swore and raised his fist, and the laughter grew louder. One of his friends pulled out a kerchief and dabbed at him in mock concern. The sequins on the kerchief glinted in the firelight.

"Look!" breathed Goldie. "It's *Olga Ciavolga's*!"

For a moment, she couldn't move or think. Olga Ciavolga would never have given up her kerchief willingly. Where was she? What had the soldiers done to her? Was she still alive, or was she—?

Tears sprang to Goldie's eyes. She brushed them furiously away—this was no time for tears—and forced her mind back to the problem. How could she let some of the museum's wildness loose? Where would she find something that was big enough to reduce the pressure, but not as dangerous as these soldiers?

There was another roar of laughter from the camp. A

prickle ran down Goldie's spine. *The kerchief. The knots. The big knots . . .*

Quickly she turned to Broo. "What if I stole the kerchief and released one of the Great Winds? Would it blow out into the city? Would it reduce the pressure enough?"

"I do not know," rumbled Broo. "Even Olga Ciavolga has never released one of the Great Winds."

Goldie stared at him, her heart beating wildly. She had no idea if it would work. It might make things worse. And the thought of trying to get close enough to the soldiers to steal the kerchief made her feel sick. What if they caught her? What would they do to her?

Don't try and push the fear away. . . .

She ran her tongue over dry lips. "I can't think of anything else to do, Broo. I'm going to try it. You'd better stay here."

The hackles on the back of Broo's neck rose. "I am a *brrrrrizzlehound*! We do not stand aside while our friends go into *dangerrrr*!"

"You *must* stay here," whispered Goldie. "So that if I . . . um . . . if I fail, you can still make your run for the Fugleman."

"I do not *like* this plan. These men are like idle-cats. If they catch you they will *tearrrrr* you limb from limb."

"They mightn't," said Goldie, although she was horribly afraid that the brizzlehound was right. "*Please* stay here."

Broo rumbled his disapproval. But then he bent his head

and licked her face with his enormous tongue. "You are as *brrrrave* as a *brrrrizzlehound*. Go well. I will be watching."

Goldie turned back to the army camp. This would be harder than anything she had ever done before. But the shadows and the bustle and noise would all help to hide her. She settled lower into the long grass. She slowed her breath. She made herself a part of the mud and the firelight. *I am nothing. I am a shadow. . . .*

Her mind drifted outward like sparks from a fire. She could sense Broo's deep, slow heartbeat beside her. She could sense a family of mice somewhere nearby, scurrying hither and thither. She could sense a dreadful, raging hunger from the army camp.

I am nothing. I am a shadow. . . .

As silent as a wisp of smoke, she drifted out of the long grass and across the bare earth. There was a wagon right in front of her. She slipped beneath it and the noise of the camp closed around her. The scrape of swords. The rumble of the grindstone. The brutal laughter of the men. She pressed herself against the wagon wheel, wishing she could crawl into a hole and disappear.

It took all her courage to creep out from beneath the wagon. Her stomach churned, but her feet trod carefully in the mud, and the little voice in the back of her mind whispered advice. *Keep to the shadows. Don't move suddenly—sudden movements catch the eye. Go through that little alleyway between the tents. Watch out! Someone's coming!*

A man blundered down the alleyway toward her, stinking of beer. Goldie faded into stillness.

I am nothing. I am the smell of smoke on the night air. . . .

The soldier shouted something that Goldie couldn't quite make out. From inside one of the tents, there came an answering shout. The soldier laughed and slapped his thigh with a noise like a pistol shot. Then, without a backward glance, he strode past Goldie and out into the firelight.

The men around the grindstone were growing noisier. Two of them had begun to wrestle and the others were roaring encouragement. Goldie crouched in the shadow of the nearest tent, watching them. Somewhere in that seething mass was the man who had Olga Ciavolga's kerchief. Which one was he?

That one?

No.

That one!

No. There were too many of them. How was she going to find him?

A whisper from the little voice. *Let your mind seek the kerchief.*

Goldie let her thoughts drift toward the soldiers. It was hard to ignore the awful hungry heat of them, but she made herself think about other things.

Winds, great and small. A cool breeze in the middle of summer. A knotted kerchief.

And there it was, like a bright spark in the middle of darkness! She could see the soldier now, hanging around the outside of the mob, thumping his fellows on the back and laughing uproariously. The kerchief was in his right-hand pocket.

Goldie slid out of the shadow of the tent, her eyes fixed on the soldier. Fear and excitement welled up inside her and she let them drift away. *No thoughts. Nothing. I'm a shadow. . . .*

The mob of men was heaving backward and forward. The shouting was so loud that she was almost deafened. The soldier, *her* soldier, strode away around the outside of the circle, and she thought she had lost him. But no, there he was again, standing with his hands on his hips and shaking his head as if he was disappointed in the way the fight was going.

She was so close now. Just a little farther. Slowly. Slowly. *Ahhhh.*

As the men fought and shouted, the shadow that was Goldie reached out its hand. Slipped it into a pocket. Closed its fingers over the kerchief—

There was a sudden yell, and the crowd surged sideways. The man in front of Goldie cannoned backward, straight into her. Her fingers lost their grip on the kerchief, and her hand flew out of the soldier's pocket. She stumbled, and fell.

She was on her feet again almost immediately. *I am noth-ing! I am a shadow!*

But it was too late. They had seen her.

Before she knew what was happening, she was surrounded by a crowd of huge, bellowing men. She shrank back from them, her legs shaking so that she could hardly stand. One of the men grabbed her hair in his big fist and hauled her up until she was on tiptoe. He peered in her face, then turned around and shouted to his fellows, "Is a leedle gel!"

The men argued briefly over what to do with her. Then two of them herded her away from the others, past the grindstone and between the wagons. "Dis way!" they shouted, and they pushed Goldie toward a fire where a dozen men shoveled food from a cauldron.

"What is dis?" growled the man tending the cauldron. "Haf you brought us our sopper?" He grabbed Goldie's arm and pinched it hard. "Ha! Not enough meat on dis one. Haf to mek her into soop!"

The soldiers guffawed loudly and urged Goldie onward. Past a row of horses, past a huddle of tents and wagons and a patch of bloodied earth where two men were butchering a goat. Goldie felt as if she was going to be sick. Her heart was a small hard lump inside her. She had failed. Soon Broo would make his run for the Fugleman, and be killed in the attempt. Ma and Pa would be lost. The city would be lost. *Everything* would be lost.

Look! whispered the little voice in the back of her mind. *There, near the wagon.*

What? thought Goldie despairingly. *What is there to look at? Everything's gone wrong!* But she looked all the same, and saw a patch of shadow that her eyes seemed to *slide* across. . . .

Her heart leaped. Toadspit! He must have been just a few minutes behind her! And now he was here! Maybe, just maybe, everything wasn't lost after all!

The soldiers herded her past more wagons, past another huddle of tents. And suddenly there was the Fugleman, in a circle of flaming torches, with Guardian Hope at his side. He was deep in conversation with another man, who looked like an officer.

One of the soldiers shouted. Three heads spun around. Goldie saw the surprised snarl on the Fugleman's face. "What's *she* doing here?"

The soldiers shoved Goldie into the circle of torches. "Stand dere!" they shouted. "Donchoo move or we shoo-choo!"

The officer, who wore a velvet coat with silver frogging, stared curiously at Goldie. His eyes were blue and cold. Goldie saw Guardian Hope whisper in the Fugleman's ear. The Fugleman raised an eyebrow and turned back to the officer.

"I apologize for this interruption," he said. "This girl is

from my city. Please accept her as a gift. My assistant assures me that she will make an *excellent* slave."

Goldie's eyes widened in horror. A *slave?* The officer murmured something. One of the soldiers grabbed Goldie by the scruff of the neck and prized her mouth open as if he wanted to check her teeth. Goldie bit him. He yelled in surprise and whacked her across the ear.

"Ow!" she cried.

"She can be a little troublesome," said the Fugleman hastily, "but I'm sure you will soon beat that out of her. Now, let's get back to business. We are agreed, are we not, that, after the invasion, *I* will be Grand Protector over the *whole* peninsula."

The officer nodded. "We are agreed on dis." His voice was deep and slow, as if he measured each word before he let it escape from his mouth.

"Of course, the new Protectorate will not be like the present one," said the Fugleman. "I think a dictatorship would suit me best."

Goldie's head was still ringing from the blow, but she stared at the leader of the Blessed Guardians in disbelief.

"As soon as I am established in that supreme position," continued the Fugleman, "I will allow you and your men to sack the cities of Spoke and Lawe, farther down the peninsula. They are quite as rich as Jewel, so you'll be well rewarded for your trouble. And if you want to take slaves, that can be arranged. I know of . . . ah . . . several children who would be *particularly* suitable."

The officer was nodding again, as if the whole idea was entirely reasonable.

He was a terrifying man, this officer. He was shorter than the Fugleman, and not as handsome, but Goldie had the feeling that, once he and his men were loose, they would be unstoppable.

She looked back at the Fugleman. Compared with the soldiers, he suddenly seemed a sham, with all his sleek importance. He was like a clockwork dog thinking he could control a pack of brizzlehounds.

With that thought, the anger rose up fierce and wild inside Goldie. The Fugleman—the man who was supposed to protect the city's children—was willing to sell them into slavery, just so that he could be dictator! And Hope, a sworn Blessed Guardian, was helping him!

She looked at the soldier on her right. He was the man with the kerchief, but there was no way she could steal it, not while he held her arm so firmly. She stared past the firelight into the shadows, trying to find Toadspit.

"So, it is settled!" said the Fugleman briskly. "How long will it take to get your men ready? A week?"

"For war, dey are *always* ready," said the officer. "We will go now."

"Now?" said the Fugleman. He seemed taken aback, as if

he had not expected things to fall into place quite so easily.

"Now is goot," said the officer. "We will surprise de city while it sleeps. Surprise is goot." He raised his hand. Behind him, a bugle sounded.

If the camp was like a beehive, the four notes of the bugle were like a stick poked into the middle of it. It seemed to Goldie that, for just a moment, everyone stopped what they were doing and fell silent. Then the buzz rose again, louder than ever. Soldiers kicked their fires to ashes, and pulled on helmets or broad-brimmed hats. Orders rang out in harsh voices. Squads of men formed themselves into columns with their muskets slung on their shoulders. Others carried swords, and some had great long pikes with wicked points.

Goldie looked around frantically for Toadspit. And there, just outside the circle of light, was a patch of deep shadow. She looked harder, and saw pale fingers twitch frantically. *Must stop them! NOW!*

The bugle sounded again. A score of drums began to beat. The soldiers began to march.

It was like watching a giant machine grind into action. Legs and arms swung in unison. Grim faces stared to the front as if they were carved out of bluestone. *A-rat-tat-tat a-rat-tat-tat,* snapped the drums. *Left right left right,* tramped the soldiers, heading toward the Dirty Gate.

The whole thing was so huge and noisy and terrifying that Goldie found herself gasping for air. Her pulse hammered in her ears. Her mind raced. She stared desperately at the soldiers and the drums and the pikes and the mud—

The mud! shouted the little voice in the back of her mind. *The* mud*!*

And suddenly, Goldie knew exactly what she must do. With her free hand, she signaled toward the shadows. *Mud!* She pointed at the officer.

There was a long moment when nothing happened. Goldie stopped breathing altogether. Then the shadows shifted and Toadspit stepped forward into the light. His arm swung. A huge ball of mud flew out of his hand and spattered across the front of the officer's velvet coat.

The officer shouted in surprise and fury. The man on Goldie's left sprang toward Toadspit, but the boy was already running back through the tents and wagons. The army of soldiers kept marching past, *left right left right,* as if nothing had happened.

The officer looked down at his ruined coat and snapped out an order. The man on Goldie's right let go of her arm, reached into his pocket—and pulled out Olga Ciavolga's kerchief.

Goldie snatched it out of his hand and ran.

RESCUE

Goldie raced between the tents with the heavy footsteps pounding after her. Her fingers fumbled at the biggest knot in Olga Ciavolga's kerchief. *Hrrrrrrrmmmmmmmmmm*, it thrummed. *Hrrrrrrrmmmm-mmmmmmm.*

Behind her, the footsteps were gaining. The bugle sounded again. This time the notes seemed to form words. *"Show no mercy! Show no mercy! SHOW NO MERCY!"*

Hrrrrrmmmmmmmmmmmmmmmmmmmm, thrummed the

knot in the kerchief. *Left right left right,* went the soldiers toward the Dirty Gate.

There was a shout right behind Goldie, and a hand grabbed her arm. She ducked and twisted away from it, and tore at the knot again, but it wouldn't come loose.

Another shout. The hand gripped her arm more firmly this time. She tried to wriggle free, but the soldier had too good a hold on her. He lifted her right off the ground so that her legs kicked helplessly in the air. He reached for the kerchief.

And suddenly there was Toadspit, leaping out from behind a wagon. He ran straight toward the soldier and kicked him hard in the shins. The soldier dropped Goldie and grabbed Toadspit. He shook the boy furiously, shouting at him all the while. Another soldier came running up, his sword drawn, his face murderous. Firelight glinted off the sharp blade. He drew it back and aimed it at Toadspit's stomach—

Goldie tore frantically at the knot. Her hands felt huge and clumsy. Her heart was leaping out of her chest. She saw Toadspit's face, white with terror. She saw the sword, swooping toward him . . .

And, just in time, her fingers found the secret of the knot. It flew apart. The thrumming stopped. The soldier with the sword hesitated.

There was an instant of silence—and the thrumming

started again. But it was no longer imprisoned in the kerchief. Now it was all around them.

From that moment everything changed very quickly. The tents, which had been sitting so quietly, began to crack and flap. One of them tore loose and flew away like a huge white bird. At the same time, the bugle and drums fell silent. The sound of tramping feet stopped. The soldier who was holding Toadspit let him go. The man with the sword turned away as if he had never had a murderous thought in his life.

Goldie grabbed Toadspit's arm and dragged him behind the nearest wagon. He was shaking from head to toe. All around them, the flapping was growing wilder. The soldiers hurried through the camp, tying down tents and settling the horses. They took no notice of the two children, and seemed to have forgotten about the invasion of Jewel.

It worked, thought Goldie. *The pressure has dropped. The war rooms are calming down.*

But the Great Wind was not calming down. It poured through the camp like a river in flood. It left the soldiers alone, as if it knew that they belonged here, deep inside the museum, and must not be loosed on the world outside. But it wrapped itself around Goldie and Toadspit like a giant hand and began to blow them toward the Dirty Gate.

It was impossible to stand against it. The children half-ran, half-staggered through the camp, past the wagons, past

Broo, who was surging in the opposite direction as if the Great Wind was nothing more than a breeze.

"Broo!" cried Goldie. "What are you doing? Come with us!"

"I am going to find Herro Dan and Olga Ciavolga!" rumbled Broo. He raised his head. His nostrils flared. "Ah, I have their scent!" And then he too was gone.

Goldie and Toadspit stumbled across the grassland and through the Dirty Gate. Ahead of them, Goldie could see the Fugleman and Guardian Hope. The wind had hold of *them* too, and they were trying in vain to turn back.

The wind slammed the Dirty Gate shut, and pushed the children toward Harry Mount. All around them, nails were popping out of planks with a noise like gunfire. Rooms *shifted* as they ran into them and *shifted* again as they ran out, as if the museum was shaking itself with relief. Ahead of them, Guardian Hope and the Fugleman shouted in protest as the wind drove them on, snapping at their heels.

The children ran across the vacant block. The water in the ditch had gone, leaving a morass of stinking mud behind it. Goldie and Toadspit slid down one side and up the other. They ran through the wide corridors, past the shattered glass cases, past the broken Staff Only door. Through the front rooms and under the stone arch into the entrance hall.

And there were Guardian Hope and the Fugleman, still just ahead of them, clinging to the open doorway while the wind tried to blow them out of the museum forever.

"In the name of the Seven, I order you to *stop!*" cried the Fugleman.

But Goldie and Toadspit didn't even slow down. They raced out the door and down the cul-de-sac with the wind howling after them. Then they stumbled out into the open—and stopped in their tracks.

The city was almost unrecognizable. Black clouds scudded overhead like an endless flock of slaughterbirds, blotting out the moon. Rain pelted down in a torrent. Trees and bushes and watergas lamps thrashed about as if they were trying to uproot themselves.

"Grab them!" shouted the Fugleman, close behind. "Don't let them get away!"

The children took off down the street with their heads bent against the fury of the storm. They dodged around one corner and then another, until they had lost their pursuers. They climbed a fence and stumbled across a private garden. The rain lashed at their faces. Somewhere nearby, roof tiles smashed to the ground.

If a Great Wind is unleashed, it will destroy everything in its path.

Goldie grabbed Toadspit's arm and pulled him into the shelter of a wall. "This is going to get worse!" The wind was so loud that she had to shout to make herself heard. "We have to warn people!"

Toadspit's eyes were dark with horror, as if the shadow of the sword still hung over him. Goldie wasn't sure if he had heard her. She tried again.

"We'd better find Sinew!" she shouted. "He's locked up in the House of Repentance. So are Ma and Pa. So are *your* parents." She forced herself to grin. "Oh dear me, what*ever* will we do?"

Something flickered deep in Toadspit's eyes. The shadow faded a little. His face was still desperately pale, but he managed to grin back at her. "I suppose we'll just have to break them out. . . ."

✿

The Fugleman staggered down the hill after Hope, cursing loudly. His wonderful plans were in tatters. And now even the weather had turned against him! He had never experienced a storm like this one, and it seemed to be worsening.

He stumbled over a branch, and cursed again. The city's lights had gone out, and everything was in darkness, except for one bright patch down in the Old Quarter, where the Great Hall shone like a faraway sun.

He heard a new sound, a distant groaning. Hope clutched at his arm. "Your Honor! It's the levees!"

The Fugleman listened. So it was! He stared into the darkness, thinking hard. If the levees broke, the Old Quarter would be flooded, with hundreds of deaths. (Such a pity, especially if his sister was among those who died!) The survivors would welcome a strong hand, someone who would take control, bring order back to their lives.

And for all he knew, this storm could be raging over the whole peninsula! In which case, Spoke and Lawe would also be ripe for a takeover.

A wave of excitement swept through him. Things were not as bad as he had thought. He didn't *need* those barbarians from beyond the Dirty Gate! All he had to do was make sure he survived the storm!

He wiped the rain from his eyes. Should he try and reach his temporary office? No, the roof might not hold, and he had no intention of crouching in the darkness like an animal while chaos howled around him.

But the Great Hall had its own watergas supply. Look at it, shining like a beacon! If the levees collapsed, the lower parts of the hall would flood, but upstairs beneath the dome would be perfectly safe.

He grabbed Hope's sleeve and pointed. "See that?" he shouted. "That's where we're going!"

"But what about the children? What if they escape and tell people what happened?"

"They'll be heading for their homes. Where do they live?"

284

"In the Old Quarter."

"In that case," shouted the Fugleman, "we needn't worry about them. If they're not dead already, they soon will be!"

༰

The House of Repentance was a squat bunker of a building with tiny windows. It appeared to be a single story, but everyone in Jewel knew that there were at least three levels of cells, all of them deep underground.

There were usually several Blessed Guardians patrolling out the front, watching passersby for any sign of Abominations. But when Goldie and Toadspit fought their way through the wind and the rain to the front steps, there was no sign of the familiar black robes.

The children staggered up the steps and through the door. It was a relief to be out of the storm, although everything around them was as black as pitch and the noise was still tremendous. Windows rattled in their frames. The iron roof screeched and banged as if it was about to peel off and fly away. Somewhere in the distance there was a groaning sound that set Goldie's teeth on edge.

She and Toadspit stumbled hand in hand through the dark hallways, searching for a staircase that might lead down to the cells. They found it by accident. They were groping their way along a wall when Toadspit's legs suddenly went out

285

from underneath him, and he fell down the first few steps, dragging Goldie after him.

They caught their balance and crept on downward. Down one long flight they went, then another, until the air grew cool and the sound of the storm was left behind. After so much noise, Goldie could hardly bear the silence.

"I saw your sister," she whispered.

She could feel Toadspit staring at her in the darkness. "Is she all right?"

"She's just like you. Of course she's all right!"

They crept down another flight. "We must be well underground by now," whispered Toadspit. "It can't be much farther—"

He froze. Goldie heard something directly below them. Toadspit's hand gripped hers painfully. The sound came again. It was the faint *thrum* of a harp string.

Toadspit jerked his hand out of Goldie's. "Sinew?" he shouted.

"Great whistling pigs!" said an astonished voice. "Is that *Toadspit*?"

A tinderbox scraped. A match flared. And there, just a few steps below them, were half a dozen officers of the militia. Their faces were grim and they stood shoulder to shoulder, as if they would protect whoever was behind them with their lives.

"Here, make way!" said Sinew. "It's not the Fugleman and his cronies. It's Toadspit!"

A long arm forced its way between the officers, followed by an awkward shoulder. And there was Sinew, harp in hand, staring up at Goldie and Toadspit in amazement. Close behind him was the Protector.

Goldie's knees sagged with relief. Toadspit jumped down the stairs and threw his arms around Sinew. "We thought we'd have to rescue you!" he said.

"Well, as you can see, we've rescued ourselves," said Sinew. "The Blessed Guardians left a little while ago, when the lights went out. Once there was no one watching us, I made short work of the locks."

He looked up at Goldie. "Are you both all right?"

Goldie nodded. "They took us to Care, but we escaped."

"I thought you might." Sinew smiled briefly. Then his face became serious again. "We can't hang around here. The Blessed Guardians might come back. And we have to rescue Broo."

"Goldie's already done that," said Toadspit.

Sinew blinked. "Oh. Good. We'll go straight to the museum then. There's no time to waste. The Fugleman must be stopped."

"We've done that too," said Goldie.

Sinew blinked again. Then, slowly, he began to laugh.

All this time, the officers had been lighting match after match, and whispering to each other and to the Protector. Now the Protector turned to Sinew and said faintly, "*These* are the children you were telling us about?"

Sinew nodded. There was a crash of breaking glass somewhere far above them. The Protector's head jerked up. "What was that?"

"It's the storm," said Goldie. "You know the soldiers behind the Dirty Gate? The Fugleman was promising them slaves and silver if they'd invade Jewel and make him dictator—"

"*What?*"

"You should've seen them," said Toadspit. "There were *hundreds* of them, with muskets and pikes and drums! All marching toward the Dirty Gate!"

"They had Olga Ciavolga's kerchief so we stole it—"

"*You* stole it," said Toadspit.

"*You* threw the mud at the officer."

"Yes, but it was your idea. And it worked brilliantly, Sinew. Splat! All over his fancy coat."

"That's why they were going to kill Toadspit," said Goldie.

Sinew looked horrified. "They were going to *kill* you, Toadspit?"

"Stab me in the guts with a sword! But Goldie saved me. She undid one of the knots in the kerchief just in time—"

"—and released the Great Wind," said Goldie.

Sinew nodded slowly. "That would reduce the pressure

nicely. So. The rooms behind the Dirty Gate calmed down?"

"Straight away," said Goldie. "As soon as I undid the knot."

"Good," said Sinew with great satisfaction. "Let's hope they stay calm—"

Goldie interrupted him. "But now the Great Wind's loose in the city!"

She stopped, watching Sinew's face for a sign that she had done the wrong thing. But Sinew merely said, "We can deal with the Great Wind far more easily than an invading army or an outbreak of plague. You did well, both of you. No one could have done better."

The Protector and the officers began to hurry up the stairs. Goldie and Toadspit didn't move. "Ma and Pa are in here somewhere," said Goldie. "And Toadspit's parents too, and some boys from Care. We have to find them."

"Blow me down," said Sinew. "How could I have forgotten? Here, I'll go and look for them. You go with the Protector. She'll have more questions for you."

Goldie hesitated.

"Don't fret," said Sinew. "I'll have them out of their cells in a trice." He waggled his fingers and grinned. "There's not a lock that can stop me. But I'll need a light of some sort."

"Here," said one of the officers, and he kicked at the wooden banister until several uprights came loose. He tore his shirt into strips and wrapped them around the uprights, and lit them. Sinew slipped away with a makeshift torch in his hand.

Goldie wanted to follow him, but the Protector and the officers were already throwing questions at her, so she bit her lip and told herself to be patient for a little while longer. When the officers heard that many of their fellow militiamen were dead, they shook their heads gravely.

"And the Fugleman?" said the Protector. "Where is he?"

"In the city somewhere," said Goldie. "He and Guardian Hope were chasing us, but we lost them."

The Protector looked sharply at the officers. "They're to be arrested on sight. Particularly the Fugleman. He's not going to get away with this."

They were nearly at the top of the stairs by then, and the noise of the storm was back full force. The groaning sound was louder than ever.

"That's the levees!" The Protector had to shout now. "They won't hold against this. And if they go, the whole of the Old Quarter will flood. We have to get people to higher ground."

"Don't forget Care," shouted Toadspit. "My sister's there."

"Care is at the top of my list." The Protector's face was grim.

"We'll have to clear this place before we go," shouted one of the officers. "We can't leave folk in their cells to drown. I'll see if I can find some keys and give Sinew a hand." And he took a torch and hurried away.

The next few minutes were a bustle of planning. Goldie and Toadspit found themselves edged out of the group as the remaining adults argued about the safest place to take people.

"Take them to the museum," shouted Goldie. "It should be quiet by now."

No one heard her. She pushed between two of the officers and shouted again, "The museum! They'll be safe there!"

The Protector and the officers stared at her for a moment, then nodded to each other and elbowed her out of the way again. "We'll have to split up and divide the Old Quarter between us," shouted the Protector. "We won't get everyone out in time otherwise."

"Idiots," hissed Toadspit in Goldie's ear. "They're going to need us."

Goldie heard a weak cry from the direction of the staircase, and turned to look. A small group of people were stumbling toward her, hanging onto each other for support. Sinew's torch lit their faces.

Goldie's heart almost jumped out of her throat. "Ma!" she screamed. "Pa!" Beside her, Toadspit's voice echoed hers. "Ma! Pa!"

THE GREAT WIND

It was a while before things calmed down. Goldie clung to Ma and Pa and cried bitter tears. "I'm sorry, I'm sorry," she said. "I didn't mean to get you locked up!" She could hear Toadspit saying almost the same thing nearby.

"We're perfectly all right," said Pa, cuddling her tightly. "A little hungry, that's all."

"But sweeting, look at your poor arms!" said Ma. "Is that a scratch? Are you hurt? Oh, let me see!"

She exclaimed over each one of Goldie's bruises and cuts,

and inspected her for signs of fever. Around them, other prisoners were being brought up the stairs with cries of thankfulness and a spattering of song, "Three yea-a-a-a-ars I rowed the galley-y-y-ys—"

By now, Sinew was pacing up and down, his face anxious. "We can't linger here!" he shouted. "We must get the weakest of the prisoners directly up to the museum. Here, you boys, I'll need your help."

The Protector hurried over. "Several of the officers are going to Care. One of the boys must accompany them, to show them where the dormitories are."

Goldie leaned back in Pa's arms. It seemed like forever since she had slept, and her whole body ached with tiredness. *But there's still so much to do.*

Toadspit's pa raised a trembling hand. He was terribly thin, and had to hold onto his son's shoulder for support. "I'll go with them! Our daughter is in Care."

The Protector shook her head. "I'm sorry, Herro—?"

"Hahn. Striver Hahn. And this is my wife, Mollify."

"I'm sorry, Herro Hahn, you'd slow them down too much. You and your wife had best go straight to the museum. Don't worry, the officers will find your daughter and bring her to you." She turned back to Sinew. "We have divided the Old Quarter between us. We must set about this business straight away. The sound from the levees is worsening and I'm not sure that there are enough of us to reach all the households in time."

"I'll help!" Toadspit shouted.

"No!" cried his ma. "You're coming with us. We'll keep you safe."

"But they need me!"

One of the officers shook his head. "We can't send children out by themselves."

Toadspit scowled. "What do you think we've been *doing* all this time? We're not *babies*!"

Above Goldie's head, the roof rattled like a mad thing. "I'll help too!" she cried.

"No!" said Ma. "It's much too dangerous!"

"She's right. I forbid it!" shouted the Protector.

Sinew laughed and whacked the Protector on the back in a friendly fashion. "Forbid it all you like! I swear they'll go anyway, the minute you take your eyes off them! And besides, we need them. They're quick and they're clever. We won't get the area cleared without them."

"But—but who will listen to them?" stammered one of the officers. "Who will listen to a *child* telling them to leave their home?"

Sinew winked at Goldie. "You might be surprised! The world we knew has changed tonight. The wildness is well and truly back in the city!"

As soon as Goldie stepped outside the House of Repentance, the wind hit her. Rain lashed at her face, and the darkness wrapped itself around her so that she lost sight of the others almost immediately. The only landmark she could see was the Great Hall, its dome shining dimly through the storm.

She struggled along the footpath, fighting the wind every inch of the way. The groaning of the levees was getting louder. She crossed Trunkboat Bridge and staggered up Temple Canal to the area that the officers had assigned her.

At the first house, a man with a lantern answered her frantic knocking. He peered at Goldie through a narrow gap in the door, his face white and frightened.

"The levees are going to break, Herro!" shouted Goldie. "You must come with me!"

The man's eyes widened. "Goldie Roth? Is that *you*?"

"Herro Oster!"

It was indeed Jube's father. Goldie had been so disoriented by the storm that she hadn't recognized the house.

Now Frow Oster pushed past her husband, crying, "Goldie *Roth*? It can't be! Oh, my dear, your poor parents! We tried to help them, but the Blessed Guardians—"

"You can't come in," interrupted Herro Oster gruffly. "We can't take the risk."

"But where have you *been*?" cried Frow Oster. "We thought you must be dead!"

"There's no time to explain!" shouted Goldie. "You have to come with me! I'll take you somewhere safe!"

Herro Oster's face turned even whiter. "Go with a *runaway*? The Blessed Guardians would eat us for breakfast!"

"Besides, it's too dangerous," shouted Frow Oster. "We'll be safer here."

"No, you won't! The Old Quarter is going to flood! You have to come! Orders of the Protector!"

Herro Oster shook his head and began to close the door. Behind him someone said, "What's happening, Pa?"

"Go back in the house, Jubilation," snapped Herro Oster. But he was too late.

"*Goldie?*" said Jube, ducking under his father's arm. "Where have you been? What are you doing here? Are you on your *own*?"

"Now see what you've done!" shouted Herro Oster angrily.

"*Listen,* Herro!" said Goldie. "Listen to the storm! If you stay here, you'll drown!"

There was a crash of breaking windows. Herro Oster's anger seemed to drain away and he began to tremble. Like everyone else in Jewel, he had been protected from every sort of risk and danger when he was a child. There had been nothing to test his courage, nothing to teach him when to stand and when to run. Now he was paralyzed with fear and indecision, and so was Frow Oster. They were afraid to stay where they were, and they were afraid to go.

But Sinew was right. Some of the wildness *had* come back into the city. As Herro Oster tried to shut the door, Jube slipped through the narrow gap. Goldie grabbed his hand and the two of them ran out into the street.

By the time his parents ran after him, Jube was standing, amazed, in the middle of howling chaos. "Look, Pa!" he shouted. "Look at our house!"

Herro and Frow Oster stared. The walls were bulging in and out as if the house was an animal gasping for breath. It was clear that they must seek safety elsewhere, or be lost.

Frow Oster pointed toward the Great Hall. "The lights are still on! We'll be safe there!"

Goldie shook her head. "No. We have to get to higher ground."

Jube was shivering, but he nodded agreement. His parents looked at him in astonishment, then, slowly, they too nodded.

Goldie dragged them to the next house, and then to an apartment, and then to another house. "Hurry! Hurry!" she shouted to the frightened faces that peered out at her. "The levees are going to break!"

Each time, it was the children who slipped out into the raging darkness first. Their parents followed close behind, trying to fasten guardchains to their sons' and daughters' wrists. But it would take more than a silver chain to keep them safe on a night like this.

Goldie found Plum and Glory and their families, and they gaped at her, then followed where she led. She found Fort and a score of other children, and they went with her, and so did their parents and grandparents and aunts and uncles.

She was no longer the only one knocking on doors. The children who had managed to evade their guardchains ran awkwardly from house to house, shouting, "Hurry, hurry, there's not much time, *hurry!*" until the frightened people inside tumbled out into the night.

At last they came to Goldie's own street. As the wind and the rain raged around her, and garbage cans and fence palings and branches flew down the street past her head, Goldie pounded on Favor's door.

"Favor!" she shouted, trying to make herself heard over the storm. "Herro Berg! Frow Berg! It's me!"

When Herro Berg opened the door at last, he stared at Goldie as if she was an apparition. "G-G-Goldie!"

There was a cry from inside the house, and Favor and Frow Berg came running. Favor threw her arms around Goldie and kissed her. But there was no time to talk. Everyone was shouting, "Hurry, hurry!" and the sense of urgency was impossible to resist.

By now, Goldie was so exhausted she could hardly stand. She stumbled forward, dragging adults and children behind her like a huge, frightened caterpillar. She wanted to rest, but the groaning of the levees drove her on. *Hurry! Hurry!*

And then she turned a corner and ran smack bang into Toadspit. He was soaking wet and there was a cut on his forehead. Stretched out behind him in the darkness was a long line of people.

When he saw Goldie, he put his mouth to her ear and shouted, "I just spoke to one of the officers! They've got everyone out of Care, and the rest of the Old Quarter's clear as well! We're going to the museum! Come on!"

It seemed impossible that the storm could get worse. But as Goldie and Toadspit and their followers struggled toward Old Arsenal Hill, the wind began to scream even louder. The rain tore at them, as if the soldiers from behind the Dirty Gate had invaded after all and were attacking them head on. Goldie blundered along in a nightmare. Across Pestilence Bridge. Past militia headquarters. Toward the safety of the museum.

They were just about to step onto Old Arsenal Bridge when a small figure hurtled out of the darkness toward Toadspit. He flinched, but then his face lit up like a hundred suns and he held out his arms. "Bonnie!"

"Toadspit!" screamed Bonnie. "Toadspit Toadspit *Toadspit!*" She threw herself at her brother, laughing and crying. Rain and tears streamed down Toadspit's face. Ignoring the storm and the sound of the levees, he wrapped his arms around his little sister and held her tight. The rest of the children from Care surged past, herded by anxious militiamen.

"Bonnie! Toadspit!" shouted Goldie. "We have to *go!*"

They hurried across the bridge with the long line of people straggling after them, and began to climb the hill. They had not gone far when Goldie heard a sound that stopped her in her tracks. Metal tore against metal. The groaning of the levees rose to a shriek.

Toadspit grabbed hold of Bonnie. "Run!" he shouted, and pushed her toward higher ground. Then he and Goldie turned to the people behind them and screamed at the top of their voices, "It's the levees! Run! Run for your lives!"

Their words were snatched away by the wind. It didn't matter. Everyone knew what the sound meant. But they could not move. They stood helplessly, clutching their families. The terrible night had finally taken its toll.

Goldie and Toadspit raced down the lines, tugging at people's clothes and screaming, "Run! *Run!*" Bonnie followed them. "Run!" she shouted.

"Bonnie, *get out of here!*" screamed Toadspit. But Bonnie ignored him. "Run! Everyone run!"

Still no one moved. Goldie grabbed Favor and shouted

right in her face, "Favor, you have to *go*! The levees are breaking!"

Favor's eyes were wide with fright, but she clung to her parents and did not move. Goldie was almost weeping with fear. Every nerve in her body shrieked, *Save yourself! Save yourself!* But she couldn't leave her best friend to die. In desperation, she pulled at the other girl's hand and screamed until her voice was hoarse. "Please, Favor! Please, Herro Berg! *Make her run!*" She could hear Toadspit and Bonnie nearby. *"Run for your lives!"*

But Favor would not move. Nor would anyone else.

And then, just when Goldie thought that there was no hope, that they were all going to die, there came a great roar that could be heard even above the sound of the wind and the rain and the collapsing levees. And out of the darkness, like a huge iron statue brought to life, charged Broo.

His teeth were bared. His eyes glowed red as fire. Someone screamed, "A *brizzlehound*!" And the whole crowd of people—including Favor and her parents—sprang to life and began to run clumsily up the hill.

The floodwater caught them halfway up the next block. It surged up behind them in a hungry wave, snatching at their legs. No one could run now, the street was a river. Mothers and fathers scooped their children up into their arms. Hands grabbed hold of anyone who stumbled. A clockwork bird floated past Goldie like a tiny metal corpse.

They were high enough to have only caught the edge of the flood, and before long the water stopped rising. As Goldie staggered out onto dry land, Broo appeared beside her for just long enough to rumble, "Herro Dan and Olga Ciavolga are safe." Then he melted away like a bad dream.

The wind and the rain seemed to ease for a few minutes then. The black clouds parted and the full moon shone through. In that moment of quietness, Goldie, Toadspit and Bonnie turned and stared at what they had left behind.

The Old Quarter was hidden beneath a sea of water. Buildings poked up out of it like strangely shaped islands. In the middle of it all stood the Great Hall. It was half drowned and leaning perilously to one side, but the lights were still on. Goldie thought—though she was too far away to be sure—that she could see two tiny figures in the glass dome. They seemed to be waving for help.

As she watched, the lights flickered and went out. There was a terrible grinding noise. Then the whole building tore loose from its foundations and floated away into the night.

THREE DAYS LATER

Goldie, Toadspit and Bonnie leaned over the balcony of the Lady's Mile. In the hall below, hundreds of people from the Old Quarter crowded around the long tables, drinking tea and chocolate from chipped mugs and pannikins. Others lay back on piles of old clothes, or huddled in groups. Their cuts were bandaged and their broken bones were set, but they were still painfully quiet. No one smiled. No one laughed. The shock of the storm had not yet left them.

The Protector was making her daily report. Her voice

floated up to the balcony. "As some of you know, the houses in much of the city were not too badly damaged, and their owners have been able to remain in them. But the Old Quarter is still flooded and the waters are swarming with rats and snakes. It will be some time before the area is properly drained. Those of us who have taken refuge here in the museum must stay a while longer, if the keepers will allow it."

Goldie raised her eyebrows at Toadspit. A week ago, any mention of rats and snakes would have sent the citizens of Jewel into a frenzy. But now people merely nodded to each other, as if they were grateful to be alive and nothing else was worth making a fuss about.

Goldie's ma and pa were sitting at the same table as the Protector. So were Toadspit's parents. Olga Ciavolga, Herro Dan (with his leg in plaster) and Sinew were there too. In the far corner of the hall, a group of Blessed Guardians muttered to each other and glowered at the militiamen who guarded them.

Herro Dan thumped one of his walking sticks on the floor. "Of course, you must stay for as long as you need to! The keepers are pleased to have you! The *museum* is pleased to have you!"

"He's right," murmured Goldie in Toadspit's ear. "Have you seen Early Settlers? It's full of vegetable gardens and fruit trees. And the thornberries in the vacant block are ripe."

Toadspit nodded. "And Harry Mount's acting just like an

304

ordinary old staircase. I went up and down it three times this morning and it took me to the same place every time."

Bonnie screwed up her nose. "How could it take you somewhere different? What are you talking about?"

"None of your business," said Toadspit, who had stopped being nice to his sister now that she was safe again.

"If you won't tell me," said Bonnie, "I'll ask Olga Ciavolga."

Goldie searched the faces of the people below. She and Toadspit had been so busy for the last three days that she had hardly seen Favor. Now at last she spotted her friend smiling up at her. She waved.

Favor waved back and signed, *Come down.*

In minute, signed Goldie.

I want to know what happened! After you ran away!

Goldie leaned farther forward so that she was hanging right over the balcony. *And I want to tell you!*

Ma must have caught the movement out of the corner of her eye, because she glanced up. Her hand went to her mouth. She looked as if she was about to leap from her seat and scream a warning. . . .

But Olga Ciavolga touched her arm and murmured something, and Ma's back straightened, as if she had remembered the night of the storm, and the way her daughter had led people to safety when nearly everyone else was afraid to move. She nudged Toadspit's ma and they both looked up. Their faces were pale, but after a moment's hesitation they waved.

"They haven't met Morg yet," said Toadspit. "That'll test them."

"Who's Morg?" said Bonnie.

"None of your business."

"If you won't tell me, I'll—"

"—ask Olga Ciavolga!" said Toadspit in a mock-whiny sort of voice. Brother and sister glared at each other for a moment, then burst out laughing.

"Your parents are doing all right," said Goldie. "Your pa called you Caution—I mean, er . . . um . . . *Toadspit* this morning."

Bonnie laughed again. "And did you see Ma's face when he said it?"

"She'll just have to get used to it," said Toadspit, but he was smiling, as if he was proud of the effort his parents were making.

In the hall below, the Protector was still speaking. "So many terrible things have happened in recent times. The storm, the flood. The bomb. Ah, yes, we have not forgotten the bombers. Whoever they are, wherever they are, we'll not rest until we find them."

She paused. Her face became grim. "But they are not the only ones who must be brought to justice. The people who were supposed to protect our children—"

Goldie saw the heads of the Blessed Guardians shoot up from their huddle.

"—have *betrayed* us!" said the Protector. "I hereby *disband* the Blessed Guardians and declare them to be an *illegal*—"

Her voice was lost in the uproar as the Blessed Guardians surged toward her, shouting. The militiamen blocked their way and forced them back into the corner. The ones who refused to go were wrestled to the ground.

"Where's the Fugleman?" cried one of the Guardians, who was being held with his arms behind his back. "He'll put a stop to this!"

Herro Dan thumped his stick on the floor for silence.

"Yes," said the Protector. "Where *is* the Fugleman? Where is the greatest betrayer of all? Bring him here and let him answer for his crimes!"

She paused dramatically. Goldie looked around the hall, half-expecting to see the Fugleman push through the crowd.

"I'll tell you where he is," said the Protector. "He's gone, probably drowned in the storm, like the rat he was. It's no use looking to him for support. Your only hope is to throw yourselves on the mercy of the city."

The Guardians began to shout again. The Protector nodded to the captain of militia. "Take them away. They will go on trial for treason, and for their treatment of the children in Care."

As the militiamen wrestled the Guardians out of the room, the Protector turned to the remaining citizens. But before she could speak, there was a flash of white and something scampered across the floor and jumped up onto her table.

"It's Broo!" said Goldie.

In the hall below, nearly everyone leaped to their feet. "A dog!" they shouted. "Watch out! A *dog!*"

Parents grabbed hold of their babies, ready to flee. Even from up on the balcony, Goldie could see their horrified faces. Hearing about snakes and rats down in the Old Quarter was one thing, but this was a real live dog, something that had not been seen in Jewel for hundreds of years. And it was *here*, right in front of them!

Only the keepers stayed where they were. The keepers— and the Protector.

Broo didn't seem to notice the alarm that he had caused. He trotted along the tabletop and stopped in front of the Protector, wagging his curly white tail. The Protector looked at him uncertainly. Sinew leaned over and whispered something to her.

The Protector nodded and turned back to the crowd. "Our—our city is changing," she said loudly, though she stumbled a little over the words. "I understand that humans and dogs lived together—lived *well* together—in the distant past." She swallowed. "I—I see no reason why they should not live well together in the future."

And to Goldie's astonishment, she reached out and gingerly patted Broo on the head.

There was a sigh from the watchers. One by one, they crept back to the tables, their faces wary. Only the babies showed no fear. They stretched out their arms toward Broo and squealed. The little dog wagged his tail and danced down the middle of the table.

He looked so funny that the babies squealed louder. Goldie saw Favor begin to smile. Broo danced in circles, chasing his tail, his eyes bright with joy.

The Protector laughed.

That was all it needed. It was as if the levees had broken all over again. A flood of laughter filled the hall, spilling in every direction and sweeping away the horrors of the storm.

Broo danced up and down the table. He jumped into laps and licked faces and hands. No one could escape him. Before long, half the children in the hall were crowding around him, arguing over who should pat him next. And even the most nervous adults were sitting back and smiling fit to burst, as if a long-lost brother had arrived on their door-step and they had suddenly remembered how much they loved him.

Bonnie was leaning over the balcony, her eyes fixed on Broo. "Toadspit, do you think Ma and Pa would let us have a dog?"

Toadspit didn't answer her. His face was gloomy. "Well, that's ruined it," he muttered.

"What's the matter with you?" said Goldie.

"You should be pleased," said Bonnie, turning around to

stare at her brother. "Everything's changing! I haven't worn a guardchain for three whole days. And now there's a *dog*!"

"That's just it. There's no excuse to run away anymore," grumbled Toadspit. "They'll expect us to be contented. They'll expect us to be *good*!" He scowled at Goldie. "I suppose *you're* going to go home and be a good little girl again."

Goldie looked down at the crowded hall. Broo was sitting on Favor's lap now, surrounded by a circle of adoring children. His tail rose and fell gently. He gazed up at Goldie, and his black eyes gleamed with secret knowledge.

And suddenly Goldie could feel the museum all around her. Its mysteries and its wildness, its beauty and its dangers, the Devil's Kitchen and Dauntless and Stony Heart, and a hundred other rooms that she had not yet seen but that were there, waiting for her to discover them.

She touched the little blue bird that was pinned to the front of her smock, and thought of Auntie Praise. *Bold* Auntie Praise.

"Go home and be good?" She grinned at Toadspit, and shook her head. "I've barely begun."

MEANWHILE . . . TWO HUNDRED MILES TO THE SOUTH

I n the middle of the ocean, a man and a woman were clinging to a scrap of wreckage. They were alive, but only just. Their clothes were in rags and their faces were bruised beyond recognition. The storm was gone, but they were both terribly weak, and they knew that they couldn't hold on for much longer. Soon the deep water would claim them.

At first, they thought that the fishing boat was a mirage. The shocked cries, the strong hands that dragged them out of the water onto the streaming deck—surely it was all just a cruel trick played by their feverish minds.

It wasn't until half an hour later, when they were swathed in warm blankets with a circle of curious fishermen around them, that they let themselves believe they were saved.

"You're lucky we saw you when we did," said the tallest fishermen, who seemed to be in charge. "Way out of our waters, we are. Blown off course by that big wind. Just turnin' south again when we spotted you."

"Clingin' to that board like a couple o' drowned rats, you were!" said another man.

"*Still* look like drowned rats to me!" said a third man, and they all laughed, a loud, booming sound.

The woman struggled to raise herself on one elbow. "Show some respect," she croaked, in a voice hoarse with fever and salt water. She pointed to her companion. "Don't you know who this is? This is—"

"No one!" said her companion quickly. He waved an apologetic hand at the watching men. "Please forgive my friend, she is confused. I am no one important." And he smiled at the fishermen. In spite of his bruises, it was a particularly charming smile. . . .

ACKNOWLEDGMENTS

Many thanks to the generous people who read earlier versions of *Museum of Thieves* and helped me make it better: Mrs. Holton's grade five class (2006), Lauderdale Primary School, Tasmania; Essie and Fin Kruckemeyer; Lyn Reeves and Helen Swain. Particular thanks to Peter Matheson, dramaturge and manuscript assessor, who has such a fine eye for a story.

Thanks also to my exceptional agents, Margaret Connolly (Australia) and Jill Grinberg (United States), and to the wonderful people at Random House Children's Books. Michelle Poploff, Dominique Cimina and Marci Senders deserve a special mention, but I am also indebted to everyone else who worked so hard on the book. Thank you!

LIAN TANNER is a children's author and playwright. She has worked as a teacher in Australia and Papua New Guinea, as well as a tourist bus driver, a freelance journalist, a juggler, a community arts worker, an editor and a professional actor. It took her a while to realize that all of these jobs were really just preparation for being a writer. Nowadays she lives by the beach in southern Tasmania with a small tabby cat and lots of friendly neighborhood dogs. She has not yet mastered the art of Concealment by the Imitation of Nothingness, but she is quite good at Camouflage.